# CLEAR AND CONVINCING EVIDENCE

A Jennifer Roby Mystery

Barbara Townsend

Clear and Convincing Evidence
Second edition published January 2016,
by Fine Nib Publishing, Wyoming, USA

Originally trade published in February 2014
by Writers AMuse Me Publishing

Cover by B. D. King

ISBN-10: 0-9972340-2-4 (paperback)
ISBN-13: 978-0-9972340-2-2 (paperback)

## Praise for *Clear and Convincing Evidence*:

In these pages, you will meet gutsy Wyoming people you will admire and enjoy spending time with. But watch out! You will also encounter some despicable folks you can't turn your back on. Nor will you want to. The murder on the mythical campus engrosses the reader from the opening page until the end as timeless themes of greed and power compete with integrity and honor. I only hope that this will not be the last Jennifer Roby mystery we see from the author.

~ Marjane Ambler, *Yellowstone Has Teeth, a memoir about living year round in the world's first national park*

~ * ~

The only thing more fun than a Western cozy mystery is one set on a college campus, a small world where anything can happen. In Clear and Convincing Evidence, Barbara Townsend sends her savvy young heroine to solve a campus murder then ensnares the campus art community, campus police, and even the top administration. All this, with only the First Amendment, her dad and grandpa, and the spirit of Walter Cronkite to light her way.

~ Julianne Couch, *Traveling the Power Line*

~ * ~

Clear and Convincing Evidence by Barbara Townsend is a compelling and suspenseful read. It is a must for anyone interested in the integrity of information that is furnished to the public and the journalists that struggle to provide the truth.

~ Susan Layman, *South Pass City and the Sweetwater Mines*

*To Robert*

# Acknowledgments

Teachers may never know their influence on students. I wish to pass my warmest regards to three University of Wyoming professors who changed my world.

Dr. Connie Currie altered my view of my writing and myself.

Ann McCutchan, MFA, focused my writing. In her upper-division English workshop class, I wrote my first fiction, a murder mystery titled *Murder at Wainwright.* That story awakened a love of writing fiction and mysteries. *Clear and Convincing Evidence* evolved from that short story.

Margaret Haydon, MFA, reached into my artistic mold and shattered it. Through her, I learned the simplicity and complications of molding and throwing clay, and how to allow my imagination to evolve. Who knew a life's joy was playing in the mud?

A hearty thank you to these Wyoming professionals who gave me their time and knowledge: Jeffrey Jacoby, owner, Schrader Funeral Home, Cheyenne; Mike Samp, Chief of Police, University of Wyoming; Edward R. McAuslan, Fremont County Coroner; and Julie Heggie, Albany County Coroner.

I thank Mary Cote-Walkden, editor extraordinaire, whose attention to detail and patience improved both this novel and myself as a writer.

# Jeanne Clery Act

After the 1986 murder of their daughter in her college dormitory room, Connie and Howard Clery successfully campaigned to pass a federal law requiring institutions of higher education to publicly disclose information such as crime statistics and threats to the public.

The Jeanne Clery Disclosure of Campus Security Policy and Campus Crime Statistics Act was enacted in 1990. The law provides for exceptions to the reporting requirements.

# Chapter 1

"You are so cranky when you're blond." Hannah laughed with caution, and hoped her teasing would lighten Jake's dark mood. His natural blond roots overpowered his black dyed hair.

He was the class jokester, a self-effacing quip at the ready, but today his melancholy bordered on despair. His eyelids were puffy like he'd been crying. The stark difference concerned Hannah.

Jake said nothing. Instead, he focused on unbolting the door to the car kiln, an outdoor ceramics furnace the size of a walk-in closet. He pulled hard on the monkey wrench to break loose the bolt securing the door to the kiln's exterior frame. The teeth slipped off the rounded head. A crescent of knuckle skin smeared across the abrasive surface. Jake clenched his fist and managed not to curse.

She held her breath as Jake groaned, cradling his scraped fist. He flicked his hand at the wrist as if to snap away the pain. His trembling hands couldn't hide the chewed ebony-polished fingernails. She averted her eyes as the unofficial leader of Colter State College's artistic world blinked back tears.

Jake gulped the chilling air before grabbing the wrench. The wind blew harder. Rotted leaves from last year swirled in chunky vortices in the courtyard's corners behind the studio. Snowflakes shot across the yard like tiny white darts; the points of ice stung Hannah's face.

The winter-like winds raged strong in Colter, funneled by the Wind River Mountains to the west. Dark clouds from the fast-approaching series of snowstorms obscured the granite peaks that loomed beyond the campus treetops.

The storms also distracted Hannah's fellow students. They had chattered more about the dirt and snow blowing horizontally past the studio's massive windows than about the clay on their throwing wheels.

Earlier, in the middle of class, Professor Alexandra Redgrave had announced that the car kiln had been fired on Sunday and was now cool enough to unload. Who would volunteer to unload it? At the hesitant silence, Alex prodded. "Everyone has to take their turn."

Hannah had said nothing; she unloaded the kiln last time. This time she wanted to make the clay on the throwing wheel submit to her will. Yet, every mound of clay she tried to coax into a bowl spun itself into a lop-sided globule. She recalled Alex's caution on the first day of class: "Some days you just can't do anything, and it's best to quit for the day." Hannah sighed and raised her hand.

Across from Hannah's wheel, Jake had been quiet and seemed particularly distracted. Every vase or bowl he threw ended up as a mangled clump. He volunteered.

"Tiffany, you too," Alex said. Students in earshot of her command watched Tiffany's reaction. She sat at the worktable at the far end of the room, away from the rows of throwing wheels. She looked away from Alex and continued her sketching.

Hannah silently cheered Alex's pointed directive while she cleaned her wheel and slid her toolbox on the assigned shelf. Maintaining a ceramics studio entailed myriad chores. When Alex called for volunteers, Tiffany never offered or simply disappeared when expected to help.

"Oh." Alex held up both hands to get the students' attention. "I hate to tell you this, but Carmen reported problems with the car kiln."

Those problems meant their work could be ruined. Students stopped to stare with apprehension at Alex. She had their full attention.

"Apparently the gas line had some sort of blockage. The temp didn't get nearly as high as we needed. Remember, we wanted cone seven, around twenty-two hundred degrees. Carmen couldn't tell what temp the kiln reached. It's not likely we'll get the stoneware we expected. There's no telling what we'll get."

At the chorus of groans and complaints she held up her hands, palms out, in acknowledgment. "I know, I know. I have pieces in the kiln too. The glaze may be dull, but we can refire them. Don't despair. Some pieces may be just fine. I've already called maintenance to fix the gas line."

Jake spun the last bolt from the door. He gripped the door's edge and slowly tugged open the kiln. Hannah thought of it as a cabinet containing a giant drawer. It had no back or sides and slid on parallel rails. On the floor, removable posts supported a tower of shelves that held the pottery. She tensed for a possible collapse. If the shelves weren't balanced, the fall would crunch artwork, ruining hours of effort.

With the drawer open, Jake and Hannah moved alongside to gaze at the ceramic pieces. She always enjoyed that first look: the surprise of unexpectedly beautiful art or the utter disappointment of a sagging or an exploded piece that destroyed its neighbors.

The top shelf displayed vases and bowls with dull finishes. The two students silently began to stack the pieces in their arms. The ceramics were still warm. The heat felt good against Hannah's cold, stiff hands. She didn't dare wear gloves for fear someone's work would slip from her grasp and shatter on the ground.

She paused to hear the tiny *ting* of the cooling and contracting pieces. A delicate melody emanated from the studio shelves. The small sound always lightened her heart. The pieces were not just inanimate objects for utility or aesthetics; they were alive and had a soul. "Life's little pleasures," she told herself.

She and Jake made trip after trip into the studio, restacking the bowls and vases on the silt-smeared metal shelves. Her bowls had a matte finish. At least her dull pieces could be refired to the necessary higher temperature to attain the preferred coating.

"Is it unloaded?" The irritant in Hannah's ceramic life walked toward the kiln, leaned against it to look inside, and seemed to pout with disappointment.

*No, you little simp.* Neither Hannah nor Jake answered. She recalled the first day of class when the uninspiring blob named Tiffany was quick to inform everyone about how her parents owned two successful art galleries, one in Denver, Colorado, and one in Jackson Hole, Wyoming. During the semester, she often spoke of the latest hot artist they represented. Within days of Tiffany's initial pronouncement, Hannah and her classmates figured out that her parents' talent had skipped a generation.

Tiffany moved in slow motion as she picked up two bowls. Every student was careful to not break another student's piece, but Tiffany moved at a sloth's pace to the studio.

*If you move any slower, pigeons will land on your head.*

"What is with all this ash?" Hannah puffed on a couple bowls and waved the thin cloud away. "Have you ever seen anything like this?" She rubbed her fingers.

Jake grunted no. He stared at his gray-coated fingertips before wiping them on his jeans.

Each time Hannah and Jake cleared a shelf, Jake's height and arm strength enabled him to remove it. Constructed of high alumina to withstand the intense heat, the shelves were heavy for their size. As they worked their way down, the wind set off billowing puffs as the ash coating thickened.

Two men, college maintenance men judging from their coveralls and toolbox, came around the corner of the studio.

"Are you Alexandra Redgrave?" the taller man asked Hannah.

"No, sorry," she replied, annoyed at being confused for a prof just because she was older than most students — and some profs.

Jake pointed with his chin toward the studio. The shorter man held the door open for Hannah and her armload of bowls. She smiled. "Thank you!"

Hannah returned to the kiln, shaking the cramp from her arm. She hefted one of Alex's smaller pieces. The sculpted face was twice the size of hers and had no eyeballs, yet the eye sockets' voids exuded life and intensity. She stared at the face and tried to put into words the intrigue it commanded. Alex was into heads and faces, carved busts on a massive scale, but the eyeless sculptures fascinated Hannah. She delivered the larger-than-life piece to her professor.

The last sculpture on the last shelf was a stylized white figurine decorated with spastic black stripes, another successful piece. Hannah's interpretation of the sturdy sculpture was of a maiden wrapped in robe. She appeared to be praying to the heavens. The sculpture's soft white coating contrasted sharply with the jagged black lines.

"Ooh, whose is this?" Hannah cried. She turned over the piece to see the initials of the artist scratched in its bottom. "T. A."

"Miss Art Gallery," Jake sneered.

"She has some talent," Hannah said with envy. She brushed her finger along the black lines and wished she were this creative.

"That's mine." Tiffany materialized at Hannah's elbow with her hand extended. Hannah thought about offering her a compliment in addition to the piece, but quietly passed the sculpture. Tiffany cradled it in the crook of her arm, grabbed another bowl off the shelf, and turned back to the studio.

Jake bent to lift the last shelf to expose the remaining pieces. He gasped as the support posts lurched at his touch then he struggled to keep the posts vertical. If they toppled, he couldn't prevent crushing the pieces below. He reset his feet to regain his balance.

"Gimme a hand, will ya? Grab the post closest to you. Hurry! Some idiot used four to hold up this shelf. The whole thing wants to fall over."

Hannah grabbed the post to hold it steady. She arched her neck to see the others. "Yup, some twit used one in each corner. Why is it so hard to remember three are more stable than four?" Hannah grabbed a teetering second post. "I've got the two that want to fall."

Jake lifted the shelf with a slow, smooth motion.

Hannah set aside the two posts. "Finally, we can get these last pieces into the studio." She blinked at the snowflakes pelting her face.

He froze. His wide eyes and motionless stance caught Hannah's attention. She followed his gaze. The floor was rimmed with vases, bowls, and another of Alex's faces. In the center lay pieces of a skeleton. A skull, pelvis, and a couple long bones were all that remained.

Hannah stared. She tried to remember if Alex had assigned any student to make such a piece or if any student made it for personal art. "Wow, these look like something you'd make. Is it yours?"

After a long pause, Jake's voice choked from shock. "No."

She thought the pieces looked strikingly realistic and reached in with both hands to retrieve the skull.

*"Don't touch it!"*

At his shriek, she yanked back her hands. Her heart rate spiked.

"I'll get Alex." Jake staggered toward the studio, still carrying the shelf.

Alone at the kiln, Hannah leaned in for a closer inspection.

Little ash lay on the floor since the firestorm within the kiln during its firing had scattered most of it. A faint residue on the floor hinted of a small figure in the fetal position. The outline highlighted the gray bones. Two long bones pointed at the pelvis. A hole more than an inch across gaped at the skull's left temple. White teeth gleamed from the spread jawbones frozen in a silent scream.

Hannah's breathing became ragged and high-pitched. Her thoughts froze as horror seized her brain. Her stomach convulsed. She ran to the trash barrel by the shed and vomited.

~ * ~

"Any thought on what this might be?" Campus Chief of Police Tom Bannister asked Hannah as she shivered beside Alex. All three stood in the shelter of the shed lined with electric kilns, protected from the wind and increasing snowfall.

Hannah pressed into Alex's side. Grateful for the comfort of the professor's arm around her shoulders, she shook her head. "I don't have a clue."

"I can't imagine exactly what it's made of," Alex said. "If it turns out it's made of clay, a good ceramic artist can make anything look authentic."

The stocky policeman jotted on his notepad, and tugged the collar of his leather jacket up to his ears. He stroked his thick mustache as he stepped out from the shed's protection and blinked as the flakes tapped his face. At the kiln, he studied the rough material of its sides. "Between this surface and this weather, it'll be tough to get fingerprints," he muttered.

He asked with a note of resignation, "Any chance the prints are less than ten years old?"

"None." She shook her head. "People have been using these tools and touching the kiln for forty years and the artwork that came out earlier has already been handled by several students."

The chief scratched his cheek as he studied the area. "Let me photograph the scene now before more snow falls. I need the photos with the area as clean as possible." He hunched forward, studying the slushy ground as he stepped toward his staff car parked beside the bungalow. The flashing lights reflected off the blowing flakes like a rainbow disco ball.

A tall, slender woman in an ankle-length red wool coat rounded the bungalow's corner and stopped short of bumping into the chief. Hannah watched as the woman grabbed one of his arms and gestured with the other. With the faintest movement, he flicked off her hand then gestured toward the kiln. She nodded then stepped tentatively to the open drawer, leaned over, braced her hands on her thighs and stared at the contents on the floor.

In a sudden movement, she tottered toward the chief. He gripped her arms, steadying her as she pressed a fist to her lips. After a moment, she nodded and he turned back to the police car and lifted a large camera from a metal case.

She whipped out her cell phone and spoke into it with great gestures.

"You feeling better?"

Alex's words snapped Hannah from her reverie of watching the woman. "Doing better, thanks." Her embarrassment spiked because of her reaction to the contents. Hannah was older than the professor and had years of military experience. She should have handled the shock better. She ran her tongue over her teeth in another effort to rid them of the film of her breakfast's reemergence then lifted her hand toward the kiln. "What do you think, Alex?"

The professor stared at the kiln as if contemplating its contents. After a huge sigh, she raised her hands as if in resolution. "It has to be hand constructed. That's all it can be. The chief'll confirm it. I'm going to see if he needs me to do anything else." Alex patted Hannah's shoulder and reached the chief as he adjusted the lens on the camera.

Hannah leaned against the shed wall and watched the woman in the red coat as she listened, nodding as if the other person could see her movements. Closing the phone with a snap, she spun on her heels, and held out a hand to stop the chief from snapping photographs. She pulled him away from Alex and stepped close to him as she spoke.

The chief's face grew red. The woman shook a finger at him as vehemently as he shook his head.

She spun away from him and strode with a purpose toward Hannah. "I'm so sorry you experienced this upsetting prank. The chief said there's nothing for you to worry about here."

Hannah's eyes narrowed at the abrupt pronouncement. Mistrust rose like the remnants of her breakfast.

Beyond the chief's car, a vehicle idled forward. A magnetic sign stuck to the van's side read *Coroner*.

## Chapter 2

Jennifer Roby hustled into the deserted *Lariat* staff room and heaved her overstuffed backpack onto the metal desk. "Poo!" She plopped onto her cloth-covered chair stained from years of spilled coffee, sodas, and snacks. With a deep breath to clear her mind from a two-hour chemistry exam, she leaned back. Sinking eyelids scratched her periwinkle eyes, dry from the strain of concentration. The maroon King Ropes ball cap bulged to contain the tangled mass of natural white-blond hair.

A nineteen-year-old journalism sophomore, Jenn was the newest reporter for Colter State College's student newspaper. The *Lariat's* staff room and the newsroom across the narrow hall were on the third floor in the Student Commons. In the Commons, students ate, drank, worked at banks of computers, and generally hung out between classes.

The red brick building had undergone a recent multimillion-dollar renovation, which rid the building of its 1940s and 1970s eclectic décor. The refurbishment did not include the floor that housed the newspaper. The staff room was long, and packed with cluttered Army-surplus metal desks, computers, stacks of books, and class papers. Sagging bookcases spilled piles of newspapers onto the black and once-white tile floor. Strewn soda cans and coffee mug advertisements furnished the only color. Windows dominated the tired room.

Jenn picked up that day's issue and studied the headline: *Massive Budget Cutbacks Coming.* Uncertainty fluttered within her about the forewarned higher tuition trumpeted in the article.

She stared out the window beside her desk. The huge windows let her snoop at the happenings in front of the Commons and around Barren Lake, a small lake — or a large pond — lined with massive ponderosa pines, at the center of the college grounds.

The wind gusted harder. A few blasts pushed the evergreens until she thought they'd snap. Horizontal snow grew so thick that the buildings on the other side of Barren Lake disappeared in the whiteness. A student chased his papers as the white eddies whirled like recyclable dervishes. Those papers won't stop till they hang up on Nebraska corn stalks, Jenn thought.

*Lariat* editor and fellow student, Manuel Whitaker, interrupted Jenn's thoughts as he marched into the room. A senior journalism student in his early thirties, Manny's black goatee camouflaged his double chins. His ample spare tire jiggled as he hurried toward her.

"Hey, Jenn."

"What's up, Manny?"

"Research and write up an article about this police blotter entry. Stroll said he wants to put a stop to this foolishness. It got a lot of people upset." Manny handed Jenn the section that listed the blotter.

*Monday, March 3: 2:33 p.m., Ceramics Studio Hamilton - Received report of skeleton in a kiln. Case was determined to be a prank.*

"Why is this a big deal?"

"A couple students uncovered it when they unloaded the kiln. It scared the hell out of 'em."

Jenn wrinkled her nose. "Yikes."

"It disrupted classes for the day — got all sorts of official types to investigate." Manny paced as he stroked his goatee. "See what you can find out from the police, who they think did it, and why."

"So we're doing public service announcements again?"

Manny snorted. "Stroll just told me 'write the damn story'."

"Want me to let you know what the police say before I write it?"

"Nope, just leave it on my desk." He turned and was nearly out the door when Jenn thought of her next question. Before she opened her mouth, Manny tossed over his shoulder, "I'm going home for dinner. Then I'll be back to finish tomorrow's edition." He disappeared down the hall.

Jenn reread the blotter. Why would the Dean of Students, Doctor Robert Stroll, mandate an article about a prank? Granted, Stroll was the department head for Student Publications, which included the college's newspaper, but he'd never ordered an article to be written for a minor story … *well, except the time the Pi Pi Pi fraternity smuggled a heifer into the Delta Omega Gamma sorority house and inserted a laxative down her throat.* Perhaps Stroll had heard of more pranks and felt the need to put a stop to them before they escalated.

She donned layers of scarf, ski cap, and parka. Feeling like an artichoke, she trudged toward her first stop. The police dispatch office in the Maguire Building was a block from the Commons. The dispatch office maintained the college's police report, where it was available to anyone who wished to read it. She wanted to find out if any more printed information on the incident existed.

She walked west in front of Jefferson Hall, which blocked the strong northeast gusts. Circling south toward the Maguire Building, she braced herself against the freezing blast as she slogged near the statue of Benjamin Franklin on his step, high in the air near the School of Arts. She laughed out loud at the red boa someone had snaked around Ben's neck and shoulders. With the boa whipping in the wind, he looked like a cheap floozy waving down students.

In the Maguire Building, she panted to catch her breath. "The police blotter, please," Jenn said between breaths. The clerk behind the plate glass window slipped the clipboard, thick with police blotter reports, through the slit in the protective glass. Jenn flipped to the previous day's report and reread the exact text that Manny had given her. This listing, however, also reflected the investigating officer's name: Chief Tom Bannister.

Odd that the chief of police would investigate such a minor incident, she thought. She had expected to see Sergeant Matt Kerry as the investigating officer. Simply thinking about the detective caused burning patches to sprout on her cheeks.

"Thank you." Jenn set the clipboard back on the counter and smiled at the clerk.

Still distracted by thinking of Detective Kerry, she pushed open the door. A gust threatened to yank the knob from her hand. She wrestled the door closed. Hunching her shoulders against the gale, she let it push her along the icy sidewalk to a small, unlabeled brick building. This was the actual police station, separate from the dispatch office that most people mistook for the police station. The building retained its homey appearance. As Jenn approached the front door, she fought the urge to knock first. She entered a tiny foyer and stamped the snow off her scuffed cowboy boots, regretting not wearing her snow boots.

"Can I help you, Jenn?"

She met eyes with the police chief's secretary, Brida Nowak. Another Wyoming girl, Jenn had liked her immediately the first time they met last semester. Like Jenn, Brida loved the wild of Wyoming and decried the surge in population and encroachment of arrogant or jaded big-city people.

"Hi, Brida, sorry to bother you."

Brida waved her hand in dismissal. "Oh, you're not bothering me. It's good to see you. It's been awhile." She took Jenn by the arm and led her down the hall. "Besides, I needed a break from all the commotion," she whispered, motioning with her chin over her shoulder.

"What's going on?" Jenn immediately wished she hadn't asked. While most of the happenings at the police station were public information, much of it was private to those involved. Dad and Grampa had impressed on her that journalists must respect a person's privacy. "Our Code of Ethics is specific in that regard."

"The announcement will come soon," Brida whispered. Conspiracy flickered in her eyes.

"Is Chief Bannister finished with the report on the prank at the ceramics studio?" Nothing happened at the police station or on campus without Brida knowing about it.

"Oh, yeah. He turned over the report to Sergeant Kerry. He's about ready to roll, but you can still catch him."

Jenn gave Brida's hands a squeeze then headed down the hall to Kerry's office.

Sergeant Matt Kerry, the college's only detective, cut a fine figure in his tailored uniform. He didn't have to wear a uniform, but Jenn suspected Kerry was so proud of his physique that no civilian attire could display it to his liking or project the image he wanted.

She paused before knocking on his open door. Kerry stood behind his desk with his back to the doorway as he checked his weapon then slipped the Glock into the holster with a practiced twist of his wrist. She took in his broad shoulders that angled to a slim waist and round buttocks. Her face burned. Kerry spun around and noticed her.

Embarrassment washed over her for having been caught leering. Jenn stammered, "Um, good morning, Sergeant. I'm Jennifer Roby, reporter for the *Lariat*."

Kerry smirked, apparently pleased he'd caught her ogling. "You're the one who wrote about the cow in the sorority house."

"She was a heifer. Do you have a moment to talk to me about one of the entries in the blotter?"

Jenn mentally thanked Manny, her editor, for making her memorize her introduction to sources or witnesses. "In the heat of battle, it's good to spit it right out so you always make that succinct first impression, no matter the circumstances or how flustered you are," he had said.

"Which entry?" Kerry still smiled; his cheekiness replaced her embarrassment with irritation.

"The skeleton found in the ceramics studio."

Now Kerry squirmed, she thought. She watched him appear to search his memory for the incident. His eyes were curious. "Yeah, it was a toy. Why?"

"Well, it's such an odd thing to do. Do you know who placed it in the kiln?"

"Nope, and no one owned up to it."

"Did you ask around ... all the students who use the kiln?" Jenn pushed. "After all, there can't be that many students who'd use it." Questions popped into her head, rapid-fire.

Kerry shifted his weight to one leg. With an emphasis to show his displeasure, he thumped his other foot on the floor. "As important as investigating a prank is, that's not the biggest thing I have on my plate. But yes, the chief did talk with the students who found it and the professor. They all stated they had no idea who would place it there." An edge in Kerry's voice warned Jenn that their conversation was drawing to a close.

"What did they look like?"

He didn't try to hide his irritation. "Like bones. That's why the police were called."

"What were they made of?" Jenn knew little about ceramics and firing a kiln, but she knew it got pretty danged hot.

"Some synthetic material."

"Why didn't it melt?"

"What?"

"Well, a kiln gets very hot," Jenn plunged into her explanation. "If they were synthetic, they would've melted and looked like mush."

Kerry's eyes narrowed.

*He's going to make up an answer because he doesn't know.*

"I don't know what they were made of, specifically. The gas line malfunctioned. The kiln didn't get as hot as it should have. That's probably why they didn't completely disintegrate or, as you say, turn to mush." He paused as he pursed his lips as if to consider the circumstances.

He waved his hand as if the movement reminded him of something. "Actually, the chief thought that they looked real because the heat altered their appearance. The heat was high enough to cause the chemicals in the plastic to fume a film residue on the floor. It actually looked like a body had lain there."

"Were they made by a student or purchased somewhere?"

With an exaggerated sigh, he rested his hand on the pistol butt. "I'm sure you can buy them off the Internet, along with whoopee cushions, cut-off hands, and other adult gimmicks."

"Have such pranks happened before at the ceramics studio?"

"No. Anything else." This was not a question, but a statement. Kerry reached for his black cowboy hat on the rack in the corner of his room.

"I was surprised to see the chief was the investigator and not you. Were you not available?" A jolt on uncertainty for asking such a question stabbed Jenn's chest.

He shrugged. "I was in Cheyenne for a conference with other campus police and security officers from around the state. We're trying to devise ways to slow the alcohol abuse on campuses. So the chief took the report and completed the follow-up."

Jenn flinched with confusion. "Do detectives figure out alcohol problems?"

A small smile creased Kerry's mouth. "Along with my seven other additional duties, such as traffic and crowd control, and parking ticket appeal." He waved his hat before settling it on his head. "The last thing I detected was the frat boys who managed to get a Smart car on top of the rival frat house's roof. You know this is a small campus. We don't have many problems here, so certain positions have multiple responsibilities."

She nodded in understanding. "Do you expect more pranks, especially since it's getting close to spring break?"

"We'll have more if they're publicized, like through the newspaper." Kerry pulled his jacket from the rack and moved around his desk. "Kids'll read about their stunts in the paper, and that'll encourage more."

Jenn understood the message: Blame the media. "So this is the media's fault?"

"Just because you can print something doesn't mean you should." He stood erect, like a statesman making a pronouncement. "The writer who hides behind the First Amendment obscures the big picture." He relaxed and approached Jenn's private space. She was forced to back out of his office with him trailing close behind. "Don't you agree, Miss Roby?"

*Yes, darn you.* She pretended to be offended and avoided his eyes with him so near. Jenn rattled off Manny's second mandatory blurb: "Thank you for your time, Sergeant."

She spun around, gave a wave to Brida on her way out, and trudged back to the Commons. The wind had slowed to a stiff breeze. The humidity had increased, causing the cold air to sting her skin as if her clothing had vanished. Classes had let out and a rush filled Maguire Street.

Jenn waited at the crosswalk until a driver noticed her and stopped. She waved as she crossed. She pulled open one of the Commons' double doors against the breeze and let it nudge her into the building. Jenn ignored the elevator and walked up the grand, curving staircase to the second floor, then the narrow, straight stairs to the third.

The clicks of Alejandro's typing were the only sound in the staff room. His desk stood at the far end of the room and faced away from hers.

Not wanting to disturb him, Jenn quietly sat at her desk, woke up her computer, started to type her article, but then stopped. The story needed the victims' perspective, yet she had no idea who to talk to. Aggravated for letting his hunkiness distract her, she hadn't thought to ask Kerry for witnesses' names. Tracking him down wasn't a good idea since he was already irritated.

She looked up the ceramics professor's telephone number on the college directory and dialed. Jenn expected to leave a message on the answering machine, but her timing was perfect; Professor Redgrave picked up on the first ring. Jenn talked low so as not to disturb Alejandro. He must have heard her anyway. He turned around and waved. Jenn waved back.

"Professor Redgrave? Could I come by your office to talk to you about yesterday's incident with the kiln?" Jenn poised her pencil to write their appointment.

"I have to leave in about ten minutes. Can we talk now?" Her voice rose as she spoke.

"Um, I don't mind. Could you tell me what happened?"

"I was in the studio during class. A student came in and told me there were human bones in the kiln. I didn't believe him, but sure enough."

"How did your students handle this shock?" Jenn scribbled Alex's quote.

"Not well. The student who told me could barely keep himself together. He actually cried. I had to send him to the clinic. The other student got sick. She recovered after awhile, though she was pretty shaken. Haven't seen either one today to see how they're doing."

As Alex talked, Jenn flipped to a fresh page and wrote as fast as she could. "How are you, Professor?"

"Me? I'm still upset. I don't know who would do such a thing. I know all my students and thought no one would pull a stunt like this."

"Is there restricted access to the kiln?"

"No. The kiln is in the courtyard between two buildings. It's mostly hidden. It's open to anyone, but realistically only the ceramics students know it's there."

"Any other students see the bones?"

"Unfortunately, yes. A few students snapped photographs of it. God, I hate cell phones. Since I didn't know what the bones were, I didn't want anyone else seeing them and kept them away." The professor's voice grew more agitated. "Then when I found out they were phony, I didn't want anyone else getting any stupid ideas."

"What were the names of the students who found them? I'd like to talk with them."

Alex paused before responding. "Who are you again?"

"Jennifer Roby, *Lariat* reporter."

A groan emanated from the receiver. "You didn't identify yourself as a reporter." Alex's voice was accusatory. "I'm sorry. I've been instructed not to talk with the press on this issue. This must be off the record."

Disgust washed over Jenn. She smacked her forehead with the heel of her fist. Distracted, she'd gotten ahead of herself. When she called, she only expected to make an appointment, which would have allowed her time to prepare her introductory statement and questions. Instead, she blazed into her questions and hadn't properly identified herself. She took a deep breath.

"I'm sorry, ma'am." Jenn sighed. "I won't print any of this. Thank you for your time." She lightly banged her head on the desk, mortified by her mistake. As she watched her fingers drum the desk, she reviewed her facts. Even after talking with Kerry she didn't have much of a story, particularly since everything the professor said was off limits. She didn't know the names of the other witnesses. She stared at the computer screen before she began to type. Within fifteen minutes her article only needed an edit.

The staff shared one printer next to Alejandro's desk. As the printer hummed to life, he turned around. "Jennifer, how are you today?"

Alejandro Nkuete was an exchange student from Cameroon, a chesty young man, short, with a face of the softest black skin and gentlest eyes Jenn had ever seen. She loved his crisp speech. He pronounced each word with solemn emphasis, as if every syllable was very important and couldn't be relegated to a lesser status. Always upbeat and happy, Alejandro made her feel the same way.

"I am fine, thank you. How are you?" She answered, matching his formal, perfect English.

"Good, very good. Thank you."

"What story are you pursuing today?" Jenn asked.

"Oh, a mystery benefactor gave the track and field club a donation of two million dollars." He nodded his head at Jenn's shocked expression. "Yes, and he donated land outside Colter for the cross-country squad. The coach and the athletic director are thrilled, especially since the short budget has hit the athletic department."

"Wow. Too bad the journalism department doesn't have that kind of luck."

"Yes, it is too bad." Alejandro pulled papers from the printer and culled his story from Jenn's. He handed over her article.

As she set the paper on the desk, she glanced up. "Oh, how's the database coming? Manny told me last week you're close to having it finished."

His bright smile flashed. "Yes. All those hundreds of hours in the haunted basement are drawing to a close. I have spent so much time in that dark place I am losing my complexion."

A snort escaped as Jenn chuckled at his joke. She wouldn't be surprised if he reported someone had been chained to the concrete wall in that dungeon. "After all that data collection, what happens then? What good do you expect to come out of this?"

Alejandro dragged a chair from the neighboring desk and sat down. "I am so excited about this project, for the *Lariat* and the college — for anyone who wishes to conduct research on the old Army post and early regional history. I went through every student newspaper in the archives starting from Issue Number One in nineteen-oh-four. The database has a line for the date, the issue number, key words of every story, and the names of the people involved."

"I can't imagine the work, Alejandro. Doesn't that get old?" She gave a slight grimace.

He shrugged. "The early issues are fascinating, and they had only one small issue a week, rather than the four we have now. I have a greater insight into frontier living, even on this tiny campus and town. Most impressive is how this college changed over the decades, through the world wars, and in social issues."

He leaned forward, shaking a finger as if reminding himself of something. "Actually, my favorite thing was finding some of the original Fort Auger newspapers. They wrote of Indian attacks and some of the illness epidemics. I made a database just of the Army's newspapers."

She smiled, soaking in his excitement. "I love older newspapers! When can I get my hands on it?"

"Well, one parameter of the project is the draft database is not to be distributed." He held up a thumb to start a count. "Step one—where I am now—is to finish putting in the information into the database until the year nineteen eighty-two. Since then, the editor tracks the issues. Step two is to marry those files. That will be easy. Step three is to include the search capability in the college's website. Researchers from anywhere in the world will be able to find the articles, though they will be required to go down to the archives to study the physical copies. The last step is to scan each page and tie that page to the search engine. There is still much to do."

"Gosh, I had no idea it was such a huge project," Jenn marveled. "It's interesting that we have a database on stories going back to the eighties. I never knew that—I never thought about it, actually."

Alejandro laughed. "For such a small newspaper, it is a huge project. It has taken me two years to get this far. Toward that end, Manuel has submitted a grant to construct a reviewing room and add more lights." His face fell. "With the cutbacks, I doubt the grant will be funded. We are not sure if my pay will be funded to finish the project." His eyes brightened. "My stipend is small, but it keeps me in tacos."

Giggling, she said, "You just sign over your paycheck to the Taco Stand?"

"Yes." He stood, pushing the chair back under the desk. "I must go. Have a good evening, Jennifer."

"Thank you, Alejandro." Jenn smiled at him. "You have a nice night, too."

She sat back in her chair and reviewed her article. She made a few changes, recommended a headline of "Prank Horrified Students" then reprinted it. She saved her article to a disk so Manny didn't have to retype it to make any editorial changes.

Jenn checked the time on the clock on the wall. Soon, she'd have to leave for news writing lab. Before heading downstairs to the food court for a quick dinner, she tossed her story and the disk on Manny's desk in the newsroom.

## Chapter 3

The next morning in the college bookstore Jenn grabbed a dreaded "blue book" — the pale blue pamphlet of lined blank pages used for some exams. Since chemistry and finite math classes were before her news writing exam that afternoon, she wouldn't have a chance beforehand to buy one.

As Jenn waited in line to pay, movement caught her eye at the Cosmetique counter near the bookstore entrance. Three young women clustered around the smock-attired specialist who was applying makeup to one of them. All three wore leather jackets, waist-length, and too short for this wintry weather. Their airbrush-tight jeans were tucked into their high-heeled boots. Perfect makeup coated their faces under the bangs brushing their eyelashes.

"Oh my gawd, Adoreé, this is, like, so you."

"Oh, you could be, like, that new artist, Stef-A-Nee."

"Oh, this will make your lips, like, so pouty."

"The girls at Gamma Pi Gamma should try this; maybe they'd be pretty like us."

The young man in front of Jenn turned and caught Jenn's eye. He rolled his eyes. She smiled as she stifled the urge to stick her finger down her throat.

"Your mother would shit if she knew you got that tattoo."

"She'd shit if she knew where!"

Peals of hoots rang at Adoreé's mother's expense. "Gawd, I wished she'd quit hounding me about everything I do."

*If she were gone, you'd wish she could hound you.* Jenn felt a sharp pang in her heart. She'd call Dad tonight, though neither would be able to bring themselves to say much. Her mother's absence touched her every day, but the grief heightened on the anniversary of her last breath twelve years earlier.

Although she tried to hide its complications, her mother's multiple sclerosis had progressed rapidly. Jenn remembered Mom's loss of balance. Then her legs wouldn't work at all. There were times she felt better, but after each improvement the symptoms worsened. Soon bedridden, Lora Rander Roby was too weak to fight off the pneumonia that claimed her life.

Squeals of laughter pierced Jenn's ears and brought her back to the bookstore. She blinked back tears as the young man in front of her gathered up his purchase and walked away.

Adoreé changed her voice to a highbrow English accent. "She asked me if I was sexually active."

"She should have asked how many." The three women shrieked with laughter as they high-fived each other.

Stepping forward to check out, Jenn tossed the pamphlet onto the counter and gave the clerk a quick nod of her head. Not hearing the clerk's "twenty-five cents," Jenn mechanically pushed a dollar forward then gathered her pamphlet and change. She'd have to hurry to be on time for chemistry class in the Learning Center, a building of classrooms on the far side of Barren Lake.

The snowfall had stopped, but the buildings acted as wind tunnels. She pushed against the gale and squinted to keep the snowflakes from stinging her eyes as she looked up at Benjamin Franklin's statue. Tucked under his arm was a drooping stuffed dog. With snow-covered fur, it looked as sad as Jenn felt.

~ * ~

After a morning of chemistry, finite math and news writing classes, Jenn slouched at a long table for a quick lunch at the Popo Agie Dining Facility. The large, south-facing windows flooded the massive dining room with sunlight reflected off the snow. The brightness was a respite from the interminable clouds of the past days.

Picking at her salad, she tried to calm her frazzled mind. She felt good, but dazed, about her blue book loaded with scribbled answers from her news writing exam. "I hate Wednesdays," she muttered to no one. Three classes and one lab crowded that day. She glanced at her watch and, with a sigh, reached for her backpack.

She hurried to her assigned spot within the rows of black cabinets in the chemistry lab then spun the dial on the combination lock on the locker that she shared with three other students. She pulled out her acid-holey lab coat — one of her father's old denim work shirts. The large lab was crowded with workstations and standard Bunsen burners. A vent hood protruded to exhaust hazardous odors, and wall lockers containing myriad vials and jars of chemicals and equipment.

The lab assistant sauntered around the room slapping worksheets for the afternoon's assignment at each workstation. Jenn pulled out her notebook and pencil, and noticed Jake Barton standing at the next counter at his assigned spot. Today he was more blond than brunette, but he wore a black lab coat covered with alien symbols drawn in silver ink. Jake was quick to help those who struggled. Jenn had picked his brain about a number of experiments. Thinly built and always pale, his face was wan, more gaunt that usual. *He must be sick.*

"Hey, Jake."

He looked over and stared at Jenn as if trying to remember who she was. Then he seemed undecided about talking to her. He turned his body and squared off like he wanted to fight. "I read your article."

His flat voice and the severe look in his eyes made Jenn's heart skip a beat. Her face grew hot. She had not yet acquired the thick skin of the older reporters and worried about negative critiques. "Oh?"

"You're wrong."

Jenn gulped and tried to ignore the embarrassment that washed over her. To calm down, she focused on her father's voice in her head: "Listen to another's perspective and learn." She tapped the counter. "My source told me the skeleton was a toy."

"Your source don't know shit."

The lab assistant standing next to Jenn glared at Jake as if to warn him about his language then handed Jenn the assignment sheet. To avoid Jake's glower, she read the assignment: ascertain the factors that affect the freezing of pure water.

Relieved to get away from Jake's intensity and criticism, she concentrated on the exercise. Through the next hour, she set up her freezing plate, dripped a drop of pure water on it then timed how long the drop took to pop, which meant the drop had frozen. To every drop after that, Jenn added more sodium chloride, and repeated the process. The more sodium chloride she added, the longer it took to freeze and at a lower temperature. *Now I see how rock salt and ice in an ice cream maker work!* She continued with more drops until the assignment was completed.

Occasionally she peeked at Jake but was careful not to catch his eye. She cleaned up her workstation and stuffed her dad's shirt back into her locker.

After turning in her assignment, Jake leaned toward her. "You need to correct your story."

No longer embarrassed, anger flooded Jenn. As much as she liked and respected Jake, who was he to make such a statement? "There's no reason to revisit the story."

Jake stepped closer. His eyes flickered with outrage. "I was there. I found it."

## Chapter 4

Clusters of students hurried past Jenn as she waited in front of the large windows at the end of the wide hall. She had the space to herself while waiting for Jake to finish his lab assignment. She stared out the windows to collect her thoughts. In the distance, Benjamin Franklin's statue stood on its step. The stuffed dog was gone, but his Superman cape waved in the wind.

Jake bolted into the hallway and flung his backpack over his shoulders. The chains hanging off his body swung in time with his steps as he hurried toward her. A few thin ones disappeared under his clothing; Jenn tried not to imagine how they were attached. While he walked, he stared Jenn in the eyes. Her face flushed cold. He looked angry, yet oddly hopeful.

"There's no way your article is accurate, Jenn. What I saw was real," Jake declared as he approached her. He stopped talking when another student walked past them to head down the stairs.

Jenn waited for the student to move out of earshot. "I relayed what the detective said. Not to be rude, but do you know more than he does?"

Jake said nothing. He looked at the floor and kicked an imaginary bit.

"Okay, I believe you're convinced the bones are real. We're talking about a kiln, which I know you're familiar with, but what makes you think they're real?" She waited for Jake to answer, but he only fingered a chain hanging from his jacket.

"Can you give me some reason to believe you know anything about fire's effect on a body?" Jenn pushed for an answer. "C'mon, Jake, you gotta give me something."

"I just know a few things about it, let's put it that way."

"Not good enough." Jenn shook her head.

He grimaced. "My uncle owns a crematory in Montana. I work for him every summer." Jake stared into Jenn's eyes and spoke slowly. "I know cremation takes place at about eighteen hundred degrees with a full flame. I know what it does to a body." He swallowed hard. "I've seen what was left after the crematory retort's gas regulator broke and didn't work right." Staring out the window, his voice cracked. "This looked just like those remains."

"So the kiln works just like a crematory?"

"Don't confuse the two. They have totally different designs and functions. The retort's flames are concentrated on the body. A kiln has flames too, but they're more indirect throughout the space." He shook his head.

Jenn studied Jake as he looked down to the floor. The quiet in the building was loud in her ears. "Why didn't you just tell me you worked at a crematorium and you've seen ... things?"

"I don't tell people because all I get are snotty comments like, 'Oh, that explains a lot'." His face turned a dark red. He blurted, "My friend is missing."

"I'm sorry." Jenn said surprised, and hesitated. "What does that have to do with my story? Where did you last see your friend?"

Jake's body swayed. He rubbed his face with his hands, seeming to need every ounce of strength not to explode. "At the Hamilton studio."

## Chapter 5

Her footsteps echoed in the deserted newspaper staff room. The room felt immense when she was alone. Jenn tossed her backpack and coat on the desk, plopped into her chair, and propped booted feet on the desk. After one lab and three classes — one with an exam — her mind needed to rest.

She pulled off the cap and tossed it onto a pile of papers that had balanced on her desk since the beginning of the semester. The pile tipped. She ignored the avalanche until it bumped the photographs of Dad and Grampa. She pushed the papers together and righted the frames. Lounging back, she used her hands like combs and ran her fingers through the platinum cascade, enjoying the sensuousness.

Jenn picked up that day's *Lariat* and inspected her headline: *Prank Horrified Students*. She studied her article then reflected on Jake. When her questioning got too specific about his missing friend, he had walked away without saying another word. An unsettled feeling grew in the pit of her stomach.

"Hey, hey, Jenny Henny Penny."

*Oh, jeez.*

Willy gyrated his way down the aisle between the rows of desks. "Got the scoop on you, Henny Penny." As he closed in on Jenn's desk, he sang a few bars of *I Need a Lover Who Won't Drive Me Crazy*. His off-key rendition desecrated a song by John Mellencamp. Willy directed the song at her, she was sure of it. He delighted in flirting with girls, although rumors flew in the newsroom that he was gay. Jenn doubted that — he just couldn't get a date. She wouldn't have minded his teasing so much, but his leering made Jenn's flesh crawl.

Trying not to curl her lip, Jenn feared Willy had heard comments about her story being incorrect, that real bones lay in the kiln. He'd rub it in that she hadn't investigated enough. Maybe so, but she didn't need to hear it from Willard Warwick, thick-skinned and foul senior reporter.

"What scoop?" Jenn kept her tone flat. The only way to get him to go away was to let him brag and satisfy his ego.

"I'm covering the big event of the decade, Blondie Bomb," Willy bragged. His long teeth and fleshy lips conjured an image of Mr. Ed, the talking horse. She expected him to stammer "Hheellooo, Jjennny."

"I'm to cover the VIPs next week. Whaddya think about that?" Willy bent over Jenn's desk, his face next to hers. The stink of his pizza dinner wafted over her.

"What are you talking about?" Sharpness threaded her voice. *Get on with it, you cretin.*

"You didn't hear? You gotta do better at keeping your eyes and ears open, Henny Penny. Ives! The suits are bringing in *the* President Edward Ives of Colter heritage and Finis Maguire, our fave Senator, to kick off the college's fundraiser. You know — well, maybe you don't — that the college is pulling out all stops to raise money. Apparently, this has been arranged for some time, but the VIPs' visit was kept quiet. All sorts of biggies are comin' from all over the country, and Manny gave me the lead."

He pushed off Jenn's desk. "Why weren't you at the announcement? Even Alejandro was there and he's the sports writer."

With a quiz in finite math, she couldn't skip the class. She hung her head.

"You gotta do better, Jenny, if you want to get ahead in this racket."

Jenn said nothing. Student reporters walked a tightrope of studying and attending class or skipping class to follow up on stories. Manny and Willy had no qualms about cutting class to chase a story. Jenn never skipped classes. If her grades slipped she might lose her scholarships. Then she'd need a part-time job, which would make time management harder and cause a spiral of stress. *Maybe I'm just not a hardcore journalist.*

"Can't have good grades and a good portfolio," Willy chastised her.

*I must have both.*

Willy sprawled on Jenn's desk and did his impression of a dead beetle, flat on his back, arms and legs raised. Jenn pushed away from her desk, her mouth tight in anger.

"So, why did Manny give me the lead, hmmm?" Willy rolled off the desk like a sea cow. He stood too close to Jenn for her comfort. "Oh, that's right. I haven't screwed up a story."

*You scum. How would you know about that?* Furious, Jenn countered. "You mean like you and that cheating scandal at the Delta Omega Gamma sorority?"

Willy leaned down, placed his hands on Jenn's chair arms and pushed his face near hers. Stale pepperoni made Jenn gag. "Those sluts lied."

"You didn't verify their stories."

Willy sighed like a tired parent being pestered by an annoying child. "They corroborated their story between themselves." He relaxed and blew her a kiss. Without another word he danced out of the staff room to the newsroom across the hall.

Jenn felt sick: disgusted from smelling his fatty Italian food breath and fearful that she had written her first inaccurate news article.

Manny interrupted her thoughts as he stepped through the door. "Dee Forbes is really upset about your article," he said in a flat tone.

Disbelief sucked the remaining energy out of Jenn. Her stomach cramped with stress and shame. "Manny, I'm sorry. I don't know why people are having such a problem with this article. What more could I have done? The police verified the bones were phony! There isn't any more to the story." Her face burned hot. She stared at her boots to avoid looking at him.

He dragged a chair from a neighboring desk. A screech echoed through the room as the flat metal feet scraped the floor.

Avoiding his intense gaze, Jenn asked, "I mean, should I print a retraction? An apology? And for that matter, why?"

"That's the weird thing, Jenn." Manny leaned forward with his elbows on his knees, his palms faced out in what Jenn took as confusion. "After Forbes reamed me, I asked her the same things, even about what we can do to make this correct. She said, 'Just drop the whole thing'. I asked her what was wrong with the article. She didn't answer. I said, 'We'll print a retraction if we were wrong,' but she said, 'Just leave it alone. Don't mention it again'. So, case closed."

"Did you tell her Stroll ordered the story?"

"Yep. She said she didn't care—I just shouldn't have printed the story. I said I work for Stroll so if she has a problem with it she needs to take it up with him."

"Oh, I'll bet that made her happy."

"Uh, no."

Jenn gathered her hair into a ponytail. "This makes no sense. All that harassment because she didn't want the prank publicized?"

"Dunno. So … drop it."

Neither said a word as the clock on the wall clacked the seconds.

"Well, okay." Jenn said, relieved to let the dead story molder in its grave, but unsettled with confusion. Jake's adamant accusation of a false story rang in her head. "Do you have another story for me?"

He tugged his goatee before he responded. "Let's give you a break for a few days."

Jenn's hope for redemption sank. She nodded her head, feeling as if she'd been fired but not knowing why.

"Don't worry about it." He abruptly stood and shoved the chair away. "We were ordered to write the story. You wrote it. I printed it."

Manny patted Jenn on her shoulder and headed toward the door. "Take it easy for a couple days. Catch up on your studies. I'll find a juicy story for you to sink your teeth into."

She appreciated the second chance, although she wasn't sure how she had made a mistake.

## Chapter 6

After her morning Intro to Literature class, Jenn tossed her ball cap onto the stack of papers slumping from two days ago. She felt relaxed, yet full of energy. On Thursdays, Lit was her only one class so she was finished for the day.

Leaning back in her chair, she studied her father's picture. The handsome man smiled back. During the Shoshone County rodeo, he wore his long hair loose, like a salt and pepper cape. His black Stetson clamped the wavy hair that framed his face. Jenn thought he was sexy, a wicked thought for a daughter. Women fawned over him. He never returned their attentions. She recalled the stilted telephone call last night with her father. He had barely spoken about her mother.

With a deep sigh, she picked up that day's *Lariat* and studied the headline: *Ives, Maguire to Kick off Fundraiser*. The campus was bustling over next week's event featuring the person who most locals referred to simply as the president of Wyoming. Jenn had never met Colter-born-and-bred President Edward Ives since he had moved to Casper years before. When he ran for president, she, along with practically the entire state populace, flooded Jackson to attend the campaign rally.

Months later, Jenn had shaken hands with the U.S. Senate Majority Leader, Finis Maguire, when he stopped by the campus. A delightful man, Maguire was probably the only politician with a fan club, Jenn thought. A flicker of a smile twitched her lips.

Opinion articles in the national newspapers highlighted the dangers of the close association between President Ives and

Senator Maguire. Jenn rolled her eyes at the writers who invoked the mental image of Ives and Maguire hunkered in a darkened Oval Office while they plotted to burn the Constitution and take over the country.

Jenn stuck out her tongue at Willy's byline. Yesterday the fat gremlin rubbed it in to every reporter how Manny had given him the lead to cover the college's fundraising events, she recalled. That lead would give him access to the president and the senator.

Voices echoed down the hall. Alejandro walked in the staff room and gently set his leather briefcase on his desk. "Hello, Jennifer. How are you today?"

"Hello, Alejandro. I'm doing okay. How are you?"

"I am well, thank you, though the cold and snow are most uncomfortable." He pulled some papers out of his briefcase, stacked them with precision on his desk, and began to type on his computer.

Manny hurried into the staff room. The previous night he had e-mailed the morning's edition to the printer and gone home. Jenn understood him not hanging around in the evening; he hadn't seen his wife and three kids in nearly three days. Long days in class and long evenings in the newsroom prevented everyone at the *Lariat* from having much of a social life.

"Jenn, would you talk to this lady? Believe it or not, she complained to me about your story. Talk to her." At Jenn's dismayed look, Manny threw up his hands. "I don't wanna hear it. I've got to get tomorrow's layout going." Manny pointed at her as he spoke to the woman standing behind him. "This is Jennifer." He disappeared into the newsroom across the hall.

The woman seemed unsure how to proceed. Jenn hid her trepidation, smiled, and extended her right hand. "Hi, I'm Jennifer Roby."

The woman looked to be in her thirties. *A professor? Professor Alexandra Redgrave?*

She clasped Jenn's hand in her own and smiled. "I'm Hannah May. I came to talk to you about your article regarding the incident in the ceramics studio. Your facts are wrong."

Jenn didn't respond right away. She didn't know how to answer. Hannah's proclamation was as adamant as Jake's had been. Jenn shook her head to clear her mind, drew from what she hoped were inherited journalistic skills, and took a deep breath. "Have a seat. What issue do you have with the article?"

"Oh, I believe the skeleton is real."

"Why is that?"

"I saw them."

Jenn sat back in her chair. Alejandro turned around to study Hannah, glanced at Jenn then turned back to his writing. Jenn said, "Please tell me what happened, and be specific."

"I'm taking a ceramics class in one of the old Hamilton bungalows—"

"So you're a student?" Jenn interrupted.

Hannah replied with a small amount of patience. "Yes. I'm taking a class in those hovels on Cheney Street by the Fine Arts building. Alex—Professor Alexandra Redgrave—said one of the kilns needed to be unloaded and asked for volunteers. It was one of those days I couldn't do anything right so I volunteered. So did Jake Barton, and Tiffany Arnold helped."

"Oh, I know Jake. He's in my chemistry class," Jenn interjected and immediately regretted it. She shouldn't divulge information, especially details that could influence the witness.

Hannah nodded. "Jake and I went to the courtyard out back, where the kilns are. The kiln was fired Sunday. By then—Monday—it had cooled enough so we could open it."

"What's this kiln look like?" Jenn interrupted. "Please bear with me. I don't know anything about ceramics."

"It's about six feet tall and almost four feet wide." Hannah stood and spread her arms to demonstrate the height and width and how to open it. "It opens like a huge drawer on rails. That's why it's called a car kiln. Well, you know Jake, how funny he always is. For some reason, Jake was depressed … upset. His hair had grown out and he hadn't dyed it black, so I teased him about it. He didn't think that was funny. We unloaded Alex's heads. Fascinating."

"Heads?"

"Alex's sculptures. She's into heads. How she constructs the eyes is mesmerizing. The sockets are empty, but she has this filament for pupils. Then, a couple of maintenance men showed up to fix the gas line. Alex had warned us that some of our pieces might not come out the way we wanted because the kiln hadn't gotten hot enough. Jake pulled away the last shelf so we could unload the bottom of the drawer."

Hannah trembled. "A skeleton—pieces of one, really—was curled up in there. We both just stared at it. Jake is always sculpting horror pieces. He's good at it, so I asked him if they were his. He said no. I reached in to pick up the skull and move it into the studio. Jake screamed at me not to touch it. Then he said he'd get Alex and left." She rocked slowly in her chair.

"I couldn't stop staring at the skull. It had a hole in the left temple, over an inch across. Things are a blur after that. The police chief showed up. He took our stories. Dee Forbes showed up; she made a lot of phone calls. I watched them for a long time. They would step aside to talk. The chief looked really pissed off. Then when the coroner showed up and tried to work, Forbes kept interrupting her. Before she finally left, Forbes told me again not to talk to anyone about this."

"Why do you think they were real? As I wrote in the article, Detective Kerry confirmed the objects were some synthetic material. It's nearly mid-term and apparently somebody was acting silly."

"They sure looked real to me." Hannah managed a slight smile. "Jake said they were real. I mean, they didn't look like the standard toy skeleton." Her voice grew louder. "The bones were gray, with pinprick holes like real bones. There was an outline of what looked like a body on the floor. What kind of jerk thinks of this sort of thing?"

Hannah clutched her shoulders with her hands, hunched forward, and shook her head. "Ash covered all the pieces, something neither one of us had seen before. All I could think of was I'd been touching cremains. I'm embarrassed to say, I lost it and I threw up."

"How did Jake react?"

"Not well. With his penchant for ghoulish sculptures, I'm surprised at his reaction. The prof sent him to the clinic. He came back to the studio after several hours. Because of the condition of the pieces, he guessed the temp reached over thirteen hundred. I thought about asking him how he knows so much about it, but I figured that's just him."

Jenn pondered Hannah's comments. "The detective, Matt Kerry, said that the heat altered the look of the plastic pieces and fused a film onto the kiln floor. It actually looked like a body had been there."

"Why was the coroner there?" Hannah prodded.

Kerry hadn't mentioned the coroner, Jenn thought. "Probably to confirm that the skeleton wasn't real. The chief can't make that decision."

Hannah seemed crestfallen, disappointed. "But Dee Forbes was adamant about keeping this thing quiet so as 'to not cause panic on the campus'. If that was the case, then why be so concerned about causing panic?" Hannah snorted. Her mouth twisted with disdain. "Toward the end, she said that noncompliance with her directive could cause my dismissal." She shook in her head as if she'd made a sudden decision. "You know, I've been around the block for many years, been in the military, and met people like Forbes before. They're sincere on the outside, but a snake on the inside. She's just too smooth."

Jenn had seen many articles by Forbes. She always seemed to have the college's best interests at heart.

A sudden chuckle spilled from Hannah's mouth. "If this was a prank, the only thing funny about this was watching the chief trying to dust for fingerprints. He obviously hadn't done that in decades. With the snow and the rough surfaces, he left a mess."

She stared beyond Jenn out the window, likely not seeing a thing. Jenn let her think. Soon, her eyes filled with tears before she looked away. "It was terrible. The outline looked like a person had been burned alive ... it was sick, even for a gag." Hannah's lips tightened. "I wished the gas had worked right. Only ashes would have been left. We would have swept them up and thrown them away."

~ * ~

Jenn sat at her desk in the silent staff room, tapping her pencil eraser on the desk. Earlier, before Hannah had left, Jenn repeated that she had reached a dead end with the story. They agreed on one thing: although meant to be funny, the gag scarred the victims.

Hannah and her story seemed credible, yet the whole story was incredible. Jenn had learned early in the semester that Forbes' orders to Hannah and others not to talk to the press were standard orders, hampering reporters' attempts to keep the public informed. College staff members followed the orders in defense of their jobs. Young and inexperienced students also complied, but older students like Hannah often defied those orders.

"What do you think, Jennifer?" Alejandro broke the silence and strolled up the aisle toward her desk.

"I can't help but think Hannah wants the bones to be real. I mean, put yourself in her place. You're minding your own business and you find this horrific thing." Jenn stared at nothing while she talked, immersed in Hannah's point of view. "This thing could give you nightmares. Then you find out through the newspaper that it was, well, for fun. Your pain, your nightmare, means nothing. Get on with your life, you foolish person." She propped her elbows on her desk, her chin on her palms.

With a sudden thought, she tossed her head. "When you were looking at the old newspapers, do you remember any article about a prank that caused the campus police or the city and county officials to get involved?"

He took a deep breath as he stared at the back wall. His eyes moved back and forth as if reading the answer printed there. He shook his head. "There were several articles about jokes. Some required the campus police to investigate, but they caused no real damage, except for that time when Benjamin

Franklin's statue was painted electric purple like an eighties' disco dancer. There was great outrage over that one. But there has never been one that started a major investigation. This one is unique." He paused. "I recall Willard said that Dee Forbes ordered students not to talk to the press when the Commons was on fire. That was not a hoax."

Last month one of the food concessions' grills had a grease fire. The Colter Volunteer Fire Department extinguished the fire quickly enough, but not before the entire building filled with smoke and sent students into the cold streets for an hour. Willy tried to interview witnesses for personal accounts in his article, but his efforts failed since Forbes ordered witnesses not to talk.

Jenn's forehead wrinkled in concentration. "Yeah, now that you say that, I remember, but what does that have to do with this?"

Alejandro leaned against the desk across the aisle and crossed his arms. "As Willard likes to say, we journalists must play the advocate of the devil. If the students are correct, what would the college gain by keeping this silent?"

Whenever he spoke, Jenn loved looking at his teeth, brilliant glossy white surrounded by the velvet black of his skin, but Alejandro's question made her forget his teeth. "You mean, if the skeleton's real?"

"Yes."

"Well, if it was real, let's say an animal, there'd be animal rights advocates all over campus and they'd make us look really bad, like we're animal torturers. But if it wasn't an animal ... then, human?" Jenn's mind went blank, unable to get past the question to the answer. She threw up her hands in annoyance. "This is ridiculous. The police said it was all a prank, so the reason to keep it quiet is so people don't think we're blowing off our studies to pull stunts, plus to keep the number of pranks down."

Alejandro nodded as he headed back to his desk. "Do not despair, Jennifer; one may never know when the story is complete."

## Chapter 7

Colter State College President Paul Hulet sat on his mahogany and leather throne behind his matching monumental desk. Ringing his dark-paneled office in "HQ" sat the college's vice presidents and staff, all awaiting the end of the interminable staff meeting.

Dee Forbes neared the end of her briefing about the U.S. president's itinerary for the next week. Her outfit was of the style that Hulet openly criticized as unprofessional and ugly: a dark gray jacket and skirt suit that looked to be two sizes too small on her slender frame. The jacket's buttons strained under her ample bosom. Her high-heeled pumps had long, pointed toe boxes as if a bell should dangle from each one. He'd ordered her to dress differently for the Ives and Maguire visit. He shuddered at the recollection of her insulted glare.

While she droned on, he forced his stubby fingers to remain still though they twitched to drum on the desk. His eyes shifted to study the results of his recent multi-million-dollar renovation of the Headquarters building, affectionately called the HQ. Satisfied, he was convinced it was rid of any lingering Old West and the former Fort Auger cavalry traditions that had permeated the structure. The small chairs that he had specifically ordered to circle his office carried the expectation that his area would have more presence. With a sinking feeling, he feared the move had backfired, that his large desk and chair made his five-foot-three-inch frame look munchkin.

"That's my briefing for the President's and Senator's fundraising icebreaker and their later visit. I'll sum up the high points."

Hulet checked his groan. She'd repeat to the group, as forcefully as they ignored her, everything she had already told them. He thought back to the office pool he'd discovered under a stack of memos that listed numerous bets on how long her next summation would last. The shortest time on the chart was three minutes; the longest was twenty-three. Rustling noises grew as the group began to sit up and pay attention. He wondered who was keeping the official time when many sneaked peeks at their wristwatches.

"Does anyone have any questions?"

At the lengthening silence, he straightened his gray pinstriped jacket and glared at his staff. Many rubbed their eyes while trying to wake up in the room's warm, stale air. A few tried to stretch without being noticed.

"Thank you, President Hulet." Forbes pronounced his name Hew-LAY. She sat in her chair and crossed her legs.

Hulet—he preferred Forbes' pronunciation—considered himself the greatest fundraiser CSC had ever seen. His chest puffed as he reminisced about how he had personally orchestrated Wyoming's favorite sons and the country's leaders, President Edward Ives and Senator Finis Maguire, to kick off his biggest fundraiser, a month-long series of events that would reach into every wallet in the state.

Only one thing threatened to spoil his plan.

"Last thoughts?"

The staff members leaned forward, ready to make their break.

"Thanks."

Staff members relaxed and headed for the door. "Dee, Tom, Bob—stay behind," Hulet called out to Forbes, Chief of Police Tom Bannister, and the Dean of Students Doctor Robert Stroll. "Close the door." Hulet paused. "Chief, tell me about the murder investigation."

Bannister was as short as Hulet. His thick handlebar mustache and barrel chest, decorated with a neckerchief tied in an outlaw knot, gave the chief more presence than his slight, concave-chested superior. The chief replied, "It's ongoing, Mr. President."

To Hulet's irritation, Bannister either openly refused to say the president's name or he pronounced it the same way as his hometown, HEW-let, Wyoming.

"Insufficient. Give me specifics."

"It's hard to ask the right questions without letting on I'm investigating a capital crime. Leads don't just come walking up to me." The edge in Bannister's voice had a reproachful quality. "I had one suspect who I ruled out. I have no other suspects or leads." Tugging on his mustache in an apparent effort to calm himself, he faced Hulet. "Per your order, Mr. President, no City of Colter police or state investigators were there to assist. I'm not happy with the examination of the scene. It was hopelessly contaminated. Between my rustiness with fingerprinting, the kiln's rough material, the decades-old tools, and the dampness from the snow, the prints I did manage to get were useless. The ground was slushy and pocked with footprints so I couldn't even see anything. The only things of any value were the photographs."

Hulet frowned at the rebuke. "Figure it out." He turned to Stroll. "Except for that imbecilic article about the prank, nothing has been in the newspaper. Keep it that way."

"Excuse me, Mr. President." A grimace creased Stroll's face. "I came up with that story. Several people saw the skeleton, and some managed to snap photos with their cell phones before the professor barred everyone from the scene. Word could spread fast. Declaring the incident a prank was a reasonable explanation. Everyone accepted it and stopped talking about it."

Hulet recalled that Stroll had graduated from Hulett-Gold Camp High School ten years after Bannister. Though Stroll acted as if the moniker was polite, Hulet suspected Stroll was being obstinate.

"Bob, that was very dangerous to make it public." Forbes inched her way closer to the president as if aligning herself with Hulet against him.

Stroll eyed her with a sour expression and narrowed eyes. "It worked."

"Point taken, Bob," Hulet said with an unwavering tone. "But no more. Anything else?"

Stroll took a deep breath as if preparing for battle. "Mr. President, I must advise you that we can't squelch this incident. We must consider the safety of everyone on this campus. We have a duty to notify the public. They have a right to know of anything that can affect their safety."

"As we discussed yesterday, Mr. President, federal law requires us to warn students and personnel about serious crimes," Banister added. "We may have committed a violation just by putting the incident as a prank in the police blotter."

Hulet's face burned at the chastisement. He scowled, in turn, at Bannister, Stroll, and Forbes. "I'm well aware of the Clery Act. We've committed no violation since the law provides an exemption if it's not an ongoing threat to students or employees."

"We don't know if that's the case," Bannister argued. "Until we verify otherwise, we must assume there is an ongoing threat. Second, keeping this crime secret is hindering my investigation. You cannot expect me to solve a major crime without asking hard questions."

"I thought your detective, not you, would be detecting," Forbes said. Her lip curled. "Perhaps he wouldn't have made such a mess of the investigation."

"Don't you drag my detective into this," Bannister snapped and grew red at her mocking tone.

Hulet pushed the fury he felt through his eyes. "The Clery Act has loopholes. If there is clear and convincing evidence that releasing the information will cause a suspect to flee or destroy evidence, then the information may be withheld."

"We don't know if releasing this information will cause the killer to run, or if he'll return to destroy evidence. If anything, it's allowing the killer to go free among us on campus." Bannister's voice grew louder. "And I can't stop him."

"Don't argue with me. There is no danger to the public. I'm convinced of it beyond a shadow of a doubt. I told you

Monday when this thing broke, keep this quiet, at least until all fundraising events are over." Hulet buttoned his suit jacket as if the issue was closed.

Forbes raised her hand as if asking for permission to interject. "This situation can devastate the fundraiser, gentlemen. There's nothing anyone can do for the deceased. The chief is supposedly making every effort to solve the case quietly. If word of this unfortunate occurrence leaks, it will only cause alarm. The president and senate majority leader's visit will be cancelled. Our donors will cancel their attendance and, consequently, their contributions." She tugged on her too-tight jacket. "Everything about this case must be kept silent."

Bannister and Stroll stared at Forbes. Her siding with Hulet on a matter of public safety clearly incensed both men.

"Afraid you won't make your bonus?" Stroll snapped. "We know your contract requires you to meet the college's fundraising goal or it's forfeited."

She turned white. "I'm above such thoughts. This is about the success of the college."

Stroll's eyes rolled.

"Nothing is more important than this fundraiser," Hulet thundered as he slammed his palms onto his desk and stood. "You know the state's oil, coal, and gas revenues have been slashed with the downturn in the national economy. The legislature was forced to slash the budgets of all higher education facilities. I mean all of them were cut, this four-year college, all seven community colleges, and even the university, by twenty percent. That's crippling."

He flipped open the cover of a thick folder and seized a stack of papers. Waving the sheaf like a sword, his voice was tight. "Without at least sixty million dollars from this fundraiser, this college will be forced to terminate programs. Every department has projected the personnel and faculty they'll be forced to furlough or cut back to part-time. Tuition will skyrocket next semester. Many of our students will be forced to stop their education." He slapped the papers on his desk. "The loss of research grants will follow. Some sports programs are projected to fold. The funds shortfall will be catastrophic. We cannot allow that to happen."

Hulet leaned on his desk, breathing heavily. He took his time catching his breath. In a quiet voice, he said, "I know this murder situation is untenable, but keeping it quiet is important, not just for the college, but also for the future of our students and the faculty." He held Bannister's gaze. "Just do the best you can."

Bannister dropped his head to stare at the thick carpet.

Hulet pointed at Bannister and Stroll. His voice rose, clipped with resolution. "This incident shall continue to be confidential, from your subordinates to your superiors and your co-workers. I will release from employment anyone who cannot follow this directive."

To Stroll, he ordered, "In the meantime, I will not hesitate to shut down the *Lariat* if the editor tries to pursue or publish anything more about this story. I don't care what the reason is. Do you all understand?"

The three staff members responded. "Yes, Mr. President."

"Dismissed."

All three turned to head out the door.

"Bob."

Stroll tensed and turned back to Hulet, who waited to speak until Bannister closed the door.

"Bob, do you understand about keeping this story quiet? Fully?"

Stroll nodded his head. "I heard you. I've had some students tell me they may have to drop out next semester. A few of my department heads are worried. But the death of a student demands a notification to the campus."

"No, it doesn't," Hulet murmured. He drew near Stroll, so close that he could smell the dry cleaning chemicals radiating from his suit. The air in the room felt hot, close. "I hate to impose this on any employee." He pressed his palms together. "Besides unemployment, I will rescind my letter of recommendation to MIT for your daughter, and your pretty wife, who is so involved in the college with her nursing studies, will find it difficult to continue here."

Stroll's face went pale. Hulet knew Jo Stroll's master's studies in nursing were fully funded through scholarships and assistantships at CSC's School of Nursing. He guessed she couldn't start over at another college. Stroll had told Hulet that his daughter had a fascination of aeronautics and astronautics, a calling that dictated MIT. When Beth received her acceptance letter from the institute she was so ecstatic, she was already packed. "What do you want of me?"

As if reassuring a frightened child, Hulet smiled a thin, tight smile. "Bob, Bob, relax. All I want is for you to keep this story out of the paper. If you hear anything on the streets, a rumor, gossip, find a way to stop it or derail it. That's all."

Stroll gulped hard and nodded. Hulet put his hand on Stroll's shoulder. "The future of this college, and your family, depend upon you."

## Chapter 8

"What about the First Amendment?" Jenn and Manny exchanged glares. She had hounded him for the past five minutes to allow her to investigate and publish more about the skeleton. Every time Manny positioned his fingers on the keyboard, Jenn interrupted him.

They were alone in the newsroom, which was across the hall from the staff room. Jenn faced him as she sat on an arm of the threadbare couch.

"Don't criticize my decisions, Jenn. When—or should I say, if—you ever get a chance to become editor, you'll have to make decisions about which stories to print and which leads you allow your reporters to follow." Manny's clipped voice told Jenn he was barely managing to keep his anger under control.

"Oh, let me guess; we don't just print the news, we make the news." Jenn imitated her journalism instructor and academic advisor, the hated Edison Sinclair, a sarcastic English goat in tweed.

"When you're the editor, you decide. Plus, we can't print everything. There's just not enough space and we don't have the money for a paper the size of *The New York Times*." Manny turned to his computer in dismissal and started to type.

Jenn sighed. Manny was right. Maybe Jake and Hannah's protests affected her. Perhaps she was too emotionally involved and had lost her objectivity, but being barred from investigating or printing a difference of opinion irritated her.

"Then how about Jake Barton's missing friend? She's important." Jenn prodded.

"I'm not going to get any work done until you go away." Manny pushed back from his computer. "I did some digging of my own. You're not the only investigator here, ya know. She left campus, on her own. She's entitled to do that."

"She quit? Why wouldn't she tell her friend?"

"Maybe they weren't that close. Maybe they had a fight. Maybe it wasn't any of his business."

Jenn granted Manny that thought. She didn't know how close they were. "Who's your source?"

He rubbed his eyes as if to press out extreme fatigue. "Dee Forbes. Will you go away now?"

"Mind if I ask around?"

"Enough, Jenn! You sound like my kids. I do mind. You could be up for the next assignment, and you don't need to traipse all over the place on a non-story. This place'll be jumping soon enough with Ives coming."

Jenn considered Manny's words. The president and senator's visit was a major deal, but his answers were too pat. "The name?"

"What?"

"Her name. What's the name of this friend who left campus?"

Manny, angrier that she seemed to be testing him, turned back to his computer. "Something French."

Jenn spun on her boot heels and headed toward the door. The nagging feeling was building in her gut. She spun back around. "Manny, is Forbes knowledgeable about every student who quits college?"

His fingers froze. He stared at the screen then turned to Jenn with a startled look on his face.

## Chapter 9

After a cup of coffee and a microwaved burrito in the Student Commons, Jenn headed for the Ives Library to search for references for an Intro to Lit assignment. The next winter storm had arrived, or at least its wind had.

She zipped her Carhartt coat and reached to push open the door. The word *Missing* caught her attention. Taped beside the Commons' main entrance, emblazoned on a red-framed poster was *Missing, Sibylle Beaufort*. Glued underneath the text was a photograph of an angelic face framed by dark hair. Long lashes surrounded soft dark eyes. *Missing since Sunday*. This must be Jake's friend, Jenn thought. The French name insinuated this was the girl Manny said quit school and left campus. Jenn made a mental note of the phone number.

Classes had just let out. Trudging to the library, she pushed against the bitter cold and the crush of students heading for the Commons. Her stomach was tense, queasy. She felt unsettled and couldn't figure out if it was the burrito, the feeling her own editor had blown off her concerns, that Jake and Hannah were mistaken, or seeing the photograph of the missing Sibylle. Although something was wrong, she was glad to let the subject drop — for now.

A blast of frigid air sucked the breath out of Jenn. She spun around to chase her cap as it tumbled along the ice until the bill stuck in a snowdrift. She tucked her cap into her coat pocket and held her wind-whipped mane from slapping her eyes and mouth.

~ * ~

Armed with a long list of book references for her Lit assignment, Jenn let the northeast wind push her back to the Commons where she found the staff room empty. As she let her coat fall from her shoulders and draped it over her chair, she mulled the missing poster and popped open a can of soda.

Its purpose made no sense. If Sibylle left campus on her own, why the need for a missing poster? Her only logical conclusion was the young woman ran away and kept it a secret so friends didn't know. Why run away and keep it a secret? Did a terrible fight make her run away? Who put up the poster, and why would Forbes know Sibylle had left campus yet allow the poster to remain?

Distracted by the questions bouncing in her head, she swallowed too much soda and choked. Hacking and wheezing from the acid burn, she managed to get the roiling syrup down the right pipe. She caught her breath and slipped out a bubbly, but silent, burp. Although no one else was in the room, she muttered, "Excuse me."

Restricted from investigating and printing any information about the skeleton or the missing girl, delving further was pointless. If she pursued the story, information might be limited and potentially untrustworthy. The bottom line was the prank just went too far, and its victims weren't happy. Then a girl left campus, and her friends weren't happy.

If the skeleton was real and a conspiracy gripped the college, why wouldn't they want it publicized? What if the girl had been kidnapped? Jenn shook her head. *This is preposterous.* The whole scenario was ludicrous. *The police said the skeleton wasn't real.*

No matter what the answers to these questions were, the bulge in her backpack reminded her she was neglecting her schoolwork. Her focus had slipped since the story had surfaced.

With a sigh, she reached for her backpack.

## Chapter 10

Dry, frigid air burned Jenn's lungs as she squinted. Campus buildings and trees failed to slow the dense fog of horizontal powder obscuring her surroundings. A row of bare lilac bushes provided some relief from the wind, a row long enough for her to catch a breath and brace herself for the next onslaught as she plodded past.

Earlier in the staff room, she had tried to study finite math. Distracted by the skeleton mystery, she read aloud from her textbooks to force herself to concentrate. She dragged out the roll-around blackboard in the staff room to write out formulas. After she confused herself for the umpteenth time, she gave up.

Now, Jenn trudged the two blocks to the college police station. Nearing the building, her nervousness grew. If Manny found out she was questioning the police after he'd ordered her not to, he would chew her out.

To dampen her anxiety, she recalled how her father encouraged her to follow her guts, her instincts. *Sometimes that's all a reporter has.*

Hannah seemed so sure of what she had seen. She and Jenn trusted Jake's knowledge of bones. At the same time, Jenn felt foolish pursuing the issue when the expert had said the bones were imitation. *Maybe this story will end quicker than I thought.*

Jenn entered the tiny foyer, relieved to be out of the fierce wind and blowing snow. She stamped the snow off her boots.

Brida was not around, odd since she controlled her domain with an iron fist. Beside her cluttered reception area, a small room with open French doors framed two dark-suited men setting up equipment. In its prior life as a home, that room must have been a parlor. Papers and campus maps covered the room's other small tables. The advance Secret Service team must have commandeered the office as their command post to prepare for the president's visit next Thursday. Perhaps Brida fled since she was no longer in control.

At the end of the hall, Jenn peeked in Kerry's office. Seated at his desk, he studied a photograph with an intent furrow across his forehead. She stepped back into the hall, removed her coat and scarf, and let her breathing slow from her strenuous walk. She tapped on his door.

Kerry jumped. His face took on an angry cast at the disruption. Seeing Jenn, his face softened.

"I'm very sorry to interrupt you, Sergeant." She hated interruptions while concentrating.

Kerry flipped over the photograph, but not before Jenn saw the blood-spattered figure.

"Is that a current case?" Jenn was shocked at the flash of brutality. The missing Sibylle entered her mind.

"Uh, no. I'm assisting on a case from another town." Kerry leaned on the photograph, arms crossed as if guarding against Jenn snatching it. "What can I do for you?"

"I'd like to talk to you about the alleged fake bones." *Yeah, that'll tick him off.*

The sergeant eyed Jenn, and she wondered if he would tell her to leave. After all, the incident was over so why waste his time?

"What makes you think there's more to this incident?" Kerry countered. His poker face gave no hint of surprise.

"Two witnesses convinced me the skeleton was authentic," Jenn responded, mindful not to give away too much.

He leaned back in his chair, eyes bright, and he stroked his cleft chin. "If they were genuine, have you considered they might have been animal bones?"

*So the bones were real.* Jenn's heart beat faster. Even if they were animal bones, the police had lied to the press. That alone was worth a story. She swallowed hard.

"What animal ... were they?" Jenn's voice broke and squeaked, but she barely noticed because she concentrated on what Kerry said.

"Can you keep a secret?" He glanced at the open door as if to assure himself no one lingered in the hall.

Jenn squinted with concentration. An epiphany nearly blinded her. "You're talking to the press on the record. No."

Kerry's eyebrows raised in surprise, apparently impressed. "Okay. The county coroner determined ..." She leaned forward in anticipation. "That the bones were synthetic ... a fraud."

Jenn felt like she'd been spanked.

"She determined after examining the bones that it was just a prank." He leaned back in his chair, seemingly satisfied he had given her the whole story. "Gee, now where have I read this information before? Oh, yes, in the newspaper, in your article."

Sarcasm would have dripped off his chin, but he swallowed first, Jenn thought. She didn't know whether to laugh from the joke, cry from the humiliation, or get angry about his teasing. "Sergeant, you're mocking me. I don't appreciate it."

"Miss Robin—"

"Roby."

"Miss Roby, I told you all this before. Nothing has changed. The bones were a replica. What is it that you want?"

*I don't know, but this isn't it.*

Kerry seemed to empathize with Jenn's hesitation. "Tell you what, if you must pursue this and verify what was found, see Susan Hawley, the Shoshone County coroner. She's the one who identified them."

*Trust but verify.* "I'll do that. I'm curious, Sergeant, did anyone order you to keep this incident quiet?"

He scooped up the photo in a sign of dismissal. "Now you're getting into departmental policy. That I won't discuss."

"So you're refusing to answer my question?"

It was Kerry's turn to get angry. His lips tightened to a slit and his eyes squinted. "Don't twist my words with your journalist holier-than-thou crap. We have standards here, something the press would do well to emulate. We follow protocol and standard operating procedures, period. That means we don't blab everything to everybody. There are times and circumstances when we keep our findings quiet, even from the press." Kerry paused to catch a breath then pushed back into his chair. "Interpret that however you wish."

Jenn knew she had overstepped an invisible boundary and wished the floor would open up and swallow her. She couldn't meet his eyes.

In a welcome distraction from her discomfort, a dark-suited man walked into Kerry's office without knocking. He stepped behind the sergeant's desk, draped a map over the paperwork, and waited, impatient for Jenn to leave.

The sergeant grew ruddier. He clenched his teeth. "Now, if you'll excuse me ..."

"Thank you for your time, Sergeant."

~ * ~

Braced against the wind to keep from becoming airborne like a small kite, Jenn felt as if she was slinking back to the staff room with her tail between her legs. Caught up in a journalistic fervor of asking probing questions, she had baited him. She had ignored that the police, in order to protect their investigations, were restricted from speaking their minds. Perhaps an apology and an explanation were in order. For now, Jenn didn't dare pester him again.

At her desk in the staff room, she thumbed through the doodle-defaced phone book. She punched in the number. "To reach Susan Hawley, the county coroner, leave a message. For urgent assistance, dial ...," intoned her answering machine. Like many sparsely populated counties in Wyoming, the county coroner's position was part time, requiring the coroner to have another job for their livelihood.

Jenn dialed the number from the message. Hawley owned and operated the Hawley Funeral Home southwest of campus. Her receptionist responded, "Mrs. Hawley would prefer to meet you in the coroner's office for your inquiry, but because of events in the funeral home she'll meet you here." She penciled in Jenn for ten o'clock the next morning.

She stared out the window to watch the horizontal snow obscuring Fremont Hall across the street. She felt relieved and looked forward to speaking with the coroner, her ultimate source. Afterward, this whole business would be put to rest.

She noticed the time and groaned. *I need a shower in the worst way.* Glancing out the windows again, she imagined the walk to the dorm. With a sigh, she layered on her winter clothing and let the wind push her to Morris Hall, her dormitory east of the Commons.

# Chapter 11

An hour later, Jenn trotted up the stairs to the staff room. The dampness on her skin from the hot shower vanished once the cold, dry air permeated her coat.

The door stood open with Alejandro editing some pages with his back to Jenn. Quietly, she pulled off her coat, scarf, and cap. He turned. "Hello, Jennifer!" His brilliant white teeth flashed from across the room.

"Hello, Alejandro. How's the sports world going?" Jenn draped her coat and scarf over her chair.

"Oh, very well. The track team is trying to determine how to spend their inheritance."

Jenn laughed. "That's great. Those sports club members have to work so hard at fundraisers just to practice their sport. It's great that someone was so generous; one less bother for them."

"Yes. They are most happy." Alejandro turned back to his editing.

She hefted her backpack to her desk, rifled through it and pulled out her Intro to Lit notebook. Finally, some quiet time to write, she thought. Jenn preferred to study here rather than her dorm room. There, the small room's sterile atmosphere felt isolating and confining, even if her roommate, Mya Cass, was in the room. When she felt lonely, she'd open the door to the dark hallway to feel as if she were a part of the world, but the open door invited boys to stop by. Their flirting was unwelcome and distracting. They were forever hanging around.

Here in the staff room, she felt a belonging with the few like-minded students and could watch the world through the giant windows. Alejandro, like most of the reporters, was considerate and didn't try to engage in chitchat while others tried to study or write. The exception was Willy. With him around, any pretense of consideration turned into the proverbial Friday night in a fraternity. Regardless, returning to the staff room was more appealing than remaining in her dorm room, even if it meant bracing against a blizzard and the possible appearance of Willy.

While the ponderosa pines around the Commons and Barren Lake swayed in a hypnotic rhythm, she thought about her day. During Lit class that morning she managed to capture most of the lecture, but her mind slipped away a few times to think of questions for the coroner the next day. There was only one important goal: to confirm that the skeleton was man-made. With that, she could satisfy her intuition, put this whole incident to rest, and not be chewed out anymore by Manny or Sergeant Kerry — a triple bonus.

This evening, she'd catch up on her studies come hell or high water. Tomorrow, she'd head home to Dad and Grampa. Once there, she wanted no pressure to study, no stress to do anything but enjoy her time at home.

~ * ~

With the last math problem solved, Jenn rubbed her eyes. She had only one more subject — chemistry — to catch up on. Her stomach growled loud enough that Alejandro must have heard it. She tossed her math book and papers into her backpack.

"Alejandro, would you like me to pick up anything for you to eat?"

"Thank you, no." He always had apples nearby.

The food court was quiet and almost deserted. Her boot thumps on the marble-like floor echoed in the cavernous space. She microwaved a burrito and grabbed a soda then headed back up the stairs, two at a time, to eat her meal before it got cold.

She sat at her desk, propped up her feet, and unwrapped her supper. She imagined the bicycle ride home tomorrow. The mercantile's clerk had reported that the storm would pass tonight then there would be clear skies tomorrow. *Great.* She'd be able to ride her bike home, a trip of only thirty-two miles, though a mountain pass of eighty-five hundred feet bisected the route. She'd pack her panniers light to make the ride a bit easier. That Jenn would ride a bicycle such a distance was an act that brought stares and guffaws of incredulity from many folks, which made Jenn respond in kind. What was wrong with bicycling everywhere, she would ask. *People have gotten so lazy.*

By the time she wadded her empty burrito wrapper Jenn felt great. Sated, sipping a cold soda, she had one last topic to study tonight. Tomorrow morning she had a short meeting with her academic advisor, and after finite math class, the coroner would put her mind to rest. Then she could head home and enjoy Dad and Grampa's company.

"Forget Ives and Maguire!"

*Oh, jeez.*

Willy strutted up the aisle, arms up and wide in a victory salute. Jenn wasn't sure if he acted this way because he had an audience in the staff room or if he acted this way when he was alone too. Probably the latter, she thought, if for no other reason than for practice in case someone happened to see him.

Alejandro watched over his shoulder. His face was expressionless. What would a foreign exchange student think of Willy's antics, she wondered.

"You can't believe the lead Manny just gave me."

*If Willy had tail feathers he'd shake them.*

"C'mon, guess."

"No," Alejandro and Jenn said.

"Okay, fine, you killjoys." He sat on his desk in the center of the room, crossed his legs as if he were a sexy secretary sitting on the boss' desk, and looked from Jenn to Alejandro, about to burst from the tension.

Manny stepped in the staff room, leaned against the doorframe, and snickered. "Spill it!"

"This morning, the cops arrested a girl in Morris Hall … for prostitution!" He threw his head back and laughed. "The cops found hundreds of dollars in cash in her closet. They arrested her roommate for pandering. Apparently, they had an arrangement. The roommate would leave whenever there was business. For keeping her mouth shut, she got part of the, um, wages."

"How was she found out?" Alejandro's hand covered his mouth, an action that Jenn took as disgust at the incident.

"The hooker would probably still be in business, but apparently some of her hall mates got tired of all the noise and traffic and complained. Can you believe it? She got caught in a sting operation with Kerry."

Willy touched his fingertips to his chin in feigned wonder and leaned toward Jenn. "I wonder how Kerry learned what he knew. Practice?"

Jenn didn't know what mortified her more: the mental picture of Kerry doing whatever with a hooker, the possessive feeling she had when Willy invoked Kerry's name, or worse, that Willy might know it. With a start, she realized what he had revealed: prostitution in the dorm—her dorm. "Which floor?"

Willy pulled out his notes, "Third. Room three-eleven."

"You live in Morris Hall, yes, Jennifer?" Alejandro asked.

All three men turned to her when she didn't answer right away. "I'm in three-oh-three." Jenn's eyes widened with shock. "That's down the hall!"

All three men hooted, and Manny and Willy urged her to tell her story. Jenn's mouth opened, but nothing came out. Finally she blurted, "Jeez, I just thought she was popular."

To the howls of laughter, Jenn covered her face with her hands. "I mean, just popular." The hoots rolled into belly laughs. She gave up; her foot had wedged further down her throat and she choked on it. Better to leave it alone, so she stopped talking.

"Is that it? You thought she had lots of friends?" Willy laughed and tried to catch his breath, his face purple.

Jenn considered herself a good girl, naïve maybe, but not a prude. "Ya know, I'm a little bit busy. Plus, the more boys that hung out up there, the noisier it was and the more I couldn't stay in my room. It was just too noisy." The more she talked the huffier she felt.

That raised more hooting. "What kind of noise?" Willy said, half teasing. He raised his right fist and pumped it.

"Talking, playing music, sometimes they'd play hall golf as they hung out."

"Something to do while they waited their turn?" Willy sneered.

"Did you know these gals?" Manny asked.

Jenn shook her head. "I don't know most of the students in the building, let alone on the floor. The staff room is my hangout. I usually go to the dorm to sleep, shower, and wash clothes. There are fewer irritants that way, what with noise, music, and interruptions." Apparently a brothel down the hall was part of the problem. She wondered if it would be quieter now. Come to think of it, the hallway was deserted this evening, she thought.

"So you didn't hear anything or know anything more than horny guys hung out in the hallway?" Willy pressed a hand to his side to relieve an apparent cramp.

Jenn shook her head. She'd only make things worse by explaining. They wouldn't understand or try to listen to her viewpoint. The story was too juicy to take seriously right now.

"They didn't get much for their money if that's all the noise they made," Willy leered.

"I hope your story will be more professional than how you're acting now," Jenn barked, tiring of the innuendoes. The thought of what was going on yards from her room made her uncomfortable. Dad and Grampa had class. While they would be shocked, she thought, they wouldn't get foul or obscene about it.

"Oh, you're such a puritan," Willy said. "Besides, see, for all your worries about earning money for school, here's an option for you. Just change the light bulb outside your room to red, and we'll be able to find out if you're a real blond." Willy leaned over and flicked her loose hair. Jenn gasped and knocked away his hand.

"That is enough, Willard. You have gone too far," Alejandro almost shouted. "Jennifer is too smart and too good for such things." He stalked down the aisle to Willy, his eyes squinting in anger. "Be ashamed. That woman and those men should be ashamed."

"Yes, that's enough," Manny said, the edge in his voice directed at Willy. "Write the story and get it to me by early evening."

Jenn was grateful for Alejandro's defense. Grateful that he had noticed and stood up for her, Manny should have stepped in sooner.

Chastised and with his bubble deflated, Willy nodded. Manny kept his focus on him, waiting for more. Willy turned to Jenn. "Sorry, Blondie Bomb, guess I got carried away."

Jenn nodded in acknowledgment, but she certainly would not forget. She caught Alejandro's eyes and gave him a small smile in appreciation. He nodded and walked back to his desk.

Satisfied that the sordid topic was dead, professionalism restored, and resigned that Willy's "sorry" was the most Jenn would get out of him, Manny walked out the door.

Jenn dug in her backpack and searched for her chemistry book and notebook. She wasn't ready to study, but the appearance of doing something might make Willy go away.

"So," Willy approached her desk as if changing the subject would make his offense vanish in thin air. "What's the story on this?" He snatched the third picture frame off her desk. Jenn reached to grab it back; he didn't deserve to hold such a treasure, but he was too quick.

"That's from my great-grandfather." Jenn stood up and reached again for the frame, but Willy held it too far out of her reach as he tried to study the words.

"He wrote this?"

"Right after the Second World War, when Grampa left for journalism school," Jenn said.

Alejandro walked down the aisle. Perhaps he could retrieve the frame or at least get Willy to stop waving it around like a keep-away ball. Willy turned to see Alejandro approach and calmed down. "All right, all right." He read the contents. He then humphed and set it down, too hard, on her desk—an act that violated her treasure. "It's a new world, Jenny."

"Only if you allow it." Jenn wiped off imaginary residue from Willy's hands before placing the frame in its position next to Grampa's photo.

Willy ignored Alejandro's presence and sat heavily in his chair. Alejandro turned to see the frame. She handed it to him; he would appreciate its sentiments.

Alejandro read aloud the handwritten words scribed in Great-Grampa's copperplate.

*"The Constitution of the United States, First Amendment: "Congress shall make no law ... abridging the freedom of ... the press ...*

*Freedom of the press: a liberty with the utmost responsibility that bestows the means to alert, influence, condemn or pardon. This power is not for the conceited or the corrupt, but for the humble and the virtuous. Your Father."*

With tears in his eyes, Alejandro handed it back. To Jenn, and as much to Willy, Alejandro said, "Great-Grandpapa was a wise man, Jennifer. Americans take such a right for granted because it is all you know. Those who do not have such a birthright can only wish for it. Others can only dream to present the truth and to receive it. To use such a power wisely is a gift as great as the power itself. I am so happy, Jennifer, that your Great-Grandpapa understood, and that you understand and appreciate such a wondrous thing."

## Chapter 12

The hallway was bare except for the stained metal chair that Jenn squirmed on. It stood outside the office of her academic advisor, Edison Sinclair. The hallway's radiators were on full heat to combat the near-zero temperatures outside. The radiators were winning this battle. She unbuttoned her sweater.

Every semester, students met with their academic advisors to discuss their next semester's classes. Jenn gripped a spreadsheet outlining her future courses through graduation.

She checked the time: ten minutes after her eight a.m. appointment. Sinclair had a reputation for being late to class and for letting class out early. Students learned to show up late too. The joke was "if you're late to class and the prof's not there to know, are you really late?"

Jenn pushed back in the chair, balancing on the two back legs. Reflecting on her argument with Manny and her conversation with Kerry yesterday, the question *why* kept popping into her head. Why didn't Forbes give a reason the article upset her? Why couldn't Kerry give specifics about the skeleton, rather than pass her on to the coroner? Why were there no straight answers for seemingly easy questions? *Maybe there weren't any.*

The door handle to Sinclair's office turned so suddenly, she started, flailing her arms to keep the chair from slipping out from under her. The advisee leaving Sinclair's office did not look happy. He ignored Jenn, flung his backpack over one shoulder and stomped down the hall.

"Come in, my girl. Be quick," a thin voice called from the office. Heart pounding, Jenn grabbed her backpack and stepped into the office of Edison Sinclair.

Also known as E. S. because he placed his initials beside his scrawled grade on papers, Jenn's advisor and teacher was voted Most Hated in her Popo Agie Communications Honor Society. Years before, some wag came up with a more descriptive use of his initials: Ebenezer Scrooge. Sinclair could, if he were an actor, play the character without virtue of makeup or wardrobe. One thing prevented him from playing Scrooge incarnate. He lacked the character's warmth.

Jenn avoided talking with Sinclair because his cantankerousness made her nervous, and her nervousness amplified her mistakes around him. Sinclair was also the department's First Amendment authority, a pit bull with reading glasses for the right to print whatever the newspaper editor desired, regardless of news value or whom the information might hurt. His mantra insisting that reporters make the news was echoed by many in the journalism department.

The first time Jenn heard his motto and every time he repeated it in Intro to Journalism, hatred, like bile, rose in her throat for Sinclair and those of his ilk. Raised in an old-school journalistic family, she had learned to state the facts then let readers make up their minds, a philosophy that made Walter Cronkite the quintessential journalist. He was her idol.

In Sinclair, Jenn noticed a bravado, a distortion of the heart and spirit of the First Amendment that sickened her. He fed the hungry minds of the most-liberal journalism students a diet of "the importance of reporting is to publish. The rest be damned".

Jenn said nothing as she handed Sinclair her list of next semester's classes and a copy of her projected class schedule through to graduation.

"What's this?" Sinclair flipped through her carefully plotted pages almost with contempt.

"That's ... that's the classes I want to take next semester and ... and that's my classes to ... to fill out my graduation requirements." Jenn's fists clenched from tension.

"You know what's best?" Scrooge squinted over his spectacles that perched on the very tip of his nose.

"Um, well, the college bulletin states that it's the student's responsibility — "

"I'll decide what's best."

While Sinclair squinted through her class list for the next semester, Jenn's eyes swiveled as she took in his overstuffed bookcases and stacks of leather-bound books covering the floor. Her nose twitched at the thick scent permeating the room — like the old folks' home her neighbor Mr. Stephens had moved into years before.

"Fine." Sinclair filled in Jenn's enrollment form, signed it and jotted the computer pass code in the margin. He shoved her form to the edge of his desk. Jenn's silent sigh of relief was cut short when Sinclair tossed her long-term projected list in the trash.

*You bugger.* She picked up her form and wanted to retreat from the room, but delayed.

"Now what?"

"Um, Mr. Scroo — Sinclair, I have some ethics questions, if you have a minute."

Sinclair made a point of sighing and looking at his watch. She watched his little act and knew she'd cornered him. Since Jenn's advisement took so little effort, he'd have time to discuss her dilemma and still be ready for the next fearful student.

"So you didn't pay attention in Ethics class?"

"Yes. I mean, no. I haven't had your Ethics class yet. I pay attention in all my classes, and in yours last semester, Intro to Journalism." Jenn stammered and offered her proof. "You gave me an A."

"I give every student an A."

She'd heard that, probably so he wouldn't receive complaints from students. She was guaranteed an A in his classes, but she still had to sit through his lectures, a misery akin to placing an electrode on each ear and plugging the cord in an outlet.

Jenn considered deserting the odorous room. Being in Scrooge's presence was exhausting and a displeasure she didn't need, but she reminded herself of her dilemma. Maybe the little troll had something to offer, she thought.

"Mr. Sinclair, I wrote an article in the *Lariat*. The bones in the kiln? You might've read it."

"Adequate reporting."

Jenn wasn't sure why, but she took that as a compliment. "I have my doubts about the conclusion concerning the bones."

Sinclair had an almost interested look on his face. "Oh?"

"Well, I've had complaints from those who found the bones that there was no way they could be counterfeit. They were very specific in what they saw. Both the witnesses say the coroner was there. Public relations told everyone not to talk with the press."

Jenn warmed up her list of reasons. Sinclair propped up his fingers under his chin in feigned interest.

"The *Lariat* editor refuses to let me print a story that things don't add up." Jenn took a breath and talked faster. "The police detective refuses to discuss the case, but tells me to go talk to the coroner. Why should I have to talk to the coroner about phony bones?"

Jenn rattled off her last item then waited for the explosion she knew would come, exposing what a fraud and a twit she was. Sinclair eyed Jenn through narrowed lids. She fidgeted and twirled a white tendril that had escaped her cap.

"So, you expect your editor to print what you demand, regardless of good judgment."

Jenn felt she had been slapped.

"Contrary to the professional's opinion, your witnesses say a skeleton is real so you decide there must be a conspiracy."

The air from her ego's balloon started to seep out.

"And Public relations telling witnesses to keep an embarrassing incident quiet is unusual."

Deflated, Jenn gulped and stared at the floor.

"I see your quandary."

If sarcasm were water, Sinclair had gills because he swam in it. Jenn hated to admit it, but she needed his bluntness. Of course witnesses were notoriously unreliable. Perhaps the emotionalism of the event meant the witnesses believed the worst. While painful, she needed the clarity that Sinclair provided. Sometimes a contrary response put things into perspective. Though she tried not to take it personally, his comments still hurt.

"Anything else?"

Jenn hated to argue. She knew he was right, but the gnawing in her gut hadn't stopped. She took a big breath and had to decide which words to use. The right ones could mean more insight. The wrong ones meant a scolding. "I still think there's something here."

The silence hung heavy in Jenn's ears.

"I'd like to track down more information, and compare the witnesses' opinions and the professionals' facts."

Sinclair's beady eyes never wavered from Jenn's face.

"Honest, Mr. Sinclair, the way the detective talked and told me to refer to the coroner ..." Jenn's voice trailed off. She waited for the waterfall of mockery. Westminster chimes donged the half hour from somewhere in the cluttered room.

"Few ... have the fortitude to question ... to seek, too busy chasing the big byline. Take care when making your comparison of facts not to divulge information between witnesses and sources. Interviewing is strictly a one-way process, my girl."

Feeling that Edison Sinclair — now no longer Ebenezer Scrooge — gave his implied approval to her opinion and his tacit consent to pursue her instincts, Jenn sat up straight and almost smiled.

## Chapter 13

Jenn squirmed in her seat during finite math in the School of Agriculture's amphitheater. The auditorium's high ceilings and broad expanses swallowed sound and any intimacy. She felt too intimidated to stand up in the vastness and shout a question to the professor. At least this location was temporary. The class was normally held in the Business Building, but the wing was closed for emergency furnace repairs.

The best part about using the Ag's auditorium was watching the young men from the state's farms and ranches walk the halls. These young men, fit and barrel-chested, wore tight Wranglers adorned with dinner-plate belt buckles. The jeans showed off their rounded backsides. She never openly ogled them, although she wanted to. They were the hottest things on campus, and they made her weak in the knees.

Today, she barely noticed them. Buoyed by Sinclair's opinion and apprehensive about her meeting with the coroner later, Jenn struggled to focus on the formula scrawled on the mobile blackboard.

She only needed to confirm the bones were not real, yet she worried there were other questions she should ask while the opportunity presented itself. Though nervous about violating Manny's directive, she was convinced she needed to follow up, if only to assure herself of the moral victory that her story was correct and that she could give a better answer to Jake and Hannah.

The professor finished his lecture. She jotted in her notebook the next week's assignment, layered on her winter clothing, and trudged to the bike racks. In winter, Jenn's combination mountain-road bike was the only one in the rack.

She removed her ball cap and pulled on her knitted cap. Her bicycle helmet didn't fit over the knitted cap so she tugged on the straps to lengthen them. Feeling like a Las Vegas showgirl with a towering headdress balanced on her head, she eyed the mounds of snow heaped by the plows that cleaned up since yesterday's storm. She'd have to push the bike as much as she rode it.

The plows had removed much of the snow from the streets. What was left, vehicles had packed to ice. Jenn gingerly pedaled her bike. Cheap and quick transportation, her tawny bicycle named "Cougar" never let her down.

Cougar also let Jenn feel a closeness to her mother. Jenn's mother had taught her to ride her first bicycle, a pink Schwinn with silver streamers fluttering from the handlebars. They lived on the dirt Ranch Road; the rocks threw her off balance, and she fell often. Mom would pick her up, clean out bits of dirt from her skinned knees, and encourage her to try again. Now every time she pushed off a curb on Cougar, she felt her mother's hand giving her a push.

The wind had stopped, allowing the cold to settle. When Jenn breathed in hard through her nose, her nostrils stuck closed. To her that meant the temperature was ten degrees or less.

Snow muffled the vehicle noise although traffic clogged the street. She took care while she pedaled. Decades-old cottonwood trees with outstretched limbs prevented the sun from warming the street. Throughout the winter, snow and ice built up several inches thick. In front of the Hawley Funeral Home she zipped up the driveway too fast. Both wheels squirted out from under her. Feeling foolish and with a quick look around to see if anyone noticed, she brushed the muck from her jeans. At the front door, Jenn locked up Cougar with her cable and stepped inside.

While she removed her coat and helmet, Jenn found Hawley's office unoccupied near the entrance. Through open double doors, she glanced into a side room—a small chapel. A plain casket, with its upper-half lid open, held a brown man in his eternal pose. The room was set up for a viewing and chairs lined the walkway, yet it was unoccupied by anyone living. No flowers decorated the room. On a pedestal, a guest book lay open, its pages blank.

"Are you here for Mister Ramirez?" A voice jolted Jenn from staring into the room. A woman, sixty-ish, plump, wearing a black pantsuit, stood in the hallway.

Jenn's mouth flitted in a quick smile. "I'm Jennifer Roby from the college's newspaper, the *Lariat*. I'm looking for Susan Hawley, the county coroner. I have an appointment."

"I'm Susan." The woman raised her hand toward the office across the hall. "I've wondered if someone from a newspaper would contact me."

Jenn's forehead wrinkled as she tried to grasp Hawley's meaning. They sat down in a sparsely furnished office. Catalogs of casket manufacturers lined one bookshelf. A rack of condolence cards and self-help coping books overflowed next to the desk.

"I prefer to conduct coroner business at the coroner's office, but I'm buried with events here and my assistant director is out on an emergency. I hope you don't mind meeting here."

"Oh, no," Jenn said. "I just appreciate you fitting me in. I'm here about the skeleton that was discovered Monday on campus at one of the Hamilton bungalows. A few witnesses told me you were there. I just need to confirm that the staging of the bones was a prank." An excitement flowed through her for reaching the end of her search.

The statement seemed to confuse Susan. She leaned forward and fixed Jenn with a stern, yet quizzical look. "What do you know about this incident?"

Not expecting such a response—a question—Jenn blinked. Now she felt confused. Why would the coroner ask what she knew before answering a simple question? Fear flashed through Jenn's mind that Susan was part of her imagined conspiracy. She pushed aside the thought. "My witnesses are convinced that the bones were real. The police detective told me you established it was just a joke. I just want to confirm that's the case." She pulled her note pad and a pen from her backpack.

"The detective, Sergeant Kerry, told you that?"

"Yes, ma'am." Jenn feared she'd said too much. Sinclair had warned her against sharing information between sources. She shook off the warning. *Kerry was a public source, and he spoke on the record.*

Susan reached into her newspaper recycle bin. The stack threatened to fall over as she rifled through individual papers. She found the edition she sought and, with a snap, showed the *Lariat* with Jenn's byline and article. "This is you."

Embarrassed but not sure why, Jenn nodded.

Susan placed the newspaper on her desk and stared at it. After several seconds, she looked at Jenn as if deciding what to say. In a soft voice, Susan said, "What you were told and what you wrote were not correct. It was not a prank. The bones were real. They are human."

# Chapter 14

"Cup of coffee?"

More automatic than desired, Jenn nodded, still too stunned to speak. Susan headed for her credenza, looking relieved that she had started the coffee pot earlier.

"Cream and sugar?"

Jenn shook her head. Susan placed the steaming cup in front of Jenn and sat down with her own mug.

At Susan's announcement, Jenn's mouth worked, but nothing would come out. Ineffective thoughts and feelings ricocheted in her head; she couldn't sort them out or collect herself.

"I know. I know," Susan said, reassurance in her voice.

"Why would they lie?" Jenn muttered. "And about a real person?"

Susan took a deep breath and glanced up at the wall behind Jenn. "I can't answer for the detective. When I was called to campus and I had checked the remains, I was told the college had information that an announcement of this incident would interfere with the investigation." Susan took a sip from her cup. "She assured me, in this case, the police would come to a resolution faster if I were to conduct my investigation quietly because they expected the killer to flee if I divulged the information. Also, informing the public would panic the campus and cause some parents to remove their children from school."

"Who told you to keep this quiet?" Jenn flinched as the coffee burned her tongue.

"Dee Forbes."

"Public relations," Jenn said with a touch of sneer in her voice.

"Yes, she told me to pass my findings only to her or to the college chief of police."

"But now you're telling me?" Jenn's comment was a question. *Why would the coroner violate a confidentiality request?*

The coroner bristled. "Foremost, I'm an elected public servant. I'm not a college employee. Second, as such, I won't lie to a citizen or tolerate being ordered to, and third, I don't publicize my findings anyway." Susan paused to take a sip of coffee. "Now, that being said, if the police chief believes the information legitimately needs to be kept quiet for public safety or not jeopardize an investigation, I would comply and simply say 'no comment' when asked about it by a reporter."

"Mrs. Hawley—"

"Susan."

"Thank you. Susan, why did you tell me, the press? Forbes said to keep this quiet," Jenn started to stammer. "I mean, I really appreciate your telling me, but I'm only wondering …"

"That's a good question, Jennifer." Susan paused. She appeared to struggle with herself as she swirled the cup and watched the coffee spin. "Off the record, after I initially inspected the bones, I reported to Chief Bannister that I believed they were human. He and Forbes stepped aside and powwowed in private. That's when Forbes came up to me and told me to keep it quiet for the reasons I mentioned earlier. The police chief didn't say anything. Frankly, I don't work for her nor am I under the college's thumb. As far as her demand that I pass information only to her or the chief, I don't plan on telling her anything. The chief is who I work with."

"Can you tell me your findings?"

"I just received the preliminary report. The remains were seriously degraded; human, female from the shape of the pelvis, likely between thirteen and twenty-four. From what little evidence was available, the manner of death was blunt force trauma caused by an unknown object. Likely, she died instantly."

*Hannah said the skull had a hole in it.*

"Obviously, I ruled her death a homicide."

Jenn trembled, but remained focused. "Was she a student? Can you tell me who the victim is … was?" Jenn hoped she didn't recognize the name.

"I won't speculate on the status of the victim, but I have information on her identity. We're still tracking that down, so for right now she's a Jane Doe."

"Who's working on finding out?" Jenn jotted frantically.

"A forensic dentist will confirm the identity." Susan set down her cup.

"Would that individual notify the newspaper?

Shaking her head, Susan said, "Publicity is not their job either."

"Do you have any idea how long before you identify her?" Jenn jotted quickly and flipped to a clean page.

Susan tossed the newspaper back on the stack. "They believe by Tuesday they'll know. We have many clues, thankfully."

"Are you aware of any other deaths or murders on campus?" Jenn searched her memory.

Susan shook her head. "I've lived in this region all my life. I even attended CSC. There have been a few natural deaths and a few accidents, but I don't recall a homicide on campus."

Jenn tried to think of more questions. She sipped her coffee. "You said when we first met that you had wondered when someone from the newspaper would contact you. If I hadn't come here, would you have contacted any newspaper?" Jenn took another sip of coffee.

Susan drained her cup. "Nope. Like I said earlier, publicity is not my job. However, as a public servant I'll answer a question if I can. I assumed your article was a way to help the police keep this quiet per their needs. Until you came, no reporter had asked me."

# Chapter 15

"Have you lost all control of your people?" President Paul Hulet stood from his huge leather chair and screamed at Robert Stroll.

Standing beside Stroll in support, Tom Bannister believed his friend wouldn't have minded the humiliation so much if Dee Forbes hadn't been standing there looking so smug.

Stroll's face reddened. "Mr. President, I can't stop someone, especially a *Lariat* reporter, from investigating. An outright order to stop would only lead to more questions."

"Or more bogus stories," Forbes sneered, referring to Stroll's prank story.

"That story stopped all interest," Stroll snapped

"Then why is she still asking questions?" Forbes shrieked as if pushing for a real fight.

"It made perfect sense to acknowledge an incident and answer it with plausible reasons. It becomes a non-issue. Honestly, I don't know why she persists." Stroll turned back to Hulet, his hands raised in surrender.

"She questioned the police detective again," Hulet roared.

Stroll and Bannister stiffened. Silence settled in the room except for the sounds of angry breathing.

"Tom, any developments?"

"A few. I have reason to suspect her boyfriend. They had quite a public row right before her death. I haven't been able to locate him, and he hasn't shown up for classes since Wednesday. I asked the Colter police to issue a BOLO — "

"What's a bolo?" The razor edge of Forbes' sharp voice scraped Bannister's nerves.

"Be on the lookout. It's the same as APB." Bannister faced Hulet. "The Colter police and the Shoshone County sheriff have received no sightings. Other than the boyfriend, I have no leads."

"Push hard on this, got it?"

"Yes, sir."

"Dee, I saw 'missing' posters of a girl around campus. Get them down. No negative publicity," Hulet said with a flat tone.

"Mr. President, I've seen those too. I recommend they stay. I'm spreading the word that she left campus, and she dropped out of college. That's the reason I came up with for her absence. Then, as people come to believe that story, the posters'll come down on their own. Otherwise without a reason, removing them will generate questions ... questions we may not be able to answer."

"Those posters make me extremely nervous," Hulet said.

"I understand, Mr. President, but believe me, right now we're better off having them up." She turned to Stroll. "But it's pure conjecture about who was in the kiln. With the story that she dropped out and returned home, there are a few who might refuse to believe it, but it's a plausible story."

"Much like my plausible story," Stroll said, his face still red from anger.

Bannister interjected to sidetrack the combatants. "Look, the story about the hooker in the dorm has certainly distracted the campus."

"Oh, God," Hulet shouted. "Couldn't your detective have waited to apprehend that slut?" Hulet glared at Bannister, who wished he'd kept his mouth shut.

He straightened and returned Hulet's glare. "Wait for what, Mr. President? Wait until the President of the United States is actually on campus then bust her? Are you telling me we should delay in arresting a criminal in our dormitories?" Bannister's chest heaved. He felt his eyes were bulging out from his head.

Hulet closed his eyes. After seconds, he opened them. "You're right, there was no choice."

Bannister took in a slow breath. Hulet had never told him he'd been right before.

"We're all on edge." Hulet sighed and leaned on his desk. "So much pressure, with the budget cuts and the stress associated with that, the president's visit, the body in the kiln ..." He pushed off and stood erect. "If we can get through the VIPs' visit, we'll be fine."

Forbes raised her hand. "When the president arrives, everyone will forget about the whore in the dorm."

"Enough. What about this reporter who keeps asking questions?" Hulet looked Stroll in the face, as if to present a challenge.

"She must be stopped, at all costs. She'll ruin everything. If you're not going to do anything about it, I will." Forbes stepped toward Stroll and placed her hands on her hips.

Stroll looked up at the ceiling as if the answer were painted there. "I'll reiterate to the newspaper editor to direct this reporter to get involved with other stories. Everything should come to naught." He faced Forbes directly. "After all, our public relations director ordered everyone involved not to talk to the press. Who would dare violate her order?"

# Chapter 16

"A roast beef sandwich and a small tea, please." Jenn placed her order at Earl's Roast Beef Sandwich Shop a block from the funeral home. While she spoke with Susan Hawley, the storm clouds had dissipated, and the sun shone, melting the snow and ice. Already the sewers were full of runoff. Jenn would have had the usual watery dirt stripe up her back, thrown by her bicycle's rear tire from the wet road, but last year her father had talked her into installing a fender. She didn't want a fender. "It's just too uncool," she had told him. Then, she figured she wasn't cool anyway.

When she had left the funeral home, she wondered about her next move. Mentally exhausted, she needed time to process the coroner's shocking information. The coffee on an empty stomach set off a bout of nausea. Lunch was what she needed.

"Were you riding a bicycle in this wintry weather?" the clerk asked as she rang up Jenn's order. The clerk was about sixty and grandmotherly. *Carolyn* was pinned to her shirt.

Polite, Jenn just nodded. She didn't have the energy to explain she rode year-round.

"Good for you!" Carolyn said. A big smile crossed her face.

Surprised by the enthusiasm, Jenn broke into a grin. "Well, thank you!" She felt lighter because of a simple exchange.

"Here's your order." The clerk pushed the filled tray across the counter.

"Thank you, Carolyn." Jenn picked up her order.

The grandmother beamed, apparently tickled that someone called her by name.

Jenn moved to a corner where there was little view. She didn't feel like watching traffic or other patrons. She wanted to be alone to think. She sank her teeth into the thick beef sandwich and savored the rich taste. As she chewed, Jenn thought about how the whole college seemed to be involved in covering up a murder. A young lady was killed on campus, and the college was perpetrating a terrible fraud on the public. Granted, the reasons sounded reasonable: not to interfere with the investigation, to prevent the killer from fleeing, and to prevent panic on campus, but they lied.

*You didn't verify.*

Jenn remembered the fight she'd had with Willy. *Oh, jeez.* His rationale for the error in his article about the sorority girls' cheating scandal was they corroborated their stories to match. She had chided him for not figuring it out anyway. Now, she'd been suckered into believing the lies many people had corroborated. She'd have to apologize to Willy, but then again, maybe not. Maybe he needed his comeuppance.

A half hour later, Jenn still rested. The lunch rush hour was over, and only remnants of meals littered the tables. What was her responsibility now? To keep quiet, especially since she had key information? If she forged ahead, would she interfere with a murder investigation?

What was being done to find this young woman's killer? Kerry didn't have a sense of urgency. Granted, he studied a photo of a blood-spattered body that may have been connected to the case, but he said that was from another town.

Maybe a little poking around might stir up some information that could be useful to the police. The logical place to start was the ceramics studio. If she dropped in, maybe she could catch another witness, maybe even Professor Redgrave, and gain another perspective. She'd have to be careful where she went and with whom she talked so word didn't get back to Manny—or Kerry.

While she cleaned off her tray and wrapper, she thought back to Mister Ramirez. Before she left the funeral home, she stood in the chapel and paid her respects. Jenn prayed to his

God to send him to heaven and protect his soul. Then she signed the guest register.

~ * ~

Jenn pedaled her bike on Cheney Street and tried to avoid sliding on slush or splashing puddles as she approached the Hamilton buildings. She thought back to her conversation with Susan. Considering all the lies she'd heard the past couple days, Jenn believed that at least Susan was honest.

Her thoughts drifted to the college staff. The more she thought about the cover-up and the systemic lies, the madder she got and the faster she pedaled.

*Did the college have a point?* The epiphany made Jenn jump in her saddle. Other than preventing the killer from running away and causing panic on campus, did the college have another reason for not publicizing the murder? If there were another reason, likely she'd never know.

Could her snooping jeopardize the investigation? She knew nothing about the direction the police were going in their search. If she interfered, would she ruin a trap the police may have set, causing a killer to go free? She cursed her ignorance. Then she cursed her inattention when the bike slid out from under her on an ice patch. This time she didn't look to see if anyone saw her fall, but she was grateful for the thickness of her winter clothing.

She coasted alongside the curb at the Hamilton bungalows. The ceramic studio was the first building in the rows of nondescript concrete bungalows that housed the ceramics and sculpture studios and professors' offices. Branded by the college president as not sexy enough for college refurbishment money, the buildings functioned only through the continuous efforts of the art department's professors and staff.

Through the huge windows, only one person worked in the ceramics studio. As she pushed open the door, rap music blasted from a dirt-coated disc player on a metal shelf.

The room was wide and shallow. Dilapidated tables, chairs, and handmade wood shelves laden with drying or finished pottery filled the left half. A table with a rotary press took up most of the center floor space. To the right, separated by a center aisle, two rows of pottery wheels faced each other, lined up like mucky soldiers after a mud-slinging battle. Large grimy windows cast variegated shadows on the mop-swirled concrete floor. Clay blobs and dirt covered everything from floor to ceiling. The smell of mud tickled her nose.

A skinny boy, apron spattered with clay and knees soaked from thrown sludge, sat hunched over one whirring wheel. His sludge-covered hands coaxed up a spinning mound of clay. A gob fell out of his hair, landed on the spinning wheel, and was flicked to the floor.

Jenn turned to the completed ceramics on shelves beside her. Vases, bowls, and sculptures of varying heights crammed the wooden shelves. Some pieces were bumpy, rough as if a child made them. Others were fine and delicate.

She peered closer to look at each piece. Small sculptures of skeletal hands and coffins littered the shelves. *Those must be Jake's.* One sculpture made her think of a blanket wrapped around an invisible Indian. Fine black lines, in stark contrast to the flawless white porcelain, spasmed across the form. *That must be the piece Hannah mentioned. She was right; the jagged marks complement the piece's delicate lines.* Jenn looked around for Alex's heads, but there were none. The professor must have stored them in her own studio.

The skinny boy stopped his wheel to scrape off the misshapen mound. Jenn yelled above the music, "Professor around?"

"Yeah, she cancelled classes." He pointed his chin toward the back door.

"Why cancel?" Jenn howled back.

"College shut down the studio."

Professor Redgrave's office-studio was in another bungalow across the courtyard. As Jenn crossed to it, she eyed the car kiln where the bones were found. *Danger!* tape draped the kiln. Black smudges dotted the kiln's door. Jenn noted there was no tape or smudges on the other gas kiln. The part of the yard shaded by the bungalow was still covered in snow. In the sun, discarded ceramic sculptures bordered the slushy path. She glanced again at the taped kiln to imagine herself finding a real human skeleton and shuddered.

Redgrave's door was closed, but the professor saw Jenn through the window and motioned her inside. "Professor Redgrave?" Jenn asked. "I'm Jennifer Roby from the *Lariat*. We spoke on Tuesday. I was in the area and thought I'd stop by. May I have a few moments of your time?"

Hands muddy from clay, Professor Redgrave nodded. "Sure. My advanced class starts in an hour. No, cancelled until next week. Call me Alex."

A clay-smeared apron, baggy jeans, and loose denim shirt didn't hide her slender figure. Her short, black hair stood up along the back of her head like a spiky halo. She was a casual professor, yet likely strict about her and her students' ceramics, Jenn guessed. Sculptures still in progress stood on large tables. Many were covered in plastic to protect the moist clay from the dry air. From what Jenn could make out through the plastic, the shapes were massive heads and faces. The carvings dwarfed Alex's short stature. The muddy smell in the room made Jenn's nose run, but the high humidity felt good on her skin. Moisture fogged up the back window where Alex worked.

Jenn sat on the corner of a wobbly wooden chair and pulled out her notebook. "I'd like to touch bases with you about what happened Monday. Do you know … the full story about the bones, or do you have any more insight into what happened?"

"Well, remember this is all off the record, but I don't think there's much to discuss."

"How so?"

"It was just a joke—a bad joke—so I guess I don't understand why you're here."

Jenn reminded herself not to say anything that would give away that the skeleton was real. "In our earlier conversation, you said you couldn't discuss the incident. Why do you suppose that is?"

"I don't want to embarrass the college, I guess." Alex continued to scrape small sections of clay from the form she was working. "Even though they were pieces, they sure looked real. Even the college representatives there thought it was a body." She giggled.

"Which reps were there?" Jenn's curiosity piqued at the professor's humorous reaction.

"The chief of police and the public relations director." Alex snickered. "She turned so white, I thought she would faint. The chief had to help steady her ... and the coroner trying to sweep up the ash ..." She bit her lips to stop a smirk.

She pressed her fingers deep into sculpture. "I'm sorry, I shouldn't laugh. Initially, it was horrifying to see. We were all so upset. It's only funny now because we thought the skeleton was genuine. With ceramics anything can be made to look authentic. My problem is that I can't imagine any of my students doing that sort of thing."

"So you know all your students?" Jenn thought about her large theater-style classes with nameless classmates.

"Oh, sure. My classes are small since our facility is small. Plus, we work together to do chores: load and unload the kilns; develop clay; clean up; move chemicals and supplies." Alex paused with her scraper barely touching the sculpture. "Usually I know what the students are working on. I thought I didn't miss much, so I was really surprised that anyone would fool around. Everyone here is serious about their work."

Alex palmed her scraper and picked up a fork. She used the tool to scratch a spot on her sculpture's forehead and spritzed the area with a spray bottle. She pinched off a blob of clay from a nearby pile, pressed the blob firmly into the scraped spot, and smoothed the area with the scraper. The new eyebrow made the face appear quite angry. As she pushed the clay with her thumbs, she looked at Jenn for the next question, but noticed Jenn watching her work. "Ever taken a ceramics class?"

"No. It's interesting," Jenn said honestly. "I don't have the imagination to do things like that."

Alex laughed. "Sure you do. It only takes a little practice. Besides, in the beginning courses you're told what to do, so it doesn't take too much artistic talent. Sign up. You'll enjoy it."

"I'll consider that. Who loaded the kiln that these bones were found in?"

Alex draped an arm across the top of the angry head, like she was giving it a hug. "My intern Carmen Ortega de la Vega loads the kilns, normally on Sundays. She told Chief Bannister she found the kiln partially loaded. All she did was finish loading it then fired it."

Jenn wondered if de la Vega told the truth about finding the kiln partially loaded.

Alex started to carve the eyebrow, then stopped and looked at Jenn. "This isn't that big a deal. Why are you still asking about it?"

## Chapter 17

The block-long bike ride from the Hamilton studio to Morris Hall was invigorating. The level street, calm wind, warmth in the sun, and coolness in the shade made for easy pedaling. *Perfect.* Jenn corralled Cougar in the bicycle security box and trotted to the dormitory.

Hurrying, she still had to pack her panniers, load her bike, and start pedaling if there was any chance to get home before dark. Though excited to go home for the weekend, her senses tingled from blowing off Manny's directive and ferreting out important information few people knew. She opened the front door and swung her backpack over her shoulder.

"Dad!"

John Roby sat in the lobby reading that day's *Lariat*. Looking up, a radiant smile spread across his face as he saw his daughter. He folded up the paper and tossed it aside. Spreading his arms wide, he scooped her up in a bear hug.

"What are you doing here? What a wonderful surprise!" Jenn exclaimed.

"Well, I decided to come get you rather than worrying about you on your bike. A section of highway was closed down to one lane because another semi flipped over." He leaned back to look at her.

"New sport jacket?" Jenn fingered the material. "Camel hair?"

"Yup. Talked myself into a new jacket." He turned, put his arm over Jenn's shoulder, and steered her to the bank of elevators.

"Good for you. You don't treat yourself very often."

They rode up the elevator in self-conscious silence and ignored the other student in the car, a young woman with too much makeup who eyed her father. Jenn felt possessive and gave him another hug. "Boy, this a nice surprise."

"I'm glad to have such a great reception." John returned the hug. "How's your semester going? Hey, what response did you get on your bones article?"

Her father's return to a terrible reality gave Jenn a fairy-tale-bursting sensation. Her simple story of a prank had evolved into a murder and a cover-up. He must have sensed a change in mood. "Everything okay?"

Mindful of the girl in the elevator staring at her father, she murmured, "Um, yeah."

They stepped out of the elevator and headed toward her room. John looked up the hall. "What's with all those red lights?"

A series of light stands placed along the hallway stood on either side of room 311. The lights gave the dim deserted hall a hot pink glow. She groaned to suppress a giggle as she struggled to unlock her door. Waving her father into her room, she waited until the door was closed before she explained the hooker.

At first, he was incredulous, then furious. After he vented for a moment, he stared down at Jenn. "You never noticed a prostitution ring down the hall?"

She recalled the teasing from her fellow reporters. "Dad, no. No. I didn't notice. I have been busting my rear end here keeping my grades up and working for the newspaper, and I'm supposed to know what's happening inside some room down the hall?" Jenn choked up. "All I know is, it can be so noisy around here I have to go to staff room to get any work done. There are times I can barely sleep here!"

Her father raised his hands and touched his forehead. "I can't believe that sort of thing could go on around here. I … I'm afraid that you might get hurt, and I don't want you exposed to that sort of thing. That's all." He placed his hand on Jenn's head and gave it a light jiggle. "Sorry, babe."

Jenn still smarted. "Well, you had a smirk on your face."

He sighed. "Yeah. I did." He snorted. "In some bizarre, sick way." Then he started to giggle and shook his head.

After another sniffle, Jenn joined in.

"Isn't there a resident assistant on this floor? Isn't she supposed to keep an eye on things?"

"Yup. It had to have been obvious to her. I wonder if the police will investigate whether she looked the other way. Maybe the RA was the lookout."

Her father flipped his long hair over his shoulder and sat on one of the office chairs at the double-wide desk in front of the window. Jenn watched as her father noticed a separation in the room. On one side, the bed was unmade. Soiled clothes lay scattered on the floor or kicked under the bed. Dirty glasses and candy wrappers hid every horizontal surface. Racy posters covered the brick wall.

On the other side of the room, John's daughter gathered clothes and toiletries. She placed them on the made bed before she stuffed the pile into her gym bag. Jenn tossed her bike panniers into the wardrobe closet and paused. She smiled and thought how cliché her actions were as she stuffed loads of dirty clothes into a duffle to wash at home.

## Chapter 18

"You've done a great job here, Manny." Robert Stroll pushed aside weeks-old newspapers and motioned for Dee Forbes to join him on the newsroom's stained couch.

Hesitating to avoid an unknown liquid smeared on the Naugahyde, she tentatively perched on the edge. "Yes, your handling of the college newspaper is stellar." Her smile split her face.

"Your award from the Associated Collegiate Press for best college newspaper was a major triumph for you — and the college," Stroll added.

"Thanks," Manny said, a little unsettled about the real reason why Stroll and Forbes had come. Usually only those directly involved with the newspaper came into the newsroom. Any other visitors came to complain.

Stroll eyed Manny as Forbes looked over the thumbtacked posters of outdated events and clipboards with half-inch-thick stacks of memos plastering the bulletin boards. Empty soda cans and coffee cups sat on every available empty spot. A few cups sat on signs declaring *The editor is not your mother. Clean up after yourself.*

Manny tensed as the silence lengthened.

"Is your reporter still asking around about that prank?" Stroll's voice rose then cracked.

"No. Why do you ask?"

Forbes twisted on the couch to gaze at Manny full in the face. "We have a concern that her reporter activities on this non-issue could cast a bad light on the college. With the president of the United States coming to launch a major fundraiser that's the last thing we want to happen. You agree, I'm sure." Her voice was soft, sweet.

"It is a closed topic for the newspaper. I don't understand your comment about her activities. I've already told Jenn not to pursue it." Manny's forehead wrinkled in concentration as he tried to fathom why they would even bring up this topic.

"Then why is she pursuing it?" she pressed.

"She's not."

"She interviewed the police detective again—yesterday afternoon." Her voice dropped to an accusing level.

Manny pulled out his chair and sat. He didn't know what made him angrier: that Jenn wasted her valuable time chasing a dead story, that she violated his order, or that he had to hear about it from Forbes.

"Have your reporter—Jennifer Roby, right?—assist Warwick on the president's visit. Apparently, you need to keep her busy," Stroll exclaimed.

Forbes slowly shifted her hand to touch Stroll's arm as if to soothe him.

Manny bristled. As editor, he assigned the work and the stories. For Stroll to demand this new assignment grated him just as much as when Stroll ordered the prank story in the first place. He had no choice to comply, but not without an argument.

"Warwick's a senior reporter. He doesn't need help with this assignment. I need Jennifer out and about; she's excellent at keeping her ear to the ground." He flicked a quick smile to show he was trying to be cooperative. "I think it's because she's all over campus on her bicycle. I've seen people talk to her just because of it."

"On a bicycle? It's still winter." Forbes' eyes widened.

To hide his anger, Manny raised his eyebrows and waved his hands to show he was impressed. "If you see a tall blond on a bicycle zipping around even though there's a foot of snow on the ground, that's her." He picked at his fingers then crossed his arms. "I'll do some remedial training, and she can take some time to concentrate on her studies. Frankly, Doctor Stroll, I have to insist that I make the assignments."

Stroll pushed his hands against the couch seat as if to rise. Forbes' hand again touched his arm. This time, her hand lingered. "Manny, I must insist your reporter stop her inquiries and follow your orders. Furthermore, you understand the impact the *Lariat* makes to the college. The campus, the city, and even the state populace reads your newspaper. Your editions influence a lot of people." She pressed her palms together like she was in prayer as if trying to impress on Manny of her sincerity. "If you publish any negative story about the college, it could adversely impact the fundraiser. You've printed articles about the cutbacks and interviewed those who will be laid off. It's terrifying for all of us. Please, do not print anything that may show us in a bad light. We need you to be on board with that."

"My job is to manage this newspaper and print the truth about what I feel the public has a right to know," Manny snapped.

"Your job is dependant upon this college. You are a student. You do not have absolute power here," Stroll almost shouted.

Manny felt his face grow cold. "You expect me to censor a major story just because it might be perceived as negative?"

"Gentlemen, please," Forbes held her hands out in peace. "Manny, listen to me. We all want this fundraiser to be successful. You agree with that, don't you?"

He stared at her, his lips tightened.

"Well, don't you, or do you want us to fail?" Her face grew red. "So much is at stake. I know of one university that has failed to meet its fundraising goal. Others have resorted to selling the naming rights for bathrooms! Is that what you want for CSC?"

Manny met Stroll's glare without flinching. "You ordered the original story to be written. She wrote it. I printed it. Why now is it a problem?"

Stroll stiffened. His face grew red. "I will not accept a flat refusal to carry out my directions, and I will not tolerate having my original order thrown at me." He pushed off the couch and approached Manny so fast that Manny leaned back in his chair.

"Let me spell this out for you, Manuel. I'd hate to pull my recommendations for your job searches or rewrite my endorsement so close to your graduation, but any refusal to follow your branch chief's directives will certainly cause me to do just that."

"Doctor Stroll! Calm yourself." Forbes cried as she struggled to escape the couch.

Stabs of fear and shock shot through Manny's heart. After graduation, he needed to get a job near his family in St. Louis. Newspaper jobs in metropolitan areas were hard to come by. His father, dying of cancer, had an expected year left to live. Without a recommendation …

"There's more going on here than you not publishing one story. Lives are at stake here." Stroll's words were clipped from anger.

Breathing heavily, Manny looked away from the manic eyes flashing before him. *Blackmailed? Censorship? Because of a story about a prank?*

## Chapter 19

Jenn and John Roby headed west on Highway 28. The lone housing development and the high plains of the Devil's Valley passed from view. By the time Colter disappeared from the rearview mirror, she had settled into her father's new Dodge Ram pickup, a 3500 Longhorn edition in deep burgundy. Breathing in the new-truck smell, she scoped the bells and whistles, standard with the deluxe package.

Repulsed by the decadence, the pleasures of such fanciness excited her. Dad had always owned a beater truck; Grampa too. Initially disgusted when her father presented to her what he bought the week before, Jenn watched his face as he drove. Since she'd been away at college this semester, he'd changed. She wasn't sure she liked the difference.

"So, what do you think of your new ... truck?" Jenn almost said "toy".

"Ooh, I like it. Check this out." He held down a button on the steering wheel. Johnny Cash's voice rose, louder and louder until she clamped her hands over her ears before *Ring of Fire* burned her hearing. Grinning, her father pushed the other side of the button and Johnny's voice lowered. "Neat, huh? It's even got an MP3 player and an electronic map."

"You don't own an MP3 player and you know every inch of this state."

"Oh, don't splash cold water on me. I thought it's time ... time I indulged myself for once."

Jenn stared out at the tip of the Wind River mountain range as she recalled his tough times. They'd lasted years: Mom's massive medical bills—paid off only three years ago; Gramma

Prudy, his own mother, dying of a stoke a year after he buried his wife; and the shuttering of his and Grampa's small county newspaper after the advent of the Internet.

Shame washed over her for resenting his splurging. "Well, if you're happy, I'm happy."

He gave her a smile, his white teeth flashing in his light brown face. Jenn wondered how he always looked tan, even in winter. She was curious if he had a drop of Mediterranean blood in his Danish body.

Her father aimed the truck toward home. Jenn asked about every bell and whistle.

As the setting sun reflected off snow-capped Granite Peak, one of the jagged pinnacles that jutted from the ninety-mile-long range, John turned off the highway onto the South Pass City Road. The rolling foothills freckled with sagebrush, junipers, and pines rose to the mountain range to the north. To the south, the Red Desert stretched beyond the horizon, punctuated by Oregon Buttes. She never tired of the area's wilderness. After a months-long absence from the view on this side of the range, she appreciated its beauty more than ever. She refreshed its picture in her mind's eye as the truck sped them toward the dirt driveway that led to the ranch house.

Christmas vacation felt like a lifetime ago. "There it is," she said under her breath as the ranch house rotated into view from the curving driveway. She felt like a little girl and wanted to squeal, "I'm home!"

They pulled up in front of the hundred-year-old log structure built by her great-grandparents. The jutting porch gave the square building more presence. The years and harsh weather had stained the logs to a dark chocolate. On the porch, a cluster of three rocking chairs was turned upside down and tied down to prevent the winter winds from catching the woven straight backs and flinging them down the driveway. The hunter green shutters always needed painting and the roof's shake shingles looked like they'd been given a perm. "They'll be replaced this spring," Dad said.

Massive yellow pines circled the old house. The branches rustled as they scratched the blue sky. Planted the year her father was born, the forty-year-old trees dwarfed the two-story log house and provided cooling shade. Every summer Sunday, the Roby family had a picnic under the tree Jenn named Prudy's Hen, so called because Gramma Prudy had pruned the trees just before an ice storm. The damage shaped this tree like a giant chicken, tail feathers and all.

The snow had melted. At seventy-eight hundred feet, the South Pass City Road was higher in elevation than Colter's fifty-five hundred feet. The temperature should have been colder here, yet in the winter the reverse was often true. Frigid air would settle around Colter and the Devil's Valley east of the Wind River Mountains. The tip of the mountain range would deflect many storms, making forecasting difficult. Either home was punished by storms or Colter was. This year, south of the mountain range had a warmer than usual winter and Colter was being pummeled by storms.

Jenn pushed open the truck's heavy steel door. Even with her long legs, the muddy driveway was a long way down. She hauled open the crew cab's full-sized back door and tugged out her gym bag and duffle bag. She wiped off the mud from her boots on the scraper mounted on the porch. "Where are the greeters?"

"They're hitting the sauce with Dad. I swear those dogs have no sense of smell."

Jenn shook her head. Too often, their two Australian shepherds, Dee-oh-gee and Gristle, would bolt to find a local female skunk, apparently to practice their herding. She took a dim view of their efforts and let them know it. Grampa would take down the metal tub out back and give them a tomato juice bath to remove the skunk smell.

The ritual became a joke. When the boys' "cologne" preceded them into the house, Grampa would roll his eyes and head to the pantry where he stocked tomato juice by the gallons. The routine led to the expression "hitting the sauce".

John grabbed the duffle from Jenn and held open the door for her.

"Oh, moose stew!"

"With fresh biscuits," Obed Roby called out as he stepped through the pantry door, wiping his hands on a towel. "I had to fix your favorite meal for your return home."

"Grampa!" Jenn dropped her gym bag and ran through the living room to jump into his arms.

"Every time I see this girl I swear she gets taller," he declared to his son.

"Is that a bad thing?" Jenn said, a teasing smile on her face.

"Not at all, dear heart. You're more gorgeous than ever. Gosh, seems like you've been gone ages."

Jenn liked to look at her grandfather as much as she liked to look at her father. Grampa looked how Dad would twenty years from now: pure-white hair, distinguished and handsome, interesting interchange of wrinkles, and sparkling blue eyes that made him look like an imp struggling to contain naughtiness. Giving him another hug, she asked, "How have you been?"

Grampa glanced at his son. By the look in his eyes Jenn couldn't tell if she was seeing sheepishness, silliness, or pride.

Furry backs bounded into the living room, jiggling and hopping. "Hello boys, do you smell better? Oh yes, you do." Jenn knelt, adult voice sliding into baby talk as the boys' tailless rumps writhed with joy. Throaty growls tumbled from their mouths.

"Well." Grampa clapped and rubbed his hands together. "How 'bout you tell us all about your semester during dinner, hmm? The biscuits will be out in a few minutes."

~ * ~

Seated at Gramma Prudy's dinner table, three generations exclaimed over Grampa's moose stew. Jenn pulled apart another steaming biscuit and slathered on butter. She held up the biscuit in salute. "This has to be the world's best food combination ever."

"Hear, hear." John swept a chunky spoonful into his mouth.

"Thank you, Jennifer. Thank you, John." Grampa turned his head and nodded as he formally thanked each one. "I must confess, at the risk of sounding conceited, I agree. So, tell us what happened at school."

To Grampa's shock, Jenn related the story of the prostitute arrested in the dorm. He looked as if he wasn't sure if he should laugh when she described the disappearance of the young men and the appearance of red light bulbs.

"You didn't notice anything?" Grampa asked.

Her spoon stopped stirring the stew. Only in her mind did Jenn throw back her head and scream in frustration. Why did everyone assume she knew what was happening?

"Dad, I'm sure Jenny was too busy to notice."

Jenn grinned at her father. "Right, Grampa, to be honest, I didn't notice."

Quiet returned to the table as everyone refilled their bowls and plates. Throughout the meal, Jenn cast sidelong glances at Dee-oh-gee and Gristle as they sat on their cushions in the corner of the living room. Barred from the dining room during meals, they licked their chops as they watched every mouthful of food disappear. Soon, one foot, then another, would scootch them closer to the wide dining room doorway. Their heads raised or lowered to find the strongest scent wafting into the living room. They tried hard to comply with their orders to remain there, straining against every muscle fiber that moved them toward the table. By the time meals were over, the two dogs had slinked inside the dining room and seemed to congratulate themselves that no one had noticed.

Jenn looked around the combined kitchen and dining room, and she realized how much she had missed the old room. At college, her dorm room's white or brick walls exuded no warmth. Only standard dormitory furniture cluttered the small space.

This kitchen was huge; L-shaped counters corralled the room. In the open corner stood Gramma's plank dinner table, nearly ten feet long, draped by her old linens. Dad thought the linens were too old and delicate to use and should be put away for safekeeping. Grampa wouldn't have any of that and insisted on using them.

Medium-dark beadboard wainscoting lined the room with burgundy wallboard above. The dark walls would have made the old room like a cave, but five years ago Grampa splurged on chandeliers and installed lights under the cupboards. The new lighting made the room warm and cozy. A spotlight highlighted the old wood cookstove, a black Majestic, original to the house. The stove's chrome was thin, worn from constant use and cleaning, but the one-inch-thick steel plates hadn't warped despite intense heat through the decades. Years ago, Grampa removed a floor cabinet and installed an electric stove that they used in the summer, but as long as the weather wasn't hot, Dad and Grampa still preferred to use the old cookstove.

Her family sated and relaxed, Jenn squirmed in her chair. Her heart rate increased. She couldn't wait any longer and steeled herself. "I need your advice."

"Shoot." Grampa reached for another biscuit.

Jenn couldn't respond right away. Her mind froze. How she had planned to start this conversation vanished. Her father and grandfather stopped eating to wait for her to speak. Concern spread over their faces and, in unison, they lowered their spoons.

"Jenny, we'll be glad to help you anyway we can," her father prodded.

She looked at her bowl of stew, hung her head, and struggled with what to say.

"Honey, you're scaring me."

"Sorry, Dad." She took a deep breath and focused on the carrot that lay on the bottom of her bowl. "Remember my story in the newspaper about the practical joke? I've uncovered something ... something really bad."

## Chapter 20

Her father and grandfather hadn't said a word while she gave the whole story of her discovery. She held nothing back: the skeleton, Detective Kerry and his lies, the meetings with Professor Alex Redgrave and the coroner who broke the news that the bones were human. Jenn choked up as she spoke of Hannah May saying that had the kiln properly fired, she would have thrown out the bones' ashes, a horrifying close call for a victim — someone's child — to be forever missing. She became angry when she told them of Manny's order barring her from pursuing the story and public affairs' order for all concerned to keep quiet, a comment that made her father and grandfather exchange glances.

When she finished telling her story, she covered her face with her hands. "I don't know what to do," she cried.

The plastic cat clock ticked on the wall. Jenn knew the men; when neither said anything it meant they were thinking. Just as they had kept quiet while she spoke, she'd learned to give them time and silence to think.

Her father spoke up, his tan face a lighter shade. "Okay, I admit, I'm having trouble grasping this." He looked to his father.

Grampa exhaled and threw up his hands. "I'm glad I'm not the only one."

Both men vented. Sometimes one talked, paced, angry, fearful, sometimes they both talked and nearly bumped into each other while they paced. They raised their voices and spoke of notifying Colter's newspaper, the *Cabernet*, and the attorney general's office, calling a police hotline, barging into

President Hulet's office and stamping on his desk, or picketing the campus. They lowered their voices and muttered about stopping payments on their alumni membership dues and the Cavalry Foundation memberships. Jenn sat quietly and watched.

Both men stopped pacing then collapsed in their seats. John looked to Jenn. "Okay, how do you see yourself handling this?"

The simplicity of his question only made her dilemma tougher. She didn't want to come up with the answer. She felt she was in water over her head. She wanted them to tell her which swimming strokes to perform in order to save herself. "I don't know." She hated that automatic response in interviewees and now she uttered it. "I don't know. The whole thing is so unreal. I don't know where to begin or if I should even start."

"If it helps, I'm having real trouble believing this murder has to be kept quiet to catch the killer," Grampa said.

"Me too, Dad." John spun his spoon on the table, his fingers a blur. "I never heard of a murder being kept quiet to make it easier for the police." He turned back to his daughter. "I absolutely believe it would hinder them. How can they ask questions? How would they get leads? This makes no sense."

"What would you do?" Jenn hoped for guidance.

"I would adjourn to the living room." Grampa stood as he started to stack bowls. "If for no other reason than to give us more time to think."

~ * ~

The table cleared and cleaned, the leftover stew tucked in the refrigerator, and the full kettle on the woodstove to boil, each took their usual seat in the living room. Jenn sat in the antique rocking chair, a birthday gift to her mother from her father, set near the pot-bellied woodstove. Dad and Grampa sat in their overstuffed recliners that faced the television. This room, like the kitchen, was vintage early 1900s. Lace curtains and flowery wallpaper topped white painted beadboard on the interior walls. The room's exterior walls were log; the wood still looked as if it had been hewn a week ago. Old photographs covered the walls. Her ancestors' eyes followed her wherever she moved in the room. In the corner, Dee-oh-gee and Gristle circled the wide cushion before lying down, each snout on the other's rump.

The television that had been as old as Jenn had been replaced by a modest-sized flat-screen. Her menfolk had been splurging with more than a new truck and a camel hair jacket.

"Maybe we're looking at this the wrong way." Grampa handed his son a Scotch in a tumbler. "Earlier, we focused on the situation. The police and college personnel are ordered to keep the murder quiet. This is something we—you—cannot control. It's out of your hands. Instead of focusing on things you can't do anything about, let's focus on your choices."

Jenn and her father sat in silence as they considered his comments.

"You're right, Dad." Jenn's father set his tumbler on the oak side table. "Let's look at your choices, hon. One, Manny ordered you not to pursue the story. Fine, you do nothing, go to class and study. Let the police do their thing—although I still can't imagine how they can investigate without asking pointed questions." Still agitated, he stood up and kept talking, arms waving. "Maybe, hopefully, they'll find the killer. Maybe not. Either way, it's not your case. It's not your problem.

"Or two, you ignore your directive and keep asking. You may uncover some tidbit the police don't have. You may even persuade Manny to publish it. The public will know about the murder and that there's a killer loose. What's the worst that could happen? The killer flees? Killers run all the time, but now the police can ask real questions and solve this thing. The college might get into trouble for keeping it quiet? Probably. And you? You may be fired from your job." He stopped talking, breathless. He faced Jenn. In a soft voice he asked, "Would that be the worst thing?"

Grampa leaned toward Jenn. "Faced with these choices, you have to ask yourself: what do you feel is the right thing to do? What actions can you live with? A year from now—five years from now—what would you regret?"

Jenn stared at the floor. Thoughts tumbled in her mind. Her father leaned against her chair and draped his arm across her shoulder. She looked up at him, then over at her grandfather. "Asking the questions is the easy part. Answering them is the hard part." Although in her heart, she knew the answer was easy. "I can't do nothing. I know too much. The public has a right to know this information."

The kettle whistled. While Jenn steeped tea, Grampa and Dad discussed whether they should approach the college or the local newspaper about Jenn's information. They agreed they would not do either. Their interference could cause the investigation—if there was one—irreparable damage. If the police had a plan of attack, their outright meddling could cause someone to get hurt.

Jenn returned to her chair and balanced a mug on her knee. "If I do anything, there's only one person I can think of to talk with before I hit a dead end. Even if I find out anything worthwhile, Manny would never publish it. He's gotten really weird about this story."

Dad and Grampa warned her, as a reporter for the *Lariat*, against taking what she knew to the Colter *Cabernet*. "Such things just aren't done," Dad said.

They talked into the early hours about the unknown woman's murder and Jenn's search for answers. She admitted she was scared. Emotionally and psychologically, she needed their support, and she trusted their judgment, their goodness. They held her, and told her how proud they were, a compliment that humbled her.

She trudged up the stairs, changed into her pajamas and crawled into bed. As she pulled up the covers, a hint of dust from the quilt wafted to her nose. Christmas vacation seemed ages ago. Keyed up yet exhausted, Jenn drifted in and out of sleep all night.

## Chapter 21

In a dreamy haze, dank fishy air washed over Jenn's face. Cold fish scales brushed her cheek. With a start, Jenn opened her eyes. Dee-oh-gee sat next to her right shoulder and panted into her face. He snaked a tongue to her cheek. Gristle lay beside her other shoulder, sniffing her pajamas.

Jenn mumbled to Dee-oh-gee, "You fish-eater." She struggled to free her arms. They were tangled in the twisted blankets, which were held down by the dogs. When her arms were free, she gave them both a scratch. Gristle's quaking rump jiggled the bed. Pleased they'd done their morning job, the dogs jumped off the bed and headed down the hall.

*Oh, pancakes and bacon for breakfast.* She threw off the covers, noticed the *9:30* on the clock, and groaned. She hated sleeping late. What a waste of a good morning, but then, she and her father and Grampa had stayed up late last night to discuss her findings on the skeleton in the kiln.

Sitting on the edge of her bed, alternately scratching and stretching, Jenn looked around her room. The cabbage-rose wallpaper still irritated her — too girly — but it would remain. The wallpaper was original to the house and, out of deference to his parents, Grampa refused to remove it. He bought plain sage-green curtains and throw rugs to tone down the paper's garish colors. Two small oak dressers belonged to her great-grandparents. On the rare occasions of high humidity, the drawers were a bear to open. A tiny closet had a once-ornate metal knob, worn smooth by decades of turning. She reached for her bathrobe, tucked her feet into fleece slippers, and headed for the bathroom to freshen up before plodding down the steep stairs.

"Want some coffee?" Dad's voice wafted up the stairs with the coffee scent. The creaking staircase was always a give-away. At the table, her father handed her a cup.

"Thank you, Dad. Good morning."

"You're welcome, and good morning."

"Where's Grampa?"

"He's taking the boys for their run. Should be back pretty quick."

Jenn giggled. "Remember when the boys herded that litter of skunk babies into the house?"

Dad groaned as he lifted the edge of a pancake to check its brownness. "I remember the stink of the mother letting us know she wasn't happy. I thought we'd all sprout a foot out of our heads with all the chemicals I had to use to get rid of the stench."

"How'd you sleep?" She sipped her coffee and flinched as the scalding liquid touched her lips.

"Not great. Kept thinking about what you found out." He flipped another pancake onto the stack and poured more batter on the griddle.

"Well, good morning, darlin'," Grampa sang as he entered.

The two boys bounded in, toenails ticking on the wood plank floor, their tongues lolling and rumps vibrating.

The fresh air smell emanated from their cold, rounded bodies. "You stink good," Jenn said to the boys as she rubbed them. "Oh, you too, Grampa," she added, laughing.

"Always nice to get a compliment." Grampa tousled her hair and limped past her.

"What happened, Dad?" John pulled out a chair for his father.

"Oh, that ol' cattle guard finally got me. My feet straddle the gaps just fine, but this morning my foot slipped. Twanged an ankle muscle. It'll be fine."

"Will it slow you down for the trip?"

Jenn perked up. "What trip?"

The men exchanged glances. "We didn't get a chance to tell you, what with your news last night." Grampa reached for a plate.

"It's no big deal. Let's enjoy breakfast first." John placed the steaming platter of cakes on the table. He moved the pitcher of hot maple syrup from the top of the wood stove and placed it beside the platter. "Dad, more coffee?"

~ * ~

"So, tell me about your trip." Jenn pushed away from the table and reached for the coffee pot. She leaned to top off Grampa's, then Dad's cup. An unsettled feeling swept over her as the two men glanced at each other. She sat down and topped off her own cup.

Dad cleared his throat and took a sip of his coffee. He flinched then blew on the liquid to cool it. He set down the cup and fixed Jenn with a look between nervousness and happiness. "Monday ... we'll be back Friday ... don't worry ... we're heading into the Red Desert ... we're not leaving the state. We're doing some spring camping since the winter's been so mild."

"Well, that's great! Sounds like fun."

Dad turned to Grampa, who leaned forward. "Jennifer, we're not going alone. Two women are going with us."

"Cool! Are you teaching them the desert?" She leaned forward, her grin widened.

Dad stood and walked to Jenn's side. He placed his arm around Jenn's shoulders. "Honey, these women are our dates."

Jenn felt her face grow cold.

Grampa took a deep breath. "We four have been double-dating for three months now."

"Jenny, we hope you'll understand that these women would never, ever, take the place of your mother or your grandmother in our hearts. Your mother — "

At the mention of her mother, she realized that her father had rejected Mom's memory for a new woman, and that he and Grampa had discarded their devotion to "we three against the world". Jenn gasped and burst into tears. She pushed off her father's hugging arm, and ran out of the dining room. She didn't stop until she ran into the old barn where she sat on a bale of hay, pulled her bathrobe tight around her, and felt her renewed loss. In the past three months while she'd been away, Dad and Grampa had splurged: new truck, new jacket, new television, new women. The men in the Roby household had moved on with their lives, leaving her stuck in the past.

Dee-oh-gee and Gristle nudged open the barn door and crept next to her. Dee-oh-gee jumped on the hay bale and leaned into her. Gristle laid on her feet and watched her. Jenn put her arms around Dee-oh-gee and leaned against him.

Despite the dogs' warmth, the morning's cold air leaking into the barn chilled her through. Shivering, she headed into the house, relieved Dad and Grampa had left the dining room.

Not wanting to face them, she slumped at her mother's piano with both boys piled on her feet. She pecked at the keys; which notes they were she didn't know. Mom loved the antique piano and allowed Jenn to stroke the velvet-soft rosewood or press the ivory keys. Mom tried to teach her to play, but Jenn only wanted to play outside. Now, Jenn regretted her refusal to allow Mom to teach her how to play the beautiful instrument.

Too many shocks this week at school and at home had shaken her. She leaned an arm on the shelf above the piano's keyboard and thought about her father and grandfather in the garage pulling out camping equipment.

They were ... well, Dad and Grampa. They were sexless creatures. They weren't supposed to have interests in the opposite sex, let alone have sex. "Yuck." Jenn wrinkled her nose, and shook her head to rid her mind of the image. *Girlfriends? At their age? What about her grandmother? Her mother?* Her mother's voice called to her father. "John-Roby!" She always called him John-Roby. If she were here, what would she say about the momentous news of her husband having a girlfriend?

Jenn clapped her hands to her face. How ridiculous she was acting. Perhaps the men in her life were not just father and grandfather. They were men. Twelve years and eleven years ago, they buried their wives, their beloveds. Since then, they had had no women in their lives. A daughter didn't count. They had earned the right to move on. They had been apprehensive of hurting Jenn and of her reaction to their good news, and she'd let them down.

She tried not to be too hard on herself. Their announcement had been a shock. At least she hadn't cursed them or insulted them. Thankfully they hadn't brought the women into the house and paraded them like prized pigs.

*Oh, God.* She'd have to meet them. Maybe she'd be back at school before they came over so she wouldn't have to see them. They'd fawn over her, cluck, and try to look maternal to make a good impression for their new men. *Too much information. Not yet.*

She sat on the floor and hugged the boys. Their rumps jiggled with excitement. They didn't care about the new women. They liked Jenn just fine. She headed to her room to change clothes before she walked out to the garage.

~ * ~

She opened the door to the garage and stepped in. Dad and Grampa were rolling out the sleeping bags to air then stood to watch her. Jenn hesitated, not knowing what to say. Dad held out his arms; Jenn hustled to him and pressed herself into his chest.

For the next hour, they sat on camp stools. As she talked about her memories and her fears, they listened, and wept for the past. They recovered, and joked about the future.

Later that evening, Grampa regaled them both with stories from his youth growing up on this ranch, stories he'd told a hundred times before, but his son and granddaughter acted like they'd never heard the stories before. Since Grampa never told the same story the same way, they did hear it for the first time. Jenn cupped her face in her hands to watch him — his eyes sparkled in his little-boy face — and delighted in his memories.

As she settled into bed, her father knocked on the door jamb before sitting on the edge of her bed. "I'm sorry, Jenny, about springing our news on you. I know how sensitive you are to your mother's loss. I should have done better about this, but I just didn't know how." He looked down at his hands. "I appreciate your good wishes. So does Dad."

Jenn sat up and crossed her arms on her knees. "I have a confession too, Dad. I don't want to meet them ... or talk about them. Not yet anyway."

"They're wonderful women. You'll like them." He smoothed a strand of her hair behind her ear.

A light smile crossed her lips. She reached out and laid her hand on his arm. "You're wonderful men. If you like them, then they must be wonderful." She paused. "I just need to get used to the idea, that's all."

He kissed her on her forehead and tucked her under the covers like he did when she was a little girl. "Good night, honey."

"Good night, Dad." She slept through the night.

~ * ~

The next day, Sunday afternoon, Jenn folded the last of her laundry, pleased to be washing clothes at home. She hated the weekly chore of lugging her dirty clothes down to the laundry room in the dorm's basement and, worse, folding her underwear in full view of boys washing their clothes. Once, one of the boys found a dropped brassiere on the floor. They passed around the bra and spent the whole time playing with it, wearing it, fitting it on their heads, and making comments about the size of the huge cups and what they held. Jenn blushed and—she had to admit—laughed at some of their antics.

"You ready?"

"Coming, Dad!" She hefted the bags and staggered out her bedroom door.

While he drove her back to campus, Jenn outlined her plan.

"I think you've got it all figured out. There really isn't too much more for you to do," he said. "This sounds melodramatic, but you have to keep this in the front of your mind as you question people. My concern—my legitimate fear—is you're not just chasing a story; you're chasing a killer." He squeezed her knee for emphasis as he looked at her.

At his words, the hair on the back of her neck stood up. She'd never considered doing anything but searching for the truth, but he was right. The killer—a real person—was not an ephemeral byline. A murderer walked the campus. He might hear of her asking questions or he could be a person she would interview. He would not appreciate her snooping.

"Anytime you feel you're in danger or have gotten yourself in over your head, call the police, immediately." Her father's voice was adamant. "Do not delay even if you feel all you'll do is embarrass yourself. Better to be embarrassed than ..." His voice trailed off and he squeezed her hand, tight. "Do you want me to stay home? That way you can call me anytime. I can get to campus in twenty minutes."

His words and his concern for her safety scared her. *Yes, stay home and away from that woman while you're at it.* The thought shamed her. "I'll be fine, Dad. I can only think of one person to talk to and it's over. If there's any trouble, I won't hesitate to call the police. I promise."

At the front of Morris Hall, her father got out of the truck and unloaded her two bags. He insisted on walking her up to her room. Before he left, he gave her a long, hard hug and kiss on the forehead. "I'll call you as soon as Dad and I get home."

He headed to the elevator.

## Chapter 22

At eight o'clock Monday morning, Jenn unlocked the staff room door and pushed it open. She threw her backpack on the desk, fired up her computer, and searched the student directory for Carmen Ortega de la Vega, the student who loaded and fired the kiln.

Rejuvenated from her time at home, bolstered by moral support and advice from her father and grandfather, she was ready for the investigation. She felt powerful enough to fight anything or anybody, Manny, in general, and Dee Forbes, in particular, be damned.

She jotted down Carmen's telephone number then dialed. After seven rings, the receiver lifted. A raspy voice came through the line. "What?"

"I'm so sorry to wake you, Carmen. I'm Jennifer Roby, *Lariat* reporter on campus. I'd like to talk with you—at your convenience—about the incident in the ceramics studio ... the bones found in the kiln?"

"Why?" Carmen's inhalation and groan exploded into a loud yawn.

"Um, I'd like to find out what may have happened, what may have led to the bones getting into the kiln ... the prank."

"Oh, sure, how 'bout later this morning? Stop by the Hamilton studio, around back."

Satisfied with herself, she headed downstairs to grab a bagel and coffee at Breakfast 'n' Lunch before finite math. She didn't want to be around if Manny came in.

~ * ~

As she sat in the Ag auditorium, her lightheartedness continued. She even ogled a few cowboy students. Maybe it was the promise of spring weather. Maybe she was getting used to the idea of Dad and Grampa's girlfriends. She shook her head at that thought. Her senses tingled as she considered the quest for the truth about the skeleton in the kiln. Chemistry was a breeze, and — bonus — the professor was to present a paper to a New York science academy on Wednesday; no class on Wednesday and no homework until Friday.

She hopped on Cougar outside the Ag building and pedaled hard to get to the ceramics studio, two minutes by bicycle if she got the green light on First Street. Breathing hard, she leaned it against the studio. Through the enormous, dirty windows, she saw a group of students clustered around the worktable and clay press. She walked around the studio to the courtyard. The snow had melted over the weekend revealing all manner of broken sculptures littering the courtyard. The cautionary banner was gone. A roaring sound radiated from the kiln, which led Jenn to believe it was running.

"Jennifer?" A loud whisper emanated from a small building just west of Alex's office. A rotund Hispanic woman motioned for Jenn to enter. "Hi, I'm Carmen Ortega Aurelia de la Vega," she said as Jenn entered a room lined with barrels and shelves filled with ceramics coated in what looked like dried Pepto-Bismol. A massive worktable took up much of the room. Covered buckets filled the space under the table.

"Hi, I'm Jennifer Roby, *Lariat* reporter." Jenn offered her hand to Carmen, who might have been in her late twenties, but dark circles under her eyes aged her.

"Didn't want to yell with the class going on," she said with a wave of her hand.

Jenn nodded, then looked around, not sure of the room's use.

Carmen noticed. "Been in here before?"

Jenn shook her head. "I don't know anything about ceramics."

"How about a quick lesson? When we finish sculpting a piece, it sits in the studio to dry. Once dry, the piece is very fragile; the slightest bump could fracture it. Then it's moved to an electric kiln in the shed." Carmen pointed out the window at the open shed. Kilns lined the walls.

"This first firing is called bisque, and the kiln's fired to almost nineteen hundred degrees. The heat transforms the clay through a process called quartz inversion. At that point, the piece becomes sturdy and not likely to break.

"This is the glazing room. After the bisque firing, we set the pieces here." Carmen pointed to the shelving unit to the left of the door.

She popped off a few buckets' lids to expose thick gray liquids. "In here is the glaze. Each one has different characteristics, like they'll produce a flat or shiny finish, plus they're formulated for various firing temperatures. We dip or brush the glaze on the bisque pieces then store them on this side." She lifted her chin to indicate the ledges littered with pieces covered with the dull pink film.

"From here they're placed in the kiln." Carmen pointed to the kiln that Jenn passed in the courtyard. "The heat— generally over two thousand degrees –causes a chemical reaction. That's when they turn to their final hardness and the glaze to its final matte or shiny surface and color.

"Over here in this room is where all the glazes get mixed." Carmen walked into an adjoining small room lined with lidded buckets and a large worktable with built-in storage bins. "There's more to it than that, but that's the down-and-dirties of it."

Jenn laughed. "I appreciate that. I'm too ignorant to be told too much. It's harder than I thought."

"It's even much more complicated when you get into clay properties and firing temperatures. Simply building a sculpture can be an engineering feat. Developing glazes is pure chemistry."

Jenn nodded as she looked around.

"So, what did you need to see me about?" Carmen said, getting down to business.

"You're the ceramics intern?" Jenn needed to know Carmen's responsibilities and her perspective of what happened that day. "Plus, I don't understand about the gas for the kiln. What was the problem? The big deal?"

"Yep, I'm the intern," Carmen nodded. "The temperature in the kiln didn't get as high as it should have because there was a kink in the gas line, and some debris apparently clogged the kink. The gas couldn't flow like it needed to, so the flame was starved for fuel." Carmen pulled out buckets and placed them on the table. "Because there wasn't enough fuel, the flame didn't get as large as it should have and raise the temp to what we needed." She opened a metal cabinet. Small glass jars, plastic pots, and paper sacks crowded the cupboard. She studied the labels, selected one jar marked "cobalt" and set it by the buckets. "It was supposed to get to two-thousand-two-hundred degrees."

"Wow. I had no idea it had to get that hot."

"It takes that high of a temp to make stoneware and for the glazes to turn to glass properly. But with the gas line kink, after nine hours, the temp just wouldn't rise."

"How high do you think it got?"

Carmen shrugged. "Who knows? Anywhere from a thousand to eighteen hundred, but even that's just a guess. That kiln doesn't have an internal thermometer. The newer ones do." She gathered measuring spoons and scoops from the shelves by the door. "I mean, the entire process takes about eight hours on a good day. So, the only thing to do was shut it down. If the gas had worked properly, those bones would've completely melted or been incinerated."

Hannah May's words about sweeping up the ashes echoed in Jenn's head.

"When the gas is shut off and the flame dies, we wait for the kiln to cool, which is usually the next day, then we can open it." Carmen flipped through a stack of papers that lay on the table. She noticed Jenn watching. "Glaze recipes." She continued with her instruction as she worked. "If you open the kiln when the interior's too hot, the shock of a drastic change in air temp can crack a lot of pieces."

"So, you loaded the kiln on Sunday?" Jenn felt her voice almost crack from nervousness. Her father's cautionary words that she might be talking with a killer reverberated. The trick was to get the information she wanted, yet not tip her hand that she knew more than she let on. If Carmen had loaded the kiln, she had to have seen the body—or was the one to put it there. Goosebumps sprouted on Jenn's arms.

"As the intern, it's usually my job to load the kiln and fire it. Students float in and out all the time. Some will help. On Sunday, Jake Barton and a few others like Tiffany Arnold were here, and the kiln was partially loaded, so I finished loading it and fired it."

"Did you look inside the kiln at what had already been loaded?"

Face wrinkled in disbelief, Carmen stared at Jenn like she had just thrown up. "No. Why would I do that? I'm not going to unload a kiln just to see what's in there. I just finished loading it."

"How much of the kiln was loaded?"

"Uh, the floor and one shelf."

"Do you have information you could share about the ... bones ... in the kiln? Do you know who'd pull a joke like that?" Jenn tugged her notepad and pen from her backpack.

Carmen nodded and concentrated on Jenn's question. "Oh God, you're not going to print my name are you? This is off the record, right?" Apparently, she had also received instructions from Forbes not to talk.

Jenn nodded her head. "Naming you wouldn't be the right thing. If anything, I'd say you're 'an unnamed source'."

Carmen threw up her hands, like she'd wanted to talk about the incident and the enforced silence was killing her. "This makes no sense! Why the hush-hush? The way the cop and PR woman acted, I'll bet they were lying!"

"What makes you say that?" Jenn saw an opportunity.

"The head cop had to help hold up the PR woman. I thought she was going to puke. The coroner was here. She had gloves on and tarps spread out. She had a box to lay out the bones just as they lay in the kiln. All of them were acting like they found the flippin' Holy Grail." Carmen flung an empty bucket to the floor.

"Did you talk to any of them?"

Carmen leaned against the table, her hand on her hip. "Chief Bannister grilled me. I even gave him the nickel tour I just gave you."

"Do a lot of people come back here or in the courtyard or mess with the kiln?" Jenn scribbled furiously.

The intern turned back to the table. "Yes, yes, and yes. The students do, of course, but some of them bring their friends or their kids. Too many of them can't keep their hands to themselves."

"So, there could be a lot of people touching the kiln or the pieces?" She looked up at Carmen.

A hiss escaped from Carmen's lips. "Yeah. I'll chew on them if I catch them. I don't want anyone's pieces to get broken."

Jenn poised her pen over her pad. She swallowed hard. "Getting back to the professionals' reactions, do you believe there was any chance the bones were genuine?"

"I ... can't believe ..." The intern seemed torn.

Jenn's face crinkled as she concentrated on Carmen's reaction. She decided to take another tack. "What is it about these bones that bother you?"

Carmen started to hyperventilate. Gasps strained from her throat.

Jenn didn't understand the reaction. *An asthma attack?* She didn't know what to do, so she patted Carmen's shoulder. At her touch, Carmen's shoulders heaved.

"This joke really upset you," Jenn said. "You ran the kiln that day." An odd comment, she knew, but she needed to keep information coming.

"Sorry." Carmen wiped her face with her hands. "It's not that. There's something else ..."

Jenn perked up, waiting to hear.

"My friend is missing." Carmen's words mirrored Jake's in the hall of the chemistry building.

"Sibylle?"

"Yes! Do you know anything about her?" A hopeful look crossed Carmen's face.

"I only saw the poster in the Commons."

"I'm so worried about her." Carmen shook her head. Jenn patted the sturdy back. Tears welled in Jenn's eyes. "I'm so sorry about your friend."

Jenn thought about revealing the truth about the skeleton, but her advisor's warning against sharing information between witnesses and sources was forefront in her mind. More importantly, if Carmen wasn't the friend she portrayed, for her own safety Jenn needed to keep that information to herself.

Carmen sniffed. "If she shows up all fat and happy for putting me through this worry, I'll kill her myself."

# Chapter 23

The end of finite math finally arrived, and Jenn stuffed her notebook in her backpack. The handful of amphitheater occupants rose en masse, split down the center, and headed for the exits. She'd tried to focus on her chemistry and math classes, but her mind wandered to Carmen and whom to interview next.

She hurried back to the *Lariat* hallway, peeked into the staff room then into the newsroom. Both rooms were deserted.

At her desk, feet propped up, she let her silver mane fall. She blew an exaggerated sigh and imagined being in a better place. She was bicycling: the spring wind tangled her hair. Her thighs burned as the pedals churned faster to reach the summit of Red Canyon, west of Colter. Flying through the steep canyon that paralleled the Wind River Mountains, antelope raised their heads to watch her whiz by. Maybe a tiny baby 'lope would toddle from its hiding place, trying to untangle its long legs. She smiled at the thought.

Her mind came back to the present. She thought back to Carmen, who loaded and fired the kiln, and the missing Sibylle. Jenn felt a shiver of fear that the skeleton in the kiln was Sibylle.

*Don't get ahead of yourself.* She forced the thought to the back of her mind.

Jake Barton hadn't been in chemistry class that morning, or, come to think of it, since last Wednesday. She sat up, dialed his telephone number to talk to him if for no other reason than to see how he was doing. As she poked the numbers on the telephone, she paused. The numbers were the same as those on Sibylle's missing poster. *He said they were friends. Maybe he's heading up the search.*

"The number you have dialed is no longer in service."

*Maybe he's not a good friend if he's already given up. Maybe he ran away.* She tapped her fingers on the desk.

Something Carmen said rang a bell. Jenn grabbed her backpack then fished around the papers, snacks, and textbooks to pull out her interview notes. Carmen mentioned Tiffany Arnold had been at the studio. Maybe Tiffany saw something. Jenn woke up the computer, entered the Internet, and navigated to CSC's directory.

She jabbed the phone's buttons. The phone rang once. A high-pitched voice breathed into the mouthpiece, "Johnnie!? I've been waiting for you to call." A giggle tickled Jenn's ear.

Shocked and embarrassed, Jenn froze.

"Stop teasing!" Her breath hissed through the earpiece.

"Um, I'm sorry. I'm Jennifer Roby, *Lariat* reporter."

The silence on the other end lengthened. To get beyond the embarrassment, Jenn decided to press on as if Tiffany had answered normally.

"I'd like to talk with you about your experience in the ceramics studio on Monday … about what you'd seen. Would you meet with me this afternoon? At your convenience, of course."

"Why would I want to talk with you?" The voice turned cold and angry. "All I did was unload the kiln. The press would just take that out of context."

Anxious, Jenn stammered, "I'm trying to get a sense of what may have caused someone to pull a prank and its effects on the people who discovered it. I assure you anything you say will be off the record."

"I've dealt with the press before. I'm not impressed with their accuracy or truthfulness."

Jenn looked to the ceiling as if the strength not to slam down the phone could be found there. "I'm only looking for the personal story. Again, all your comments will be off the record."

~ * ~

Jenn hurried to meet Tiffany in the basement of the Student Commons. Tiffany had made it clear she didn't want to talk to a reporter and Jenn feared she wouldn't wait long.

The Commons basement, fresh from its renovation, was a maze of hallways that opened to a massive airy room. In that open area a beer bar, the Tap Lounge, stood in the center. Against the wall was the glass-enclosed Billiard Room. Throughout the basement, students studied, slept by the gas fireplaces, or sat at the tall counter that overlooked an interior eating area. Though in a hurry, Jenn tried not to slam her boot heels too hard on the tile floor. Each heel's *clump* echoed through the large room.

At their decided-upon meeting place, Tiffany slumped on her barstool overlooking the seating area. Short and chunky with a receding chin, Tiffany's yellow bottle-blond hair hung just past her shoulders. Leopard print Capri pants exposed thick ankles and strapless high-heeled pumps. Jenn suppressed a grimace.

"Tiffany? Thank you for meeting me." Jenn said, breathless, as she threw her backpack on the floor. She smiled and extended her right hand in greeting. "Jennifer Roby, *Lariat* reporter."

Tiffany gave a smile more like a curled lip. Her fingertips brushed Jenn's hand.

"I'll keep this as short as possible. I'm sure you're busy." Jenn fished out the interview notepad. Tiffany made a point of studying Jenn's faded jeans and worn Carhartt coat. Jenn tried not to care, but she pulled back her feet so her scuffed boots weren't so noticeable. "What did you notice out of the ordinary a week ago Sunday at the ceramics studio?" She flipped the pages in her notebook to find a blank one.

"I didn't see anything Sunday," a petulant voice said. "My father owns two art galleries. One's in Jackson Hole. The main gallery is in Denver. I live there. I helped Daddy set up a show opening for Ty Albert. He's my Daddy's discovery." Her nose and voice rose as she spoke. "I wasn't even in Wyoming that weekend."

Tiffany's sneer of "Wyoming" grated Jenn. She thought of Wyomingites' pet insult for Coloradoans: *Freakin' Greenie*. A deep breath calmed her irritation. "Really? I was told you were in the studio that morning."

Tucking her chin into her chest as if someone were ready to strike her, she insisted. "I was in Denver. I won't even work in Hamilton except when I'm forced to in class. My daddy had a contractor build me a studio, complete with my own kiln."

"Why would anyone say you were at the studio Sunday if you were not?" Jenn prodded.

"Mistaken possibly. Lying probably. Carmen's jealous of my talent."

Jenn watched Tiffany's chin sink into her chest, a movement that reminded her of the toad that had once loved her garden. Its throat stretched as it croaked a ribbit sound.

Tiffany's mention of Carmen being a liar reminded Jenn that Carmen had partially loaded the kiln. Perhaps she did more than partially load it.

"What can you tell me about her?"

Tiffany humphed. "She's a know-it-all. Demands we load the kiln just right while she hovers, nitpicking. 'Clean up after yourselves in the glaze room.' 'Put everything back like you found it.' She's like everyone's uptight mother."

"Would she have any inclination to play a joke to scare students?"

"Oh, yes, the prank. I read the story in the paper. Yeah, Carmen could do that. She's a two-faced backstabber." Tiffany leaned toward Jenn. "Carmen seems very nice, seems like she's trying real hard." Tiffany glanced over her shoulder to ensure no one was listening. "She's not. A few weeks ago, in the glaze room, I hadn't yet cleaned up a splash of glaze on the floor. She told me if I didn't clean it up right then, she'd break all my greenware, and no one would ever know."

"Greenware?"

"That's clay that hasn't been biscuit fired."

"Biscuit?" Jenn recalled that Carmen said bisque during her ceramics lesson.

Tiffany's sigh spoke of her impatience with Jenn's ignorance. "Fresh clay that's been fired once is called biscuit ware. Then it's glazed."

Flustered by Tiffany's impatience, Jenn wondered if there was a side to Carmen that was violent ... violent enough for murder? By her own admission, she loaded the kiln. Even Jenn thought Carmen should have seen something, especially a body, in the kiln.

"I heard you helped unload the kiln. Did you see anything suspicious or out of the ordinary?"

Tiffany paused, but her lip curled as if she was concentrating. "No." She reached for her purse. "Are you done?"

"I appreciate you taking time from your busy schedule to talk with me. Do you have any other information about Carmen, or anything you might think is important?"

"I don't know." Tiffany fidgeted. "I heard her tell one girl she needed to, like, help her make clay or she'd kick her ass." When Tiffany looked directly at her, her second chin had disappeared. A slope of soft skin draped from narrow chin to chest.

"Make clay?" Jenn thought nature made clay. All people had to do was dig it up.

Tiffany gave Jenn a look of utter contempt for her ignorance.

"Look, Tiffany, I don't know anything about ceramics. I know you're an expert ..." Jenn said, disgusted she had to feed this woman's ego to keep her talking.

"To make clay usable for ceramics, we combine several ingredients. It's not like we just go dig it up or anything."

*You freakin' dough-girl-Greenie.*

Tiffany stood up. Jenn needed to get the interview back on track, fast. "So, you think Carmen is capable of violence?"

"Oh, yeah. A lot of students are afraid of her. She's unstable. Swears in Spanish."

"Well, I've only spoken to Carmen once. She seemed very nice. She was upset and concerned about her friend, Sibylle. You may have seen the 'missing' posters?"

Tiffany began to gather her things. Her chin tucked back into her chest. *Ribbit.* "Some friend. Carmen once insulted Sibylle and said she'd kick her ass."

"What made Carmen say that?"

She rolled her eyes, "Carmen had a big thing for Jake, but he had a hard-on for Sibylle. Are you done? I have an event at my sorority."

"Do you think Jake Barton could be violent?" Jenn wanted as much information out of Tiffany before she walked away. She had the feeling she'd have only this one chance.

"He's just weird."

*Not as weird as wearing Capri pants in winter, you twit.* "Have you heard him threaten anyone?"

"I heard that he threatened to kill his girlfriend." Tiffany had a look on her face that made Jenn think she was being helpful, but just enough so Jenn would get off her back.

"Do you know why he'd say such a thing?" Jenn choked off a gasp.

The rounded shoulders shrugged.

"May I quote you about what you heard?" Jenn asked. In a flash, she recalled telling Tiffany everything she'd said would be off the record.

Tiffany eyes grew wide. Her mouth flung open like Jenn had slapped her. "Hell no, you can't!"

Now it was Jenn's turn to feel slapped. She swallowed hard and forced herself to stay forthright. "That's right. I already said that your comments were off the record. I'm sorry." A compliment and a distraction might calm this shallow woman. "Your parents are successful gallery owners. They must be a great source of inspiration to you."

Tiffany paused then she slowly slouched on the stool. A slight smile flitted. "Yes. They are."

Jenn smiled. "Do their two galleries have a focus for their artwork? A particular medium?"

A tinkling laugh fell from Tiffany's growing smile. "Oh, yes. Mother is a famous ceramicist. She's sold work as far away as Berlin and London."

"Is your father an artist too?" Jenn relaxed. She was actually enjoying the change in Tiffany.

The smile grew. Tiffany's eyes shone. "Sculpture is his concentration. You've seen his most famous piece, I'm sure, the public display in Tokyo called 'Nippon Drapery'?" She turned to face Jenn. "It's a monumental steel structure," she prodded.

Jenn suppressed a grimace. She slowly shook her head. "I'm sorry."

Tiffany waved a hand. "Well, it's a big deal." She paused. "I hope someday they'll show my own work in their galleries."

"Does their success put a lot of pressure on you?" Jenn was shocked to see Tiffany's eyes well.

Tiffany blinked hard and nodded.

Uncomfortable with the stress her question apparently caused, Jenn decided to hearten Tiffany. "I saw your black and white ceramics piece. It was beautiful. How did you make it?"

Tiffany's eyes bulged. Her lips pursed. "So, that's what this is about. You just want to steal my technique!" She snatched her Gucci purse and faux leopard-skin jacket and clicked away like a worst-dressed poodle.

## Chapter 24

Jenn threw her backpack on her office desk in the staff room. Stalking up the three flights of stairs, one step at a time, hadn't taken the furious edge off her anger. *What a stuck-up bitch.* Trying to calm down, she rubbed her hands over her face, hard. She stared at her father and grandfather's photos and wondered where they were and what they were doing. *That's a bad image.*

She dug out her notepad and picked up the keyboard before kicking her booted feet onto the desk and leaning back in the chair. She may as well be comfortable while she wrote the article that would expose a murder and a conspiracy to the entire campus.

As she typed, she paused at Alex's, Carmen's, and Tiffany's words. They had bucked Dee Forbes' order to spurn the press, but their comments were off the record. Each could face repercussions, particularly Alex as an employee of the college. She left out their names.

Jenn wanted the story ready to hand to Manny as soon as he arrived to put together tomorrow's edition. Years ago, Grampa told her one way to get what you want from a boss was to have all your information ready. "You want a soda machine in your office. If you ask your boss, 'Can we get a soda machine?' it's easy for him to say no. Instead, ask 'Can we get a soda machine in the office? Here's the rental cost. The soda company will stock it. Here's how money we'll make since I've asked if others will use the machine. The electricity cost this much, but the bill can be paid with the machine's proceeds. It can sit in this unused space.' You see? Make it easy for your boss to say 'yes'."

Manny entered the staff room just as she printed her article. With no preamble or greeting he ordered, "Jennifer, come with me."

Jenn knew she was in for a tongue lashing, but her article would explain why she violated his order. He couldn't be mad at her after he read it. She followed him into the newsroom.

He slammed the door behind her. "What the friggin' hell are you doing?"

"Manny, I know you're ticked, but hear me out—"

"I will not hear you out. I'm getting reamed from more sides than I can count. Did you not understand my order to drop the bones story?" His face flushed dark red. "I could fire you right now."

She couldn't meet his eyes. His last words gave her pause. She recalled the talks over the weekend with Dad and Grampa, took a deep breath, and plowed ahead. "Manny, I spoke to the coroner. She confirmed the bones were real."

Manny's eyes narrowed, but he didn't speak.

"They were bona fide bones—of a girl. This whole prank story has been a lie."

He froze. His face was a blank. His hand, as if attached to a disembodied arm with a mind of its own, floated around behind him in search of a chair. It found one. He sat.

She kneeled in front of him and gripped the arms of his chair, encircling him. "Manny, I've exposed a cover-up, of a murder—probably a student. Everybody I've talked to said the college told them to keep it quiet."

Manny remained silent. His face grew pale, almost gray. Jenn let him process the revelation. He closed his eyes, inhaled, and held it. After he exhaled, he opened his eyes, but still didn't look at Jenn.

"Manny?"

More to himself he muttered, "That explains a lot of things."

Not wanting to give him too much time to remember he was chewing her out she offered Manny her article. "I wrote it out, all of it. We can put it on the front page—a scoop."

In slow motion, he took the paper from Jenn's hand without looking at it or her. "I have to review it first." His voice was flat, expressionless.

Jenn stood up. "Yeah. I know it's a shock. It was for me too … still is. It's all in there. Are you going to read it?"

"Yes."

"I'll stay while you read it." She wasn't the only one who knew this huge secret, and she felt exhilarated to share the moment.

"No. Go home, Jenn."

"I want to stay with you while you read it."

Manny's head snapped up. The frightened look in his eyes alarmed Jenn. "Go home."

Unnerved, Jenn turned to leave. "Um, okay. Call me if you have any questions?"

Manny nodded. "Hold on. How many people have you told about this?"

"You're the only one."

"Even when you interviewed all these people? No hints?"

"Nope. I just pretended I was asking about the prank." She felt a flush of pride in uncovering a murder without revealing what she knew.

Manny seemed relieved. "Don't forget: Forbes' and Stroll's secrecy orders still stand. Say nothing about this to anyone. Got it? There's a lot at stake here, not just now, but after graduation. I mean it."

"Yeah, until tomorrow. Then everybody will be talking about it." With a wave, Jenn headed out the door, puzzled and unsettled by Manny's behavior.

~ * ~

Manny stared into the depths of the unkempt room, but he didn't see any of it. He didn't move as he read the article. He never moved for several minutes more.

At the recycle bin, he lifted a handful of discarded papers, inserted her sheets in the pile, and replaced the handful.

He picked up the phone receiver and stabbed at the button with a preset number. "Doctor Stroll, I'm sorry to bother you so late ..."

## Chapter 25

"What the hell is this?" Jenn screamed at Manny as she approached him from behind in the newsroom and flung the newspaper on his desk.

Manny picked up the paper and tossed it into the trashcan.

"Answer my question." Jenn fished it out. She displayed Tuesday's headline: *College Initiates Cutbacks*.

"Can you be more specific?"

"Don't be snotty." Jenn felt her face burn. "What is going on here? Human remains are found in a kiln on this campus, and you don't even print it? Don't you give a damn about informing the public anymore?"

Manny shot her an angry look. "You don't know what's going on here."

"I know you're suppressing this story, my first scoop. You're censoring an important public service announcement. For the life of me, I can't figure out why."

"Never question my journalistic integrity," Manny almost yelled.

Jenn stared into Manny's eyes. The hard look in his eyes matched hers. "I am questioning your journalistic integrity." The words exited Jenn's mouth with great care and a push for effect.

Manny advanced toward Jenn so quickly, she stepped back. He stopped just short of bumping into her. Each glared at the other.

"How long have you two been married?" A bright voice boomed through the newsroom. Jenn stepped back from Manny as he retreated from her.

Willy Warwick bounded into the room and headed for the angry couple. Willy's eyes fondled Jenn's body as he slapped Manny's shoulder. He plopped on the foam cushions as they protested with a loud *psssh*, spread his arms onto the back of the couch, propped his feet on the broken coffee table, and ignored the falling pile of old newspapers. His wide smile forced Jenn to turn away from his horse teeth.

"Well, aren't you going to ask me my big news? Or would you prefer I join your little tiff?" Willy leaned forward and looked at Jenn. "We could make it a threesome."

Jenn's lip curled. She spun to face Manny.

"One guess who's been picked to interview Ives and Maguire? Me! I'm going to interview the prez and the senator! Congratulate me. Come on." Warwick grinned and looked from Jenn to Manny.

Jenn whispered so Willy couldn't hear, "I could go to the *Cabernet*." She would never go to City of Colter's newspaper, but she wanted to see his reaction.

Manny grabbed Jenn by the arm and marched her into the hallway.

"Bye, bye, Henny Penny," sang Willy.

Manny slammed the door shut behind him. In the dim hallway, he kept his voice low so it wouldn't echo and so Willy wouldn't hear.

"Jennifer Roby, let me give you some lessons, some journalistic advice. You're just a sophomore. You haven't had enough classes to be as smart or intuitive as your editor, because, right now with your skill level, you're such an amateur you oughtta focus on fiction."

Jenn gasped as if she had been punched. Her face burned in embarrassment.

"First lesson, if you ever—ever!—go to the competition when you're working for another newspaper, neither paper will trust you." Manny gripped Jenn's arm and shook it for effect. "You will lose all integrity. Each side will consider you a traitor.

"Second lesson, in your article you wrote some key words: 'off the record' yet you included enough hints that anyone could figure out who your sources were. Do you understand what that means?" Manny pushed his face close to Jenn's. The anger boring from his eyes would have pierced hers, but she looked away. "Answer me."

Frozen from humiliation, Jenn thought she knew what he meant, but apparently not what was affecting Manny. She could only shake her head.

"It means what they said is for your ears, not your eyes. Those little words forbid us from printing such descriptions. It's strictly confidential. You must protect their identities at all costs. Anything less would violate everything sacred about journalism." Manny released her arm. His chest heaved.

"Is there any of it we can print?" Jenn gulped, trying not to cry, ashamed of going too far too fast and for getting so wrapped up in the events she hadn't thought through it all.

"Oh, sure, let's see, an unnamed source said something we can't print because the reader will figure out who they are, but that something was verified by another unnamed source. I'm talking about something really important. Just believe me." Manny's sarcastic voice stabbed at Jenn's feelings. "Whatya think about that?"

At Jenn's silence, he continued his tirade.

"Third lesson, there are things happening that you don't know about. Trust me on this: people's lives are at stake."

## Chapter 26

In the corner of the Commons' seating area, Jenn faced the wall. Her head felt like it weighed a ton as it lay on her crossed arms. She stared at the wall without seeing it. Maybe journalism wasn't her calling. Thinking back through the past seven days, all she could see was how she'd screwed up, made people angry, and made herself look and feel foolish. Her mistakes could have tragic consequences, interfere with police business and meddle in innocent people's lives. Inexperience was no excuse just because what she knew was important. Manny hadn't made it any easier. He should teach her before going off half-cocked, rather than after, when his lessons bordered on cruelty.

Colter's low humidity had dried her bagel to a puck, but she didn't care. She broke off pieces and ate them. She didn't taste the raisins or the cinnamon. Next week was spring break. Cougar would take her home. The exercise would do her good while she escaped the mess she'd made. During that week off she needed to reassess her life's calling.

Dwelling on emotions and self-pity didn't help to break the funk, but perhaps considering the facts would. She asked herself, what mistakes had she made? Okay, her article didn't get published, so no one's trust had been violated. She learned a painful lesson about on and off the record. Jenn searched her memory, but couldn't come up with anything else. Of course, she violated Manny's do-not-investigate order. He had been so angry he could barely stammer for her to stay out of his sight for a while. If she pursued the issue any further he would fire her.

Feeling better, but not much, Jenn gathered her belongings, tossed the trash, and wandered to the main floor. Since the *Lariat* offices were her home away from home, she didn't know where to go.

On the Commons' main floor, a row of strategically stationed tables, placed so the maximum number of students would walk by, stood covered by brochures, pamphlets, baked goods, or banners. Non-profit organizations pushed their agendas or favorite causes. Members of the organizations clustered behind the tables.

Self-conscious of the eyes that watched her, she studied which agencies were represented and what they pushed. The Pi Pi Pi fraternity sold misshapen muffins and undercooked cookies. Students for Tolerance, the campus gay and transgender organization, displayed awareness pamphlets. A county volunteer fire department sold tickets for a rifle raffle. Their table enjoyed plenty of attention. At the last table, the Delta Omega Gamma sorority touted *Free Tibet*. Three sorority members, one of whom was Tiffany Arnold, staffed the table.

Curious, Jenn decided to see if Tiffany would recognize her and how she would act. Maybe she would talk more about the students in the ceramics class.

*"If I hear you pursued this story, I'll fire you."* Jenn ignored Manny's words in her head and pretended to read the brochure. She thought of a question about the Tibetan people as an excuse to start a conversation. She opened her mouth to ask, but stopped short. Jenn recognized the other two young women at the table as the two who lingered at the makeup counter in the bookstore; one of them had complained how her mother hounded her.

A cute young man stopped next to Jenn, and started a conversation with the women behind the table — not much of one, Jenn thought; more like an introduction to flirting. The three girls pointedly ignored Jenn, their attentions focused on the guy. Disgusted, she tossed their brochure on the table and walked away.

"Jennifer!" A voice called out, too loud. Jenn turned to see Tiffany skirt the table. She still wore Capri pants, only this time the pattern was tiny flowers. The tight pattern didn't hide the saddlebags that afflicted Tiffany's thighs.

"Tiffany." Jenn wanted to curl her lip. She couldn't guess why Tiffany would act so cheery after she'd stalked away yesterday.

"Listen, I'm sorry about how I ended your interview yesterday." Tiffany spoke the last words too loudly. "When you questioned me about the story for the *Lariat*, you asked me about a topic I'm very sensitive about. You see, I've had my ideas copied, and in the art world, copying someone's work is a cardinal crime."

Why Tiffany talked so loud became clear when the other two girls and the cute guy stopped their flirting to watch Tiffany and Jenn.

"So, during your interview when you asked about my artwork, well, it brought back bad memories. Can you appreciate that?"

"Certainly," Jenn kept her voice flat.

With a quick glance at the women and man behind her, Tiffany cried, "And I want to disclose the best news ever to you as a reporter. The art department reconsidered my BFA application and approved it!"

Jenn nodded as she mulled "reconsidered". "Congratulations. Your parents must be proud."

Tiffany clapped her hands together. "Yes, they are." She touched Jenn's arm and declared, "You're welcome to include my name in your article. You understand, don't you?"

A wave of disgust washed over Jenn. *You freakin' phony.* Yesterday, Tiffany had sneered at Jenn and acted superior. Now, she was actually sucking up. Behind Tiffany, the other two girls looked at Jenn, up and down. One even leaned over the table to take in her scuffed boots.

Sick of it all, Jenn stared at the other two girls until they turned away. She let the disgust show on her face then turned to Tiffany. "I understand everything."

## Chapter 27

This is not good, Jenn thought, to let someone tick you off so much that it's easy to do something bad. She walked, tentative, into the staff room to find it deserted, as was the newsroom. Relieved, Jenn pulled out her notebook and dialed a telephone number.

"If you can make it here in twenty minutes, the coroner will be able to talk with you," the secretary said. "Otherwise, she'll be gone for the rest of the day."

"I'll be right there."

Jenn threw her backpack around her shoulders while she ran for the stairs. At the bike rack, hurrying, she misdialed the numbers on the combination lock three times before the lock released. She pushed off and pedaled fast toward the coroner's office, running through a couple stop signs. Slipping on the ice wasn't a worry; the weekend's warm, sunny weather had melted the ice and snow.

As Jenn approached Main Avenue, the last major cross street before the funeral home, lines of traffic moved east and west. Squeezing the brake handles to slow for the stop sign, the bike continued its momentum. Panicking, she squeezed the handles harder. Cougar couldn't stop.

Zipping past the stop sign and into the intersection, a dump truck bore down on her, its horn blaring.

Jenn screamed and flung herself to the pavement. She and Cougar skidded to a stop as the truck's locked wheels flashed inches from her face.

Gasping, in shock, she curled in a ball as cars whizzed past her.

"Are you all right? Didn't you see the stop sign?" The driver yelled as he ran toward her.

Jenn struggled to untangle herself from Cougar. The man pulled off the bike and flung it aside. She pushed herself off the ground. Her legs wobbled, but she managed to stand. With trembling hands, she righted Cougar and leaned against it for support.

"My brakes ... they didn't work," Jenn gasped. "I don't understand."

The man pointed to Jenn. "You scraped your leg."

Head quivering, she inspected herself. Her blue jeans' pant leg had nearly scraped through. Her right arm ached. Her sleeve was torn. Amazed she had no abraded skin, her leg and arm pulsated to the pounding beat of her heart.

Jenn squeezed her brakes' handles. The brake cables had no resistance. Not comprehending, she could only stare.

"Here's your problem," the man pointed toward her handlebars. "The cables have been disconnected. Did you forget to reattach them?"

Jenn shook her head, unable to speak. *Who would disconnect my brakes?*

"Wow. Somebody's really ticked off at you."

~ * ~

Cougar rolled to a stop on the funeral home's driveway. Jenn placed a foot on the ground and grimaced at the pain shooting up her leg. Soreness swelled throughout her body. The shock of the dump truck's tires skidding before her eyes was wearing off, but the nagging fright that someone sabotaged her brakes lingered.

Shoving aside her anxiety, she limped to catch Susan Hawley before she left. Jenn leaned the bike against the building; she didn't lock it and hoped the low crime rate in Colter would hold this one time.

Gasping for air as she pulled open the mortuary's door, a wheeze escaped. *Oh, great.* Asthma threatened to close her throat. It constricted only when she pushed so hard she had to pant for air. The stress of her accident set off the attack.

While Susan Hawley talked on the phone, Jenn concentrated on breathing in through her nose and exhaling through her mouth. Throat muscles constricted and cramped. Her entire body wanted to spasm. She tried to relax, not wanting to interview Susan while gasping for breath or being stiff from pain. Susan hung up the phone and waved for Jenn to enter.

"Thank you for seeing me, Susan, especially on such short notice." Jenn said, still puffing.

"No problem. I don't have much time though. Oh my gosh, what happened?" Susan stood and took in Jenn's scraped pant leg and torn sleeve.

"Someone disconnected my bike's brakes. I had to lay my bike down. A truck almost hit me." Saying the words out loud and realizing how close she came to death, Jenn fought back tears and shivered.

Susan sat next to Jenn and laid her hand on Jenn's shoulder in comfort. "Are you all right? How can I help you? Do you know how such a thing could happen?"

Her mind couldn't keep up with Susan's questions. "I think I'm okay." She gave a small laugh. "I'll feel this tomorrow," she joked although pain coursed through her body now.

"Do you think it may have been someone's idea of a prank?"

"Bad joke." The word "prank" brought her back to the reason for her trip. "I was wondering if you know anything more about the bones in the kiln."

"Oh, yes. She has been identified."

Jenn shivered harder and winced at the surging pain. "Who was the victim?"

Susan opened a file on her desk. "Sibylle Beaufort. I'll spell it for you."

Jenn's thoughts jumped elsewhere as the missing poster swam in her mind. *Something French.*

Either Dee Forbes lied when she told Manny that Sibylle had left school, or Sibylle had actually left campus seemingly for good and returned. Jenn blinked back tears. She had perceived a bond to this pretty girl she would never meet.

"What can you tell me about Sibylle and what happened to her?" Jenn cleared her throat to break up the lump.

"She was an exchange student from France." She tapped the file folder on her desk as her lips tightened. The file tapping stopped. Her brow furrowed.

"What is it?" Jenn prodded, alarmed.

"I'd been told students had photographed the remains. With social media nowadays, the need to notify the family was great. The Dean of Students agreed, and he obtained for me her family's contact information. I notified her parents just a bit ago."

She drummed the folder with nervous fingers. "A trusted friend of mine is fluent in French, and he translated the notification. The poor parents already knew of her being killed." She stared at her desk and murmured, "Damn immediate communications nowadays."

Jenn paused as an unsettled feeling spread in her gut. She cleared her throat. "Can you tell me how you came to verify the victim was Miss Beaufort?"

"Her boyfriend filed a missing person's report last Monday. He gave the police the name of a local dentist who capped her teeth a few months ago. The dentist gave me her records. The remains were seriously degraded, but the jaw and teeth were intact enough for the forensic dentist to make a comparison and an ID."

"Who was her boyfriend?" Jenn's pencil was poised above her notepad.

"I don't think I should answer that. It may be pertinent to the case."

"Do you have any idea how or why she was killed? Any idea who did this?"

"The police chief and I just got back from her dorm room, but we didn't find anything that pointed to a reason." Susan straightened a pile of papers on her desk. "To be honest, if we did, I couldn't tell you right now. Besides her clothes and study materials, she had only a few miscellaneous things like notes about the Colter French club, the script for the college's *Kiss Me Kate* production, a Jackson ceramics show brochure …

you know, that type of thing. She didn't have much in her room."

"Did the chief say if he was making progress on the investigation?"

"I'm sorry, Jennifer. No comment."

## Chapter 28

"What can you tell me about Sibylle Beaufort? I'd like to write a story about her. Maybe it'll make someone come forward with information." Jenn decided she could forge ahead with questioning. Her research was not about the off-limits skeleton in the kiln, but for Sibylle's obituary, although she dared not let anyone know that.

"That'll be great!" Carmen de la Vega clapped her hands.

Jenn settled on the rickety stool in the corner of Alex Redgrave's office.

After she had left the coroner, she rode back to Morris Hall and changed out of the torn clothing. Bruises bloomed on her thigh and upper arm. Her entire body ached. After checking her brake cables—again—she swung by the studios on the chance Alex or Carmen might be available to talk. Luck was with her; both were working in the office. The women had brightened because someone was taking an interest in the missing Sibylle.

Alex leaned on the latest giant head, one whose face seemed to find something hilarious.

"How well do either of you know Sibylle or her work habits? Was she in the studio often?"

Alex took a deep breath. "Sibylle's a French exchange student and so sweet. I don't know her real well. This is my first semester teaching at CSC, so I haven't gotten to know everyone as closely as I'd like." She looked at the floor. With the toe of her shoe, she traced a line in the dirt on the floor then walked to the window on the other side of the room.

"What were her habits—when it came to her ceramics?" Jenn stammered, and felt like a fraud. She knew full well what happened to Sibylle, but couldn't tell them to ease their minds. But then, the truth of how she died might be harder for them to bear. For now, they had hope.

"Sibylle's in the beginning class, but she had ceramics training in France, so her skill level is advanced. She often does things that new students don't have to, such as firing a kiln." Alex's office phone rang in the next room. "Excuse me." She stepped into her office that adjoined the studio.

Carmen shoved a toolbox out of the walkway. "She's from the same area in France that my grandmother came from about seventy years ago: Aquitaine. Grandmamma taught me a little French. Sibylle told me she didn't feel so homesick when she could speak French and reminisce about home. She and I are always here on Sundays, and she helps me load the kiln. She even likes firing it, so it surprised me when she wasn't here that Sunday."

"On that Sunday, when Sibylle should have been in the studio, what else do you remember?"

"You mean, more than I already told you?" Carmen appeared confused.

"Well, after our talk, did you remember anything else?" The muddy smell tickled Jenn's nose. She sniffed back a sneeze. Her nose started to run, and she took sneaking wipes at the drips.

"You keep asking me the same questions about that Sunday. I would have told you, so just drop it already." She sighed and shook her head.

Alex returned to the studio, her eyes large, mouth agape. She walked slowly and put her arm around her funny-face sculpture. "Sibylle's gone."

Jenn tensed and shivered, expecting Alex to burst into tears about the horrible death of her student.

"She went back to France."

A wave of disbelief swept Jenn.

"What? She didn't tell me!" Carmen cried out.

"Who was that, if you don't mind me asking?" Jenn stammered.

"Um, Dee Forbes, college PR." More to herself she murmured, "I don't understand why the registrar didn't call."

The three women were silent as they absorbed this news.

"Why would she leave and not bother to tell me?" Carmen choked back a sob.

"Or me. Forbes said that Sibylle found the campus too dangerous. She felt she had to leave immediately. She dropped out of school. Forbes is calling all her instructors."

"Unsafe? Did anyone ever threaten her?" Jenn asked. "Did she have any enemies?"

"Not that I've heard." Alex said. "I can't imagine anyone thinking this campus is anything but safe."

"Nobody had better talked bad about her or threatened her. I'd kill them myself." Carmen spoke so emphatically that both women stared at her. "Hey, there's nobody nicer than her. I loved her." Carmen wiped the tears from her face.

"She was supposed to have been here that Sunday to help you load the kiln. Could anything have happened around that time ... to make her leave?" Jenn knew the truth, but needed any information Carmen had.

"Quit focusing on that Sunday. You don't know if that had anything to do with her leaving," Carmen snapped. "It was just the same thing, people floated in and out while I was here, being it was the weekend."

"That's right, you said Jake and Tiffany were here." Jenn said, trying to calm Carmen.

Alex turned from the window to face Jenn. "That's different. On the weekends, Jake usually works in the print studio and Tiffany usually works at home."

Jenn wondered if Carmen was mistaken or lying about who had been here. *"Carmen's a liar."* Tiffany's words echoed.

"Is there anything either of you feel is pertinent, a reason why Sibylle ... left?"

After a pause, Carmen took a deep breath. "Sibylle's pregnant."

A shiver went through Jenn. *Motive.*

Alex spun, her mouth flew open. "No! I had no idea."

"She made me promise not to tell anyone until she announced it, but since she's gone, there's no reason to keep it quiet."

"Well, she shouldn't have been in ceramics." Alex grimaced. "I wish she had told me. I would have recommended she drop the class." Turning to Jenn, she explained. "We work with so many chemicals, this class may not have been safe."

*The class wasn't safe for her anyway.*

Carmen shrugged. "I did tell her, Alex, but Sibylle refused to drop a class she was already enrolled in. Then she said her mother didn't stop her pottery when she was pregnant, so why should she?" She tugged at her chin as she recalled the conversation. "Though she did tell me later she intended to skip the next semester's ceramics class, just in case."

Jenn carefully watched the two women, silent, lost in their own thoughts.

With a big sigh, Alex turned to Carmen. "Well, if she left, then I need for you to take down her show."

Carmen grimaced. "Any idea where to put it?"

The professor poked at the clay sculpture beside her, movements that seemed to give her time to think. "Just box them up and stash them in my back room. They can stay there until she tells us how to ship them back. Be careful with that basket; the flowers are incredibly thin."

"Sibylle has a show?" Jenn asked.

The prof nodded as she continued to prod the clay. "She just had her second art show opening—when was it?" Alex looked to Carmen. "Sometime in February. It would come down in a week anyway. This show was to celebrate her acceptance into the BFA program."

Jenn brightened. "Oh, like Tiffany! Where is the show? I'd love to see it."

The intern turned toward the door. "Since I'm heading there now to figure out how many packing boxes I need, I can show you."

"Oh, thank you," Jenn said as she stuffed her notepad in her backpack. She stood from the chair and flung her pack over her shoulder.

With her hand on the doorknob, Carmen paused. She jerked back to affix a stare at Alex. "Did I tell you about the paper I wrote for a Women's Studies class a few years back? Only a few states track the cause of death of pregnant women. In those states, they discovered that almost twenty percent of these women were murdered." She almost glared at Jenn. "Can you believe it? Murder is one of the leading causes of death in pregnant women."

With a faraway look in her eyes, she said with a quiet voice, "Sibylle told me her boyfriend was very upset when he found out she was pregnant. They got into this huge fight in the dorm about it."

"Who is her boyfriend?" Jenn recalled Tiffany's words about a threat made on Sibylle's life.

"Jake Barton—the guy who wears black."

## Chapter 29

The rounded buttocks shrink-wrapped in black tights swayed. The young man's mesmerizing oscillations distracted Jenn from seeing the stand. She gasped as she reached for the wobbling ceramic vase. She gripped the piece until it stood still on its podium. Her heart raced thinking she could have ruined someone's work. Glancing around, she'd have to watch where she walked. The art department foyer was a field full of diversions, podiums of sculptures circled by whirling dancers clad in varying amount of clothing, all of it skin tight.

Carmen laughed. "You have to watch out around here. There's all sorts of happenings." She lifted her hand to point out a collection of banners hanging from the ceiling on the other side of foyer, their edges about five feet off the floor. A student hurried through the foyer and, focused on the book in his hand, ducked as his head brushed a bottom edge.

She pointed to the room's far corner. "Sibylle's show is over there."

Jenn skirted a young woman in purple tights as she sank into splits. Carmen said, "Our building holds the art department and the dance and theater departments. It's real sporty in here in bad weather. The band will squeeze in here and practice."

About ten white stands of varying heights stood in a circle. Some of the pieces were tall bowls of clay, more vase-like, so thin that the sides defied gravity. Taped to the two walls were sheets proclaiming *No Photography*.

"There's the basket that Alex talked about." Carmen's hand waved, indicating the far side.

The porcelain flower basket was filled with white cut flowers. The ceramic stems and leaves were so perfect her mind refused to accept they weren't green, a disorienting effect. Studying the white bow fastened on the handle, she fully expected that if she tugged at the dangling ribbon it would untie. Jenn barely breathed, afraid even the softest puff would disturb the delicate petals.

"Amazing, isn't it?" Carmen's voice was filled with awe.

"How does she get the handle to arc so high like that when it's so thin?" Jenn whispered.

A snort erupted. Carmen shook her head. "I've watched her position other handles this thin. I swear she hypnotizes it to stay in position."

Jenn reluctantly pulled away and stepped to each podium. She froze at the sight of one piece. A foot-high sculpture differed from the others in the collection. The soft curves flowed around a stylized figure. Jenn recognized the strong similarities to the sculpture she'd seen in the ceramics studio that Hannah May described as belonging to Tiffany Arnold.

Carmen materialized at Jenn's elbow. "Yeah, I know," she said as if she read Jenn's mind. "We all feed off each other's creativity. That's realistic, but we have to dig into our selves, our hearts, and develop our creativity."

Jenn turned to Carmen. "Isn't there ever a chance of plagiarism or copying?" Tiffany's angry words about copying others' work being an offense resonated again.

"I've seen it, but it's usually a matter of degrees. We are inspired, but we have to make our art our own."

"What would Alex do if she ever decided someone had ripped off another's work?"

The muscles in Carmen's jaw worked in her chubby cheeks. "It'd be ugly." She turned to face Jenn. "An F for the class. If it was bad enough, dismissal from the art department. They could be tossed from the college too, if the cheating was chronic." Carmen stared at the piece for several seconds. "That some people seem to get away with it really makes me furious."

## Chapter 30

Jenn stared into the depths of the staff room without seeing it. The shocking things she'd learned spun in her mind, each overriding the others. Sibylle was pregnant by Jake Barton. Carmen accused her of cheating. Sibylle had been killed. Forbes was adamant about covering it up.

For tension relief, she glanced at Dad's photo, but a note and a compact disc caught her attention. She picked up the note, recognizing Alejandro's precise handwriting.

*Jennifer,*

*I made you a copy of the tracking file for the Lariat newspapers from 1982 to present. You may find inspiration in the articles.*

*Alejandro.*

"Well, how thoughtful," Jenn murmured to the empty room. Holding up the CD, she considered the possibility of articles written about people she'd interviewed. "It's a long shot," she said. She slipped the CD in the computer, and started typing in names.

Minutes later, she pushed back in her chair, and ran her fingers through her hair. Fatigue weighed on her body. She held up the paper scribbled with a few dates and volume numbers. Before she could talk herself out of a descent to the unrenovated portion of the basement, she flung herself out of the chair and grabbed her pack. "To the dungeon."

The basement's steel door squeaked as if she were in a horror movie. Jenn grimaced at the jarring sound. She flipped the light switch. Dimness burned through the darkness. She grabbed the flashlight that always stood beside the door then listened, straining for the sounds of the ghosts known to prowl there, knocking on shelves when nervous students least suspected it. With a quick glance for fleeting shadows said to wander down here, she forced herself forward.

She rifled the stacks of newspapers to find the copies she sought. The first article, Forbes' hiring from a Colorado firm, was an announcement and held no useful information. A second report highlighted a charity fundraiser. The photograph showed two women, one of them Forbes, flexing their arms, muscles straining against tight sleeves. "A self defense class for local children, taught by Dee Forbes and Lauren Aldridge, was such a success they intend to repeat the class. Thirty Colter children attended the weekend event called 'In Defense of Children'."

Jake's art show celebrating his BFA acceptance a year ago was a small write-up. No photograph accompanied the article. Jenn noted that Willy wrote the article. "Come on," she murmured in irritation.

A photo of Tiffany Arnold's sorority in a chorus line was captioned, "Members of the Delta Omega Gamma sorority kick up their heels after winning the Homecoming dance-a-thon competition." Jenn studied the list of names, then the faces until she found Tiffany in the back row.

Carmen was not named in any article.

Two articles about Sibylle were in two newspapers a week apart. The first article was her BFA art opening. One photo showed Sibylle with her hand encircling the Indian maiden sculpture. Another photo showed her gripping the handle of her flower basket sculpture as if she were going to lift it. The pretty girl smiled for the camera. "My classmates inspire me," she was quoted by Willy in his article. Jenn snorted. "I see she gets two photographs, Willy."

Pulling out the second newspaper, below the fold on the front page, a photograph depicted Sibylle beside a large man. Behind them stood four people, likely students. Jenn read the caption aloud. "Sebastian Sommer, CSC French teacher and French Club faculty advisor, and members of the club congratulate Sibylle Beaufort as the club's new president. 'An exchange student from the Landes region of France, Beaufort brings an authentic flair to our program', he said."

Jenn stared into the dimness. "He can tell me more about Sibylle." Quickly, but carefully, she stuffed the newspapers back into their original places. She grabbed her backpack and dashed out for Fremont Hall.

~ * ~

Scanning the doors in the hall that housed the foreign language instructors, Jenn found Sebastian Sommer's. She peeked in the open door. The rotund man with a bowling-ball head stood, leaning over his desk as he flipped pages of a newspaper. He sniffled as he studied each page.

"Professor Sommer?" Jenn tapped on his door. "I'm Jennifer Roby, *Lariat* reporter. May I have a moment of your time to talk about Sibylle Beaufort?"

Straightening up, he stared at Jenn. To her surprise, a tear dribbled down his cheek. "I'd love to, my dear. Please." His hand swept toward Jenn, then to a chair.

"I hope this is a good time." Jenn sat on the offered chair, tentative because of his apparent distress.

"This is the perfect time." He blotted his swollen and running nose with a tissue. "I'd love to talk about her right now, although I must insist this be confidential and off the record. I have been warned."

"Wonderful, thank you." Jenn had heard the "off the record" refrain too often these past days. She pulled out her notepad. "How does she interact with other students and what are her current work habits?"

He shook his head. His chin trembled. "Don't you mean, how *did* she interact with others and what *were* her work habits?"

Jenn swallowed hard. Like Alex Redgrave, he must know that Sibylle's returned to France. She nodded. "Although she's gone, I find her very interesting. I'd like to find out more about her."

"She was beautiful, inside and out. She cared about her fellow students. She made herself available to my French students, helping them through the difficult grammar sections.

She had a way that was calming and patient." Another tear trickled, and he swiped at it. "Please forgive my emotions. This is extremely upsetting."

Uncomfortable, Jenn nodded. "I think I can understand. It must be hard to lose a good student who's a good person."

"A beautiful life, cut short by the cruel hands of fate," Sommer murmured.

Jenn, stunned by his choice of words, stuttered "You know about her ..."

He nodded as he twisted a tissue into a rope. "I was one of the first to know of her passing."

"I'm so sorry, professor," Jenn muttered.

"Thank you, my dear. I've never had to make a death notification, and for it to be about a beloved student ..." His face tightened in a grimace as a sob escaped. His fist pressed to his mouth. "The poor parents." He choked off a hiccup.

Tears welled in Jenn's eyes as confusion rose in her mind. "So you made the notification with Susan Hawley?"

He breathed through his mouth as he dabbed at his running nose. "I've never heard of her. I made the call on behalf of the Dean of Students and the Public Relations Director." He flipped another page of the newspaper.

Now, total confusion swam in her mind. Perhaps Stroll and Forbes called the parents to offer their condolences and assistance after the initial notification, she thought. But Hawley said the parents already knew when she called.

"Did her parents know she'd been killed when you called?" She focused on his face, trying to understand the sequence of events.

He shook his head. "No. Doctor Stroll and Dee Forbes directed me to their office about an emergency. They placed the call and I notified the parents she'd been killed." He took a deep breath and, for the first time, directly gazed into Jenn's eyes. His eyelids were so puffy his eyes were almost obscured.

With a quiet voice she said, "I can't imagine how hard it is to tell parents of the death of their child, especially to murder."

He studied another page of the newspaper. "It was unbelievably hard, but it was an accident, not murder."

Jenn felt the blood drain from her face. "An accident?" she whispered. "How could that be?"

"Miss Forbes said Sibylle had quit school and was returning to France when she was rear-ended on the interstate near the Denver airport. The vehicle burst into flames."

Jenn felt as if the room was spinning.

Sommer slammed his hand on his desk. Jenn gasped and jumped in her seat. He looked to her, anger erasing his grief. He flipped the sheets back to the first page and studied the headlines. "I have studied every page of the Denver newspaper and not one mention of the accident."

## Chapter 31

Darkness had fallen as thick as the fatigue weighing on Jenn as she stared out the big windows in the staff room. The wind blew harder as the next wave of March snows approached. Silhouetted by distant streetlights, the bare branches of the deciduous trees waved at Jenn. The massive pines swayed like Old Finnegan after he'd visited the Shamrock Saloon. The lights beside the frozen Barren Lake cast ghostly shadows on the blowing snow.

She thought of Sibylle's parents and the notification. I can't imagine their despair, she thought. That Stroll and Forbes lied to them about the cause her death was disgusting. Anger rose and displaced the fatigue. A resolve emerged. She'd figure this out. It was time for truth.

Shoving her chair from the desk, she paced. The names of those she'd questioned revolved in her mind: Carmen, Alex Redgrave, Sergeant Kerry, and Susan Hawley — all twice; plus Tiffany and Hannah. She'd spoken with Jake Barton, too, but not in-depth. When they first spoke, Jenn had been too ignorant of the facts to ask hard questions, and he had walked away when her questions got too pointed.

She thought back to her decision not to tell Alex and Carmen that Sibylle was dead, burned in their kiln. It wasn't her place to make such a public announcement ... a terrible pronouncement could give the women nightmares. Upset that Sibylle had left without telling them, at least they were relieved that she was safe at home.

Her normal pacing of the long floor of the newsroom took exactly fifteen steps. Tonight, without thinking, she spun around at the thirteenth step and winced. The stabbing pain throughout her body from skidding off her bicycle reminded her to take care even when walking. *Why would anyone disconnect my brakes? If someone thought that was funny ... I could have been killed.*

*"People's lives are at stake."* Manny's warning repeated. *"You're not just chasing a story; you're chasing a killer."* Dad's words echoed.

She shook her head to dispel them. Only a few trusted people know I'm investigating, Jenn thought. Disconnecting my brake cables was just a bad joke. If she had been killed by that dump truck, who would have notified Dad? And would he have been told the truth?

Spinning on her heel, she considered the information others had given her. That snotty little witch Tiffany gave Jenn much-needed background on relationships in the ceramics studio. Carmen had seemed nice and genuinely concerned about Sibylle, but had a threatening, mean streak. Jake had the motive: he didn't want the baby Sibylle carried. Jake had the means: he knew how to load a kiln. He had the opportunity, but would he take the chance to kill his girlfriend knowing Carmen would arrive at any moment? Jenn doubted that. If he wanted to kill her, there were ways that were private. Did Jenn doubt his guilt because she didn't want to believe it?

*Means, motive, opportunity: Who else had them?* Jenn's heart skipped a beat.

*Carmen.*

She had the motive and the means. She was jealous of Sibylle's relationship with Jake. She knew about the pregnancy and must have realized that she would lose Jake forever because of the baby. She had a nasty streak, and she acted on it.

She had the opportunity while the kiln needed to be loaded. Likely, the studio would be deserted, except for her quarry. She'd have all the time she needed to kill Sibylle, load the kiln, and fire it to destroy any evidence. When Jenn questioned her, the emotional breakdown was relief from the stress of the murder and her guilt. *Convenient.*

If anything went awry with her plan, all Carmen had to do—which is what she did—was claim the kiln was partially loaded by someone else. Anyone had access to the courtyard and the kiln. Everyone knew Carmen loaded and fired it. Her fingerprints and her personal evidence were naturally everywhere. Her whole plan for committing murder was to hide the act in plain sight. *The perfect crime.*

Jenn breathed hard, her pain forgotten. She'd solved a murder, and had figured it out without divulging any information. On top of that, someone in the college—who and why she didn't yet know—was covering up the crime. Following up with Sibylle's professors to inform them that she'd dropped out and left campus was a nice touch. Dee Forbes was involved.

She glanced at the time: quarter till six. She clapped her hand to her forehead. News writing lab was in fifteen minutes. She'd have to skip it. Professor Stephenson would be ticked. He made it quite clear he expected everyone to show up—every time, but this was different. She had solved a murder and would blow the incident wide open. He'd understand. She paused, thinking how she sounded like Manny and Willy when they skipped class for a story.

Would the police chief be in? She had to report her revelation. Manny would have to print her story. She stuffed her notebook in her backpack and collected her coat. Her hands shook.

*"You didn't verify."*

Her breath caught and her muscles tensed. Her own words to Willy wilted her spirits.

*Trust but verify.* "Jenny, verify every source, no matter how much you trust them or how much you want to trust them. Ensuring accuracy is your prime role." Her father shook his finger at her while he spoke.

*Rats.*

Her mind spun through those she'd spoken with. Hannah could corroborate. She, Carmen, and Jake were all ceramics students in the same peer group. Alex wouldn't do; she might only speak kindly of her intern. For that matter, Carmen would behave differently when the professor was around, so Alex wouldn't know how Carmen really acted around students.

Jenn rifled through her backpack for the pad of interview notes, flipped through the pages, and found Hannah's phone number. Reaching for the receiver, she paused, wondering if she should tell Manny that she'd solved the case. After that, the only thing left to do was call Hannah for confirmation.

Earlier, Manny had threatened not to publish her story. He refused to even mention it. He'd fire her if she pursued the investigation. Manny was part of the cover-up. She was on her own.

"Hannah? Jennifer Roby, *Lariat* reporter. I'm sorry to disturb you. Do you have a few minutes for a phone interview? I just have a few quick questions."

"Not a problem." Hannah's lips smacked as if she was eating dinner. "Just so you know, we may get cut off. I'm in a place where I'm not getting good cell phone reception."

"I'll try to keep this quick. Would you say that Carmen de la Vega was vindictive? Would you agree with that?"

"I would not agree with that, but then I've never had an issue with her. The intern keeps the place clean. Carmen is very particular about the studio and the glaze room. It really ticks her off if you don't clean up after yourself. Glaze is messy and with so many students in a small space, it's real easy to trash the place. It ticks me off too, when some of these young'uns don't clean after themselves."

"Have you ever heard anyone complain about Carmen?"

"A few. Mainly those she's chewed out."

"Would she threaten them?"

A small dog yipped in the phone's background, frantic. "Tippy! Hush. Can't you see I'm on the phone?"

Jenn rolled her eyes.

"Um, I hear the slobs whine about her, but who cares what they think, y'know?"

"Do you think Tiffany Arnold has anything against Carmen?"

"Tiffany doesn't like anyone who's not in m' lady's social class." Hannah spoke with a British accent. "I think the feeling's mutual. Once I heard Carmen chew on her in the glaze room for leaving a mess, and said she'd break Tiffany's stuff if she did it again. Even though what she said was bad, actually I rather liked it."

"How so?"

Hannah laughed. "You'll think I'm petty, but Tiffany's an irritant. She thinks she doesn't have to pull her own weight, making clay, unloading the kiln, that sort of thing. Any time she gets her comeuppance, I like it."

Jenn smiled into the phone. "Hannah, are you aware of any relationship between Carmen and Jake Barton?"

"No way. Those two! Sit."

Jenn paused. *I am sitting.* She shook her head. *Stupid dog.* "No, I mean do you know of anything going on between those two?"

"Oh. I know Carmen likes to hang around him, is always complimenting him. She likes to pull his chains." She laughed at the double entendre. "They meet in the studio to work on joint assignments, although they both have independent study projects."

"How was—is—the relationship between Sibylle and Carmen?" Jenn winced at the past tense word.

"Ooh. Oh-kay. Mutual tolerance society."

"Really? You don't think they're close?" Jenn set her elbow on the notepad to hold it down while she jotted.

"Sibylle's a cute little thing, very shy, and she's a fantastic ceramicist. When she's not around, Carmen makes anti-French comments that, in my opinion, are aimed at Sibylle. Now, accidents happen in the studio, and I hate to say it, but once Carmen moved one of Sibylle's greenware sculptures—that's a piece that's dried clay. It's very delicate at that stage. She cracked it. If you're careful moving a piece and it's well constructed, there's no reason for it to break. Sibylle is very conscientious about making sure her sculptures are sturdy or building her sculptures on a base of some sort so it's easy to move."

"Is there anything else about Carmen's personality that you think is pertinent?"

"Other than what I told you, no. To be fair, she takes good care of the facilities and the glazes. On a side note, I know she's proud of her Spanish heritage, which I think is nice. It's melodic when she introduces herself with her full name: Carmen Ortega Aurelia de la Vega." Hannah laughed. "So, how many middle names do you have?"

Jenn snickered. "Just one: Rander. It's my mom's family name. It's the old way of naming kids, using the mother's family name as the child's middle name."

"That's neat—Jennifer Rander Roby; nice ring to it. Jenniferanderoby."

As if she stood in the same room, Jenn's mother called to Jenn just as she had always done. *Jenniferanderoby.*

*Mommy?* Jenn thanked Hannah for her time and broke the connection.

~ * ~

Jenn sat with her head on her folded arms. Hannah's voice, how she spoke, the rhythm of her words and terms, her slight Minnesota-Scandinavian accent, sounded like Jenn's mother. With her father and grandfather moving on with their lives, the unexpected sound of her mother's voice smothered her in a blanket of loneliness.

She sat up, squinting at the pain of a pounding headache. Rummaging through her backpack, she pulled out a used, rumpled tissue and blew her nose. Her stomach grumbled. She hadn't eaten since an early lunch, so she fished out a snack bar.

Thinking back to her conversation, Hannah's information changed the situation, but only a little. She confirmed the things that Tiffany had said. Jenn was convinced of Carmen's guilt, but the delay gave Jenn time to reflect before heading to the police station.

Staring out the window at the deserted street and frozen pond below, her eyes refused to focus as she unwrapped the bar. The treat sucked up what little moisture was in her mouth and clumped. It clung to her teeth and tongue. When the mass stuck in her throat, she choked. Trying not to spew the chunks, she retrieved a water bottle from a side pouch on her backpack. The stale water washed it down.

She blew her nose on a corner of the used tissue and stood up with great emphasis. She paced the floor and considered Hannah's comments, or at least the part that didn't make her cry.

## Chapter 32

"Got any bourbon in that drawer of yours?" Robert Stroll held out an empty coffee cup and grinned.

Tom Bannister rubbed his face. His stomach churned. "I wish. It's been a long day."

"How're you doing, my friend? You hanging in there?" Stroll replaced the cup on the credenza and returned to the seat in front of Bannister's desk.

Bannister shook his head. "I've never been in such a nightmare. I'll be better after the president leaves campus after the icebreaker tomorrow night, and especially after his second trip on Saturday."

Stroll's eyes never left Bannister's face as if he were studying his long-time buddy. "The preparations for the visits are shaping up? I see they've already restricted the access into HQ, and the streets are blocked up to highway twenty-eight."

"Yeah. It's been a lot of work. There's a bit more to be done tomorrow before his arrival. My officers and the city and county boys have been great. The Secret Service have it down to a science. They're not so bad. They do their job and expect everyone else to do theirs. It's just too bad the murder happened at the same time." Bannister noticed Stroll's pale face. He looked like he'd lost some weight. "How's it going on your end--keeping the murder quiet?"

His eyes shifted to stare at the wall beyond Bannister's shoulder. "The reporter's busy with other things. The editor's on board with keeping it quiet. That's one problem that's over with." Rubbing his chin, his gaze returned to focus on

Bannister. "Do you think Hulet's right? About keeping the murder quiet?"

An immediate "no" nearly burst from Bannister's mouth, but he choked it down. He thought about his answer. "I see two sides to the answer. On the one hand, as a law enforcement officer, we need to get real investigators involved and publicize it so I can get more information from the public before the case gets cold. As an employee of this campus, I think we're required to let the public know." He pushed back into his chair and spun an envelope laying on his desk.

"On the other hand, I know what the law says," he continued. "There are loopholes that allow us to keep the murder and the investigation quiet, valid ones to be sure, but I think in this case the loopholes are just a convenience to suit Hulet's purposes ... too many for my acid stomach."

Bannister spun the envelope faster. He slapped at it and looked up at Stroll. "I know if I violate his orders, I'll be out of law enforcement. You know he's got a long arm in this state. I'm not ready to end my career, but this is wrong. It's eating me up. We have a victim who deserves justice and a society who would demand I solve this as quickly as possible, if they knew about."

Stroll remained silent. He rested his chin on his fist, his eyes fixed on Bannister. Seconds passed.

"Maybe Hulet is right," Bannister blurted. He clapped his hand to his stomach as bile rose in his throat. "I can't believe he could be right about anything. There is no threat to the college or the locals. Very likely it's just one scumbag taking care of a personal problem. I got a name for his problem, Sibylle Beaufort."

"Progress!" Stroll brightened.

"Yeah, finally. The coroner showed me a picture. Beautiful girl. We checked her dorm room. Nothing." He leaned forward and braced himself with his elbows on his desk. "Then we got a breakthrough. The resident advisor over at Bridger Hall told me about the fight between Miss Beaufort and her boyfriend, Jake Barton, another student. The little prick's run off."

Stroll leaned forward in his chair. "So, is he your guy?"

Bannister grimaced in concentration. "Looks like it. One fact is nagging at me. That Monday evening, Barton came to the police station and submitted a missing person's report. Of course, he may have called attention to her disappearance to help him look innocent. By him pointing out his girl was missing, he might think that would cause me to look in another direction."

"Still, it's a huge step." Stroll shoved himself out of the chair and paced around the room. "Damn, Tom, you don't have any more Wyoming Whiskey? We cracked it open only last week."

A chuckle fell from Bannister lips. "No, Bob, I don't. What a disaster at the ceramic studio last week. I've never screwed up an inspection so bad. The scene was contaminated, snow had melted all over the kiln so it was soaked. I felt like a halfwit applying the fingerprint powder with the brush. The moisture clumped the hairs to a mass. I looked like that ape who slaps paint on a canvas." He groaned and covered his face. "That whiskey is too strong of a temptation. I took it home." He paused. "I got good photographs though."

"Well, what does Kerry say? What are his thoughts, ideas?" Stroll fell back into his chair.

He hesitated. He looked Stroll square in the face. "He has no ideas."

"None? He's a smart guy. He has no suggestions?" Stroll's face crinkled with disbelief.

Exhaling a deep breath, he said in a soft voice, "He has no idea, Bob. I didn't tell him."

The quiet hum of the room grew loud in Bannister's ears as the silence stretched on. He tapped the envelope on the edge of the desk. Finally, he said, "I lied to Kerry. I told him that the coroner said the bones were plastic and that's what I wrote in the report I gave him. I told him to investigate. I basically said he had to take his precious time to chase the perpetrator of a joke." Bannister's voice cracked, and he avoided Stroll's eyes. "Kerry was ticked off about it. I had hoped he would find something out by happenstance. He's young and the kids seem to talk easy with him, but he didn't look into it. I don't blame him for blowing it off, what with everything he's involved in."

Stroll leaned forward and placed his elbows on his knees. His head hung low. "Why not bring him into this? I think that would be okay with Hulet."

Bannister nodded. "I could have told Kerry the truth. I could have told him to pretend that the bones were the result of a prank, but investigate for real on the sly. The way I figure it, if the worst happens and this mess blows up in our faces, the heat coming down on this department will be unbearable. This way, I'm the only one going down. No one in my department knows, not even Brida. If everything comes to light, all I can do is explain my side and hope everyone understands."

Stroll nodded. "I get it, Tom. I tried the same thing." At Bannister's furrowed brow, he said. "You know that article in the *Lariat* about the prank? It wasn't just to explain the remains and stop any gossip; I had hoped it would generate some information for you."

Both men chuckled. "Too bad it didn't work," Stroll shook his head.

Bannister picked up the envelope and fingered the paper. "The worse thing about all this is, if Hulet is wrong and someone else gets hurt because the college wasn't as forthcoming as it should have been, I'll never forgive myself."

He stared at a wall plaque made by his little grandson, Tommy. The wood plaque was shaped like the Wyoming cowboy and bucking horse—sort of—and the plaque refused to hang straight. After all, the boy was only seven. In handwriting remarkably like the boy's father's, Tommy had traced and filled in with red crayon the words *Cowboy up.* Bannister's throat tightened.

He inhaled deeply and sat up straight in his chair then affixed Stroll with a resolute stare. "I'll only tell you, but I'm giving Hulet until the president leaves after his second visit. If I haven't solved this case by then, I'm going to hand him this." He extended the small envelope to Stroll.

Hesitating, Stroll reached for the envelope. He glanced at Bannister, then slid out the paper out and unfolded it. His eyes moved as they scanned the paper. "Oh, damn, Tom."

*President Hulet,*
*With regret, I submit my resignation.*
*Tom Bannister*

## Chapter 33

Tight muscles relaxed as the hot water streamed down her sore body. Steam caused the spreading purple splotches on her right arm and down her right leg to pulse in time with her heartbeat. In the communal shower rinsing off lather, Jenn felt full of energy. Surprisingly, she slept hard last night and in her own room in her own bed.

The previous evening, after recovering from her talk with Hannah May, Manny had come in the newsroom to work on the next morning's edition. They didn't speak. To avoid the chance of a scolding, Jenn escaped to Morris Hall. The dorm was unusually quiet, almost eerie. Perhaps the hall mates were partied out or had left early for the coming spring break. Even Mya hadn't returned until late then went straight to bed. Jenn didn't care why the floor was quiet. She was thankful for the peace and the solid night's sleep.

Hannah's voice during their phone conversation had made Jenn's mother materialize and brought a yearning bubbling to the surface. After returning to her dorm room, Jenn had clung to a favorite photo of her mother, the photo where she cradled Jenn on her lap before the MS diagnosis, and cried.

When she woke this morning, Jenn felt peace, as if her mother was near. The feeling was not the usual painful one, but rather that her mom was smiling at her, cheering her on. Jenn felt joy. She was very lucky to have such a wonderful family, even if one member was only in spirit. Perhaps she was ready to move on, like Dad and Grampa.

Jenn shared this bathroom with twelve other girls, but this morning she had it to herself. The towel squeaked as she wiped off the foggy full-length mirror and studied the image. The hot shower loosened her sprained muscles from the bicycle crash the day before, but the dark bruises contrasted to her pale skin. Otherwise, a slender figure stood in the mirror.

Dad and Grampa often said she looked like her mother. Staring at her mother's image in the mirror, Jenn finally believed it—although she still thought Mom was beautiful.

Tugging her favorite cable-knit sweater over her head, she thought about her meeting this morning with the police. When it was over, they would know everything she knew. She would demand answers about the cover-up.

Then, she would demand Manny print the exposé, although she wasn't sure what to do if he refused. I'll cross that bridge when I come to it, she thought.

She slipped on her coat. As she hefted the overloaded backpack, she yelped at the strain to her sore arm. At the elevator door, she wondered if she'd missed the start of spring break. Not until she got off the elevator on the main floor did she encounter another student.

Rolling Cougar from the security cage, Jenn ensured the brake cables were attached, squeezed the brake levers, threw over the uninjured leg, and pushed off. A freezing rain had rolled through during the night. The temperature had dipped enough for snow to dust the ice. She took care to avoid icy patches. That'll cause lots of car accidents, Jenn thought. The shadow of Morris Hall and the forest of pine trees kept the snow and ice solid. With great balance, Jenn pushed the pedals, and the bike, toward the campus police station. Her tight muscles relaxed as she pedaled.

At the intersection of Maguire and First Streets, Jenn stopped at the red light, one foot on a pedal, the other rested on the curb to hold up the bike. While she sat on the bicycle saddle, a red Audi TT Roadster stopped beside her. Jenn glanced over. *Sexy car.* The female driver stared at Jenn. Used to stares while riding her bicycle in wintry weather, Jenn turned away and ignored the driver.

Thinking about the mystery at hand, she considered Carmen and Sibylle's desires for the same guy. Did one woman know about the romantic interests of the other? That was likely. All three worked together in ceramics, either on projects or running a kiln. How did they act when they were together? How did Carmen act if she thought Sibylle had copied another's work?

The traffic light turned green. Jenn pushed off the curb then seized the brake handles hard to avoid the Audi that turned right in front of her. She gained control of Cougar with a sideways slide just as her front wheel bumped the sports car's back quarter panel. The car zipped past and sped up the street. She caught sight of a green and white license plate and screamed, "You freakin' Greenie!"

Heart pounding, sore muscles cramping, Jenn tried to calm herself. Grateful the brakes worked this time, she pushed the bike backward until she could lean her foot against the curb. The front wheel appeared to be true. At least this time there was no damage to the bike or to her. She let the traffic light go red. Grimacing at re-straining her muscles, she breathed hard. Recalling the Audi's vanity license plate, Jenn deciphered it: county 65, NV ME. *Vanity being the key word. Gag me.*

The warnings from Manny and her father haunted her once more. She shook her head to dislodge her paranoia.

Come on, common sense, that witch was just a bad driver, she thought. She forced her mind to go blank while she rested until the light turned green, then she pushed the pedals to rid her body of pumping adrenaline. Turning back to her task, she still wasn't sure how to approach the police about the cover-up. After all, possibly the cover-up really was to make the investigation easier and more productive. They may have a method to their madness that she wasn't privy to. Perhaps a softer approach might be better.

Coasting to the police station, Jenn carefully balanced the bike as it glided toward the door. The station had no bike rack so she leaned Cougar against the building.

This time Brida was in, but she faced two black-suited men. Her attention floated from one to the other as both spoke to her at the same time. *Secret Service?* Jenn waved to her.

Brida rolled her eyes. "He'll be back this afternoon," she called out as she pointed to Kerry's closed office door.

Jenn waved her thanks. Chief Bannister's office was down the hall on the right. She didn't have an appointment, but since it was early, she hoped the chief was in and free. He was on the phone.

She leaned against the wall outside his office. Mesmerized by the original cut-glass doorknob on the secretary's door, she heard the plastic click of the chief's receiver as it hit the phone base. She tapped on the door jamb. In a brighter voice than she felt, she said, "Good morning, Chief. I'm Jennifer Roby from the *Lariat*. May I have a few moments of your time?"

Chief Bannister frowned under his mustache, sighed, and remained seated. "I can give you a couple minutes, Miss, uh …" He waved his hand for her to enter, as he studied the tall young woman leaning in his doorway.

"Roby. Jennifer Roby." She glanced at the stacks of papers and folders that teetered on the desk and the credenza. "Chief, I'd like to talk with you about the bones found in the kiln at the Hamilton bungalow. What can you tell me about them?"

He stiffened. "Oh, uh, Miss Roby, isn't it?' The chief asked pleasantly enough.

*He's going to either lie or blow me off.* Jenn got mad. "Yes, Chief. I have some questions for you about the corpse in the kiln." Jenn spoke the last words loudly, hoping that the Secret Service agents would hear and force him to provide answers.

Bannister turned red. He waved his hand for Jenn to close the door. Now, maybe he'd give some real information.

Each stared with set jaws and waited for the other to speak. He knew Jenn knew the truth, she was sure of it. Jenn decided not to wait. "Why, Chief?"

The chief seemed taken aback by her simple question. He waved his hand for her to sit down. "Why don't you be specific?"

The chief wasn't going to dump out all the information for her to sweep up. *Enough of the pussyfooting, the lies, and the half-truths.* "Let me tell you what I know, Chief. I spoke to Susan Hawley. She told me the bones were human. She told me the victim's name: Sibylle Beaufort. You know about her because she said you two went to Sibylle's dorm room. She also said that Dee Forbes ordered her to keep this quiet. What are you doing about solving this case, Chief? Why is this murder being covered up? Why did your detective lie to me and to the entire campus about a murder?"

The chief paused and stared at the wall behind her. His gaze was so intense that Jenn turned to see what he was looking at. A bucking horse hung crooked on the wall. When Jenn turned back the chief was staring at her.

"Miss Roby, there are ... issues surrounding this investigation. If you continue to investigate, there could be fatal consequences."

*Fatal consequences.* She didn't know what she expected from him, but this wasn't it. She remembered thinking that there may be aspects of the investigation she wasn't aware of. Apparently, that was true.

"Fatal, yes, Chief."

"I misspoke. I meant disastrous." Bannister blushed.

"Maybe not. In the past two days I've had what may be two attempts on my life. Yesterday, someone disconnected the brake cables on my bike. I was danged near run over by the proverbial dump truck. It missed me by a foot only because I laid the bike down." Jenn shivered at the memory. "Then, on my way over here, a red Audi nearly ran me over. She was so close, I bumped her car with my bike tire."

At this, Bannister leaned forward and studied Jenn. "Could the Audi incident have been an accident, someone just not paying attention and didn't see you?"

"No. She stared at me before she cut me off."

"She?"

"Yeah, it was a woman. I couldn't see her very well because of the window's reflection. It was a red Audi sports car, Colorado vanity license plate, county sixty-five, 'en-vee me'."

Bannister's red face lost its color. "She may have made a mistake."

Feeling like he was disregarding her complaint and she'd get no action, Jenn decided to return to the purpose of her visit. "Chief, I have knowledge and proof of a cover-up on this campus, a cover-up involving a murdered college student. What do you recommend I do with this information?"

The chief studied the top of his desk as he stroked his handlebar mustache. "I can't recommend anything for you, Miss Roby. You must choose your own course of action."

Jenn was stumped. His flat answers didn't help her, stop her, or give her any guidance. She'd try another tack certain to get him talking. "Chief, I have solved the murder. I have a person with the means, motive and opportunity to kill Sibylle."

The chief's eyes narrowed as if he was deciding whether she was fishing for information that he refused to give. "Please continue."

"Carmen Ortega … Aurelia de la Vega." Jenn flipped through the interview notepad's pages. "She's a CSC student, an intern in the ceramics studio. She did it," Jenn said proudly.

"Why do you believe this?" The chief twirled a ringlet of his mustache.

"Two sources suggested she and Jake are romantically linked, yet he's dating Sibylle. Carmen was jealous of Sibylle, and the fact that Sibylle was pregnant sent her over the edge.

"Carmen had the whole ceramics studio to herself, with the exception of Sibylle. She killed her, put her into the kiln, and fired it, hoping to destroy all evidence. She admits she fired the kiln, but of course, that's her job. No one would think her actions were odd. Hiding in plain sight—it's the perfect crime!" Breathless, Jenn sat back and waited for the chief to dash out of his chair, gather his officers, and head out to arrest Carmen.

The chief nestled back in his chair. "So, Miss de la Vega was in love with Miss Beaufort's boyfriend, but Miss Beaufort stood in the way. That's her motive?"

Jenn nodded, not understanding why the chief was confused about this simple point. "A crime of passion."

The chief's lips upturned into a little smile. He leaned forward. "So, you're saying that a leopard can change its spots?"

Jenn's brow wrinkled in concentration and confusion.

"Miss Roby, the crux of your theory is that Miss de la Vega lusted after Miss Beaufort's boyfriend, correct?"

She nodded.

"Are you aware Miss de la Vega is a lesbian?"

Jenn sat, stunned. She was embarrassed, then mortified. She leaned forward and buried her face in her hands.

With a father's gentle patience, Bannister said, "Miss Roby, you seem like a dedicated young lady. You want to do the right thing. I believe that. You may be an investigative reporter, but please leave any real investigating to the police."

The chief's sympathetic advice, meant to make Jenn feel better, made her feel worse. She wished he would chew her out and tell her what a dolt she was. Frustration and humiliation tried to drip from her eyes, but she blinked them back. She sniffled as quietly as she could. After a moment, she sneaked a peek at the chief.

He had leaned back in his chair, a combination of slight amusement and encouragement on his face. Jenn wasn't sure if that look angered her or comforted her.

"Well, don't I feel stupid." *Lay it out for both of us to acknowledge.*

"Don't. You made a good case. Had Miss de la Vega been heterosexual, we'd have considered her a strong suspect for the very reasons you mentioned. Your only mistake was not knowing she was gay. If you found out all this on your own, your investigation skills are noteworthy."

"Chief, is there anything you can share with me?" The question was more of a plea, an appeal for her to have something to work with. Now that they both knew the truth, she still wanted to pursue the story, and hoped the chief might give her the information — and permission — to do that.

"Do you know, or have you heard of, Jake Barton?"

Shock spiked through Jenn's body. She had considered Jake to be the killer, but that was when the story wasn't real, when her fairy-tale imagination was working. Hearing the chief of police ask about him drove the reality into her heart. Did Jake knock up Sibylle, then knock her off?

"He's in my chemistry class."

"Have you seen him lately?"

"Not since last week." With her meddling in this case, she had to be honest to avoid any appearance of impropriety or obstruction of justice charges later.

"Any idea where he might be?"

"I don't know him very well." She shook her head, gathered her belongings, and stood to leave. "Thank you for your time, Chief."

"A red Audi, you say?"

## Chapter 34

Hours after she left Bannister's office, Jenn stomped to her desk in the *Lariat* staff room. Angry and tired, she hurled her backpack on her desk and collapsed on her chair. Distracted by her embarrassing performance in the chief's office, the possible attempts on her life, and being inattentive in chemistry lab while she watched for Jake, she had burned her left hand on a Bunsen burner. She took slow breaths to calm herself, absentmindedly picking at the bandage the lab assistant had wrapped around her hand.

She picked up a folded note on her desk.

*Jennifer,*

*Heard you're still investigating. Wait for me. We have to talk.*

*Manuel*

What fresh hell is this, she thought. Manny never used formal names unless he was perfectly livid. A flush of fear washed over her. Would he fire her for trying to solve a murder and a cover-up? A sense of self-righteousness poured over her fear. The irony of being in trouble for pursuing justice and being made to feel guilty for that pursuit infuriated her. With too much force she flung the crumbled ball of paper, which hooked left and knocked over an abandoned can of soda. Thoroughly exasperated, she snatched paper towels from the women's washroom down the hall. She wiped up the spilled soda, smashed the towels into the trashcan's overflowing pile then yelped after bumping her sore leg. Jenn laid her head back on her chair with a sigh.

"Well, well, Henny Penny."

*Oh, jeez.* "Willy." *Show no emotion. Maybe he'll go away.*

In the lengthening silence, Jenn lifted her head and watched him stack his books. He moved slowly, not the usual Willy. She considered asking him what was wrong, but decided against it. He'd tell her all about it. She laid her head back on the chair.

Jenn counted to sixty. She sneaked a peek at him just as he turned to look at her. She turned her head away so he wouldn't know she had been watching him, but he was too quick.

*Great, here it comes.*

Willy didn't say a word.

Outright nosy now, Jenn lifted her head, and watched Willy as he packed his things in a box. *Is he moving out?* She wanted to find out, but didn't want to talk to him — or listen to him. To urge him to talk, but on a different subject, she thought of a question she'd wanted to ask him for a long time. "Hey, Willy, do you trip over saying your name with all the w's: Willard Warwick?" Jenn guessed others had asked that question before so it wouldn't be really nosy if she asked. She didn't care if the question offended this offensive guy.

Willy barely turned his head. "Yeah."

"Oh. Thanks."

Willy didn't say anything, but continued to pack his belongings.

"Are you okay?"

At this, Willy stopped packing and turned to Jenn. "I quit the paper."

Jenn sat up. "You quit? But why? You're going to interview the president and the senator on Saturday!"

Willy finished packing his box. He swung his backpack over his shoulder, slid the box under an arm, and stopped by Jenn's desk. "Let's just say, the fascist Secret Service doesn't appreciate my opinions."

Jenn didn't know what to make of that. She wasn't going to ask for specifics. "Sorry, Willy. Good luck to you."

Willy's eyes caressed Jenn's body one last time. He gave a silent whistle then walked out the door.

Settling back into her chair, Jenn felt flustered by Willy's sudden departure. Though she wouldn't miss him, she wondered which *Lariat* reporter would have the opportunity of a career to interview President Edward Ives and Senator Finis Maguire. That lucky reporter wouldn't be her. She had caused too much trouble.

She reflected on the past two days—peace when she thought of her mother; terror at almost being hit by a car; humiliation from the police chief; relief she'd aced her news writing exam; pain from burning her hand in the chemistry lab; and glorious silence in the newsroom with Willy forever gone.

Staring at the ceiling and reliving the investigation of Sibylle's murder, she realized Manny's note and Stroll's threat of censorship didn't matter. Her investigation was over. The only remaining issue was whether Manny would fire her.

At a dead end, she'd interviewed everyone involved. She had no other leads. Either witnesses told her everything or they told her nothing. She'd almost matched the police in investigating a murder and identifying a suspect.

With the full day, the quiet room, and her feet up on her desk, Jenn felt sleepy. Her eyelids closed and her jaw relaxed. Her breathing slowed.

A shuffle at the door brought Jenn to full awareness. She rolled her head expecting to see Manny. No matter how much he chastised her, she would demand answers of his involvement in censorship and a murder cover-up.

Black clothes accentuated a white face. Large, dark circles set off glassy eyes. Unable to move, unable to breath, she stared at the figure.

Jake Barton stared back.

## Chapter 35

"Jenn, can I talk to you?" Jake's hoarse whisper broke Jenn's shock.

"Jake! What happened to you?" Jenn stammered. Mindful he might be a killer, she tried to appear as his concerned friend. She pulled out a chair for him, but placed the seat a safe distance away.

"I heard you were checking into what happened to Sibylle. The police think I had something to do with her disappearance." He waved his trembling hands over his black clothing. "Everybody thinks it's crazy for her to love someone like me, but I swear I didn't chase her away. I love her." His eyes implored her to believe him.

Speechless, Jenn felt too stunned to think of questions. *Some journalist.* She decided to let Jake talk. After all, he came to her. "Will you tell me everything you know?"

Jake leaned forward in his chair, head in his hands. He ran his fingers through his short bi-colored hair. "Can I trust you? I mean, will you believe me?"

His poignant questions calmed and softened her shock-frozen heart. She leaned forward in her chair and held his gaze. "Jake, I'll believe you if you're honest with me," Jenn said in a soft voice. "I'll do all I can to help you. How about you start at the beginning?"

He shook his head, which seemed to weigh a ton. "I don't know where to start." He shivered as if a dark secret wanted to boil over from its black kettle.

"Okay. How about if I ask you some questions? Maybe that'll get you started." Jenn reached for her interview notebook. She didn't want to divulge information that only the killer would know.

She decided to ask the toughest question. His reaction would set the tone whether she could believe him and trust him not to hurt her. She took a deep breath. "Jake, I heard Sibylle was pregnant, and that you didn't want the baby. The gist is that's why she … left."

His lips trembled. "That's true. I didn't want the baby. I'm not ready for a baby. I knew it was her choice, but I didn't know how to convince her about what to do. For crying out loud, I didn't know what to do!" Jake's head collapsed in his hands. "She told me in the lobby at Bridger Hall … in the lobby. Can you believe it?" He stared out the window at the dusky light, and shook his head.

"Why did she tell you there?"

"I didn't know then, but I've thought about it nearly every waking minute since. I think she was afraid of me. Afraid of me." Tears welled in Jake's eyes. "Somehow she needed to tell me in a public place, like I might hurt her if she told me privately."

"I heard it was quite a scene."

A small smile flitted on Jake's face. "Small campus. Word gets around. Yeah, I went nuts. I accused her of cheating on me because I'd used condoms." He picked at a fingernail that had been chewed to the quick. "One must've had a hole."

Jenn didn't know how to proceed. Either Jake killed Sibylle at the kiln and was acting as if she's still alive, or he was innocent and thinking she left because of their fight.

"Did Sibylle return to France because of your fight? Do you know where she is now?"

Jake's reaction startled Jenn. His shoulders shook. He heaved. Fearing he was going to throw up, Jenn reached for a trashcan. His heaving escalated to sobs.

She waited, letting Jake get out of his system whatever would come boiling out.

"Sorry," Jake whispered and wiped his face with his hands. He tried to speak again, but a wave of grief overcame him. "Last Monday, after I found the bones …" he stammered. "I made a missing person's report at the police station." He started to rock.

Jenn watched. She'd brought him as close to the kiln as she dared.

"When I unloaded the kiln ..." Jake gulped lungfuls of air. "The bones you said were fake ..."

Jenn's heart skipped. She shivered, wondering if he would confess.

"I keep thinking ... keep wondering ... keep worrying." Jake's rocking increased. "If those were ... hers." Jake doubled over and started to weep again.

The crash of realization resounded in Jenn's mind. His admission shocked her. His grief touched her. If he were guilty, why was he here and not on the run? If he were innocent, how could he act otherwise? The fact that he thought the bones were Sibylle's, a bizarre and macabre confession, convinced Jenn of his innocence.

*"Take care not to share information between witnesses and sources. Interviewing is strictly a one-way process."*

She made a decision. Jenn leaned forward and laid her hand on Jake's shoulder. "Jake, I'm very sorry, but there's something you have to know."

## Chapter 36

"We have a problem." Dee Forbes yelped an octave higher as she addressed her audience in Hulet's palatial office. Earlier, she had made frantic calls summoning Hulet, Robert Stroll, and Chief Tom Bannister to convene an emergency meeting about the latest developments in what she now called "the Hamilton Incident".

She stood in her high-heeled pumps, stockings wet from tramping to Headquarters in the remaining snow. "I just got a call from the coroner, Susan Hawley. She wanted to know what was happening with the investigation, and when she might receive information on the progress."

Forbes glared at Bannister as if to impress upon him that her message was the reality. "I told her—again—that the police were still keeping the investigation quiet because they were convinced their suspect would hurt others if word got out that there was indeed a body in the kiln. I think she was fishing for information."

Bannister threw up his hands. "So what? Your point?"

"I'll tell you so what. Hawley said someone came to her office asking questions about the bones."

Stroll lowered his head and rubbed his eyes with his fingertips.

"That's right, Bob. Not only did Hawley tell her the truth, she told the whole truth. The person Hawley told was your reporter, Jennifer Roby. Now Roby knows everything. What do we do about it? We have to stop her."

Each man was silent.

"And not just what do we do about it." Forbes looked at Bannister and Stroll, her face purple with rage. "I sure as hell want to know how Roby even thought to go to the coroner."

Defenseless against her fury, the men hung their heads as if each were the guilty party. From his peripheral vision, Bannister noticed the other two men raised their heads to stare at him.

"You! What did you tell her?" Forbes' stance grew wider, her expression menacing.

Bannister swallowed. He'd been caught, but he had mixed feelings about Forbes' announcement. Maybe now the story would become public, and he could investigate in earnest. "Roby asked Sergeant Kerry about the skeleton. She had a suspicion something was wrong. Where her suspicion came from, I don't know."

"Kerry must have tipped her off." She shook her fist as if she'd punch him if he were in the room.

"He didn't tip off anyone," Bannister shot back. "She basically accused him of lying. All he told her was the coroner made the determination of the bones' condition. Roby must have taken it upon herself to speak with Hawley."

"You talked to her too." Forbes shifted her stance as if to fight him.

A bolt of shock coursed through Bannister at the possibility that Forbes had a mole in his department. He forced his voice to stay steady as he turned to Hulet. "She came by my office this morning."

Forbes took a step towards Bannister. "What did you tell her?"

"Nothing. She told me she knew about the remains and Miss Beaufort's identity. She said she had solved the murder, but I cleared her suspect last week."

"You divulged information? You're under orders to keep this quiet. What the hell were you thinking?" Forbes took another step toward Bannister. Hulet held up his palm to stop her advance. Her hands clenched.

Disgusted with feeling like he was being scolded like a schoolboy, Bannister advanced on her. "Dee, Kerry's comment was innocent and based upon ignorance. Why shouldn't he refer her to the source?" He glared at Hulet. "That's the problem with keeping a situation like this a secret. Things don't always go the way you want." He turned back to Forbes. "Lying is not my forte. How sad it is for all of us that it is yours."

Forbes opened her mouth to give a response when Stroll stepped forward, hands in the air in a plea for peace. "Look, this is a non-issue. Anything Roby finds out will not go anywhere."

"How?" Forbes' sharp voice jabbed like a syringe piercing flesh.

Stroll took a deep breath. "Anything she writes will be disposed of. It'll never make it into print. Without it going to print, the story is so preposterous no one would believe her."

Forbes crossed her arms, shifted her balance to stand on one leg, mouth tight, and studied Stroll. "What if she were to uncover the entire story about us?"

Stroll hung his head, like a father tired of his children's arguing. After a pause, he turned to her. "Even if she were to uncover the whole story, anything she writes will not go anywhere. You heard from the *Lariat* editor's own mouth that he will fully cooperate in this matter. Roby has already written a second article about this incident. The editor shelved that article. He will continue to thwart any attempts of hers." Stroll made a closed-zipper move across his mouth, shifted his weight to one side and crossed his arms to mirror Forbes' posture. "She has been rendered silent."

Hulet had been speechless throughout the shouting match. With a flat voice he said, "I will shut down the *Lariat* should your editor attempt to renege on his agreement and print anything about this incident."

Forbes apparently wasn't convinced. "What if she were to go to the *Cabernet*? You First Amendment types never give up."

Stroll's face reflected differing emotions. Bannister thought that if Stroll felt proud of himself for being a First Amendment type, with his suppressive actions against the *Lariat* he should be ashamed of himself.

"She'd never go to the *Cabernet*. No matter how big the scoop, she'd never jump to the competition. No newspaper would give her a job after that."

Forbes seemed satisfied, although she was still on her guard. "Perhaps I should impress on her again not to proceed any further."

A revelation of fear shot through Bannister. "What do you mean, 'impress on her again'?"

"I have too much riding on this fundraiser to just step aside and allow it to be ruined. You just worry about the investigation." She held Bannister's gaze.

Grim scenarios of Forbes' activities spun through his head. Unease crept over him.

"This college has too much depending on this fundraiser," her voice rose. "It'll be a disaster if she lets this incident become public knowledge. The president's visit will be cancelled."

"Oh, knock it off," Bannister yelled. "If the president cancels a trip every time there's a murder a week before his arrival, he'd never visit a major city."

He breathed hard, trying to calm his jangled nerves. Stroll raised his hand to cover his smirk. "This situation has nothing to do with his personal safety or the safety of the expected crowd. You only believe the exposure of the murder will affect the fundraising."

Everyone turned to Hulet, who stared at Bannister before he spoke. "Fair enough. What's going on with the investigation?"

Clearing his mind of Forbes' threats against Roby, he replied. "Mr. President, our main suspect is the victim's boyfriend, student Jake Barton. I've discovered that Miss Beaufort was pregnant, and that they fought over her condition. Witnesses say he threatened her. Barton has classes in the Hamilton buildings and he's a hotshot ceramic artist. He knows all about kilns and was in the ceramics studio the day it was loaded and fired. That gives him means, motive, and opportunity."

"What does Barton have to say?" Hulet asked, tight-lipped.

"I can't find him. I issued a BOLO. He hasn't been to class and he's not returned to his dorm room. He has family throughout the state, so he may have skipped the area."

"What copeze is bolo?" Forbes snapped.

"I've explained this before: be on the lookout. Try to keep up."

"Keep pushing. We need this solved, quietly." The firmness in Hulet's voice screamed "now". "Anything else?"

"Secret Service's preparations are nearly complete. The bulk of my force is working with them for security. Traffic barricades are up. Emergency communications have been expanded. You already know about the restricted access to this building and the immediate area," Bannister said.

"Anything else?"

"Oh," the sharpness of Forbes' voice stabbed the air as she raised her hand. "I removed all the 'missing' posters around campus."

Stroll addressed Hulet. "We notified Miss Beaufort's parents in France."

Hulet's eyes squinted as if considering the call's ramifications. "What did you tell them?"

Forbes shrugged. "I just said after she quit school she'd been killed in an auto accident and got burned up. The coroner said to me during the call earlier that she would arrange to ship the remains back to France. I've notified the girl's professors she dropped out and returned home. That should end all interest in her."

"You lied to the parents?" Bannister's throat was tight. Anger squeezed his head so tight it threatened to pop. He pushed his fingers into his eyes to stem an impending explosion.

"Tom, I understand your shock," Stroll's voice was soft. "They know their child is dead. As hard as that is, don't you think it would be easier on them if they thought it was an accident?"

"This would ensure the murder doesn't get picked up on the wires," Forbes added.

"Anything else?" Hulet's voice had a quiet, yet sharp edge. After a pause, he rolled his shoulders and took a deep breath as if to shed stress. "I know we have stressors at every turn. Tension is high. Budget cutbacks have begun. We've had the murder of a student. We must keep that quiet to assure a successful fundraiser."

He stared at the far wall. After several seconds he started as if remembering that his staff stood in his office. His voice trembled, "In a few hours, a crucial event commences with the arrival of the president and the senator. The eyes of the country will be on us. Everything important to us hinges on its outcome. The fundraising events can end our financial problems. We must maintain our sense of calm."

Silence hung in the air.

"Dismissed."

The three headed for the door.

"Chief."

Knowing what to expect, Bannister winced. He turned around, not wanting to hear the door close behind him.

Hulet approached Bannister like a priest wanting to impress his sincerity and infinite patience on a member of his flock. "You may have violated my order of silence in this matter."

His grandson's voice chirruped in his head. *Cowboy up!* He squared off to Hulet. "You may have violated federal law with your order."

Hulet recoiled. His face went from white to red, and he drew close to the chief. Hulet spoke slowly, with great emphasis. "If you caused this incident to become public and adversely impact the fundraiser, I will fire you. You will never work in law enforcement again."

In a flash, Bannister thought of his resignation letter in his desk drawer. He also spoke with great emphasis. "If another person gets hurt because you prevented the public from being warned, you will be fired. You will never work in education again." His boot heels gouged the deep carpet as he spun around. He didn't bother to close the door.

## Chapter 37

Jenn wrung out another paper towel into the women's lavatory sink. Silence had returned to the staff room after Jake's screams faded.

How easy the movies or television made telling horrible news to a friend, a spouse, or a patient. How cavalier the speaker appeared when he broke the news of a loved one's death, or the patient's impending demise, as if the speaker gave the verdict that their houseplants had aphids.

She broke the news to Jake as gently, but firmly, as she could. Years ago, Grampa told Dad that giving bad news benefited both sides when told with the bluntness of fact, the clarity of truth, and the gentleness of a good heart. Jake had no doubt of her facts, truth, and sincerity.

Having spoken to others about Sibylle's remains and her murder, Jenn ignored her racing heart and pretended that this message was another horrible rehearsal. "The coroner confirmed her identity," Jenn said. He couldn't doubt the message's authenticity. "Sibylle died instantly. She didn't suffer."

The hardest part was watching Jake's reaction. He rocked in his chair, moaning. "No. God." Tears poured down his face and the rocking increased. "*No!*" Screams erupted, piercing the silence of the room. His girlfriend, pregnant with his baby, was dead ... murdered. Compounding the horror, he had witnessed the grotesque insult to her body. He had vomited in the trashcan by Jenn's desk.

Jenn gathered a pile of wet towels and returned to the staff room then handed them to him. She looked away so he could cool his burning face with some privacy. After he had wiped his face clean, he wiped again with a fresh towel.

She tried to look away from the pain in Jake's eyes, but couldn't. "Do you have any idea who might have done this to her?"

He sighed heavily, ran his trembling hands over his head, and stared at the floor. The black nail polish was gone. His fingernails had been chewed past the quick. "I have no idea. She wouldn't hurt anybody."

Jenn gave him another moment to collect his thoughts. "Jake, do you remember anything about that Sunday?"

Jake moaned. "That morning I went to work in the print studio, which is the next building down from the ceramics studio. I saw Sibylle go in. She's always there on Sundays. She liked having the place mostly to herself. Except for Carmen, it was usually quiet. I wanted to apologize to her about our fight, to reassure her I loved her and would respect her decision about the baby, but I saw someone I didn't want to talk to go into the ceramics studio. I didn't need the extra irritation and an audience so I stayed in the print shop for about an hour. I couldn't take not seeing Sibylle, so I went to the ceramics studio. Carmen told me she never showed up." Jake choked on his last words.

"Was Carmen this person you didn't want to talk to?"

"No. I like Carmen. She's a nice gal. She just doesn't put up with people's crap."

Jenn needed a break from the tension. She gave a quick smile. "You know, I had Carmen pegged as the person who did this."

Jake straightened in his chair. His mouth flew open.

"I thought she did it because I'd been told she was infatuated with you. When she found out Sibylle was pregnant, it drove her over the edge, and she ... killed Sibylle. I had it figured out until the chief of police told me ..." Jenn felt too embarrassed to continue.

"Carmen is a lesbian." Jake almost smiled. "She's the treasurer for Students for Tolerance on campus. You didn't know that?"

She shook her head.

"She attended the concert of that gay singing group--Wall's Flowers—last year. Remember that whackjob preacher from Texas brought his toadies with him to protest? They brought in riot police to disperse them with fire hoses." Jake shook his head at the recollection and almost smiled.

"I remember that, but I didn't know Carmen was involved."

"Well, she was a part of the event's coordination." Jake wiped his face with another paper towel then shook his head. "Do you have any idea why this is being kept quiet?"

"The chief of police told me there were things going on he couldn't divulge. He said if I kept investigating there could be fatal consequences."

"Fatal? That's already happened."

"Then he said he meant disastrous, but you know, I've had some ... questionable things happen to me since yesterday." Jenn described her two close calls.

Jake's head dropped to his hands. "Oh, my God, Jenn, what is going on around here? How does Dee Forbes figure in this? She was running around telling everyone after we found ... Sibylle to keep this quiet."

"The coroner said Forbes ordered her to keep it quiet too, that if it were kept quiet the killer wouldn't flee or hurt someone else, and to prevent panic on campus." Jenn mimicked the chief and coroner. "It's crazy."

She recalled a question she'd asked Jake earlier, but they were distracted before he answered. "Who was this person you said you didn't want to talk to at the studio?"

"This loser. She's a Greenie who thinks she's hot stuff, but she's a fraud: Tiffany Arnold."

Jenn felt the blood drain from her face. Jake was the second person to say Arnold had been at the studio that morning. *Tiffany lied. Why?* Jenn cleared the lump in her throat before she could ask, "Why would you call Tiffany a phony?"

"I've had ceramics with her. She couldn't work a piece of clay if she knew the Hope Diamond was in it." Jake rubbed his eyes.

An image of Tiffany's beautiful sculpture popped in Jenn's mind. "I've seen a piece of her work. It was wonderful. I saw one very much like it in Sibylle's art show, but wasn't it Sibylle who copied Tiffany's work?"

Jake's reddened eyes held Jenn's steady gaze in a glare for several seconds until she shrank back at the thought of a serious misjudgment. In a voice softened by choked-off fury, he said, "Make no mistake. Sibylle had the creativity of a master. She's the one who developed that sculpture. She made an entire series of them last year. A Billings gallery bought all she'd let them have. She kept that one piece that was in the show because it was a sentimental favorite of hers."

"I'm sorry, Jake," she whispered, feeling shame at her belief that Sibylle had cheated. She had wrongly interpreted Carmen's anger at copying to be directed at her.

She watched Jake as he paced the aisle. He spun and slapped at hand on Jenn's desk. "Sibylle took a field trip to an art opening at a Jackson Hole art gallery last Friday. She told me that night she'd seen works exactly like the ones Tiffany brings to class, and there were other works like her own, only the artist was not Tiffany. Sibylle was going to talk to Alex — Professor Redgrave — about it."

"Do you remember this artist's name Sibylle saw in Jackson?" Jenn felt out of breath. She reached for her keyboard and tapped the keys to access the Internet. She wondered if Sibylle's things had been packed yet. Perhaps the brochure on the ceramics show that Susan Hawley mentioned might still be in her belongings. She must verify the gallery Sibylle visited was the same gallery that represented this artist.

Jake's head dropped as he searched the floor for the answer. His head lifted, "Ty Albert. Sibylle told me his artist statement stated he was a CSC graduate, but I don't remember that name."

Tapping furiously on the keyboard, Jenn wondered if Albert had an artist's website. "Jackson Hole Fine Art by Arnold. Proprietors, um, Kirstell and Stephan Arnold, featuring artist Ty Albert," Jenn called out as the site appeared. Jenn reread the woman's name. "Kir... Crystal? Chrystyll." *Oh, Jeez.*

Jake jumped from his seat to lean over Jenn's shoulder. Dark blue cursive text scratched the violet background of the gallery's home page. Teeming with photos of abstract art paintings that looked like squished puppies eating overripe fruit, a few photos appeared out of focus. Links floated over the screen.

"Tiffany's parents," Jake said with a sneer at the proprietors' photos. Father was chiseled, salt and pepper hair, a wide smile framed perfect teeth, and dressed in a pinstriped three-piece suit. Good looking, she thought. Mother was a reflection of her daughter, yellow bottle-blond hair with dark roots, and a receding chin that accentuated a third chin. Her über-chic clothes screamed "I know art."

Jenn's mouse chased down the floating *Meet our artist* link. She clicked it. As she waited impatiently for the large photo to download, Jenn stole a glance at Jake. His eyes riveted to the screen, the muscles in his face were so tense they almost creaked.

The photo finally downloaded. Jake pushed his face close to the screen and studied the artist's portrait for several seconds. "I'll be damned."

"What? What?" Jenn cried.

"What do you see?"

Jake's question confused her. Studying the photo, she recognized the artist's wide smile framing the perfect teeth of his father perched atop the receding chin of his mother.

"Ty Albert is the Arnolds' son!" Leaning back into her chair, she looked at Jake to confirm her suspicion.

"That son of a bitch is Ty Arnold," Jake almost yelled. "I remember him now. He interned at the ceramics studio a couple years ago—a real prick. Had talent, but boy howdy, his ego was the size of the Winds." Jake stood up and shoved his hands into his pockets. "He'd slam anyone, even beginners, if their stuff wasn't avant-garde." Jake waved his hand in a jaunty manner. "But why call himself Albert?"

"That's easy." Jenn was confident she had this right. "Mommy and Daddy taking care of Baby since he can't make it on his own. They own an art gallery, but it wouldn't look good to showcase Baby's work, so they change his last name then present the artist as their discovery."

"You're on to something. I'll bet they dropped Arnold and used his middle name."

"Let's see his work." Jenn clicked on the *Master Albert's Gallery* button. A banner at the top of the screen proclaimed Ty's show had moved from Denver to Jackson Hole two weeks before. With the thumbnails downloaded, the page displayed small photos of his ceramic art. All the white sculptures had gentle curves with implied lines that made Jenn think of a group of Indian women.

"I've seen these before," Jake's voice grew louder. "But not in no art gallery."

Jenn noticed one piece that looked familiar and clicked on the thumbnail photo to enlarge it. She gasped at what looked like a blanket wrapped around an invisible maiden.

*Tiffany cheated, and Sibylle found out.*

Jake began to pant. "Big Bro must have given Baby Sis his work to glaze, fire, then show. That would explain why her work was either shitty — because she did it herself in the studio in front of everybody — or brilliant because she showed his work. Damn it." Jake turned from the computer and paced, too angry to grasp the bigger picture.

"Jake, was it common knowledge that Sibylle worked at the studio on Sundays?"

He nodded.

"Tiffany must have gone to the studio to persuade Sibylle not to report her to the prof ... or to threaten Sibylle if she did."

Jake turned to stare down the aisle. He started to tremble.

The college regarded academic cheating as a most serious charge. To falsely accuse someone of cheating was almost as serious an offense as the actual crime. She'd already been wrong, big time, in this case, so she challenged the potential of Tiffany cheating.

Pointing at the piece floating on the computer screen, she asked, "But none of Ty's pieces have horsehair. How or why would Tiffany add a horsehair decoration to his work?"

The instant the question left her mouth, Jenn knew. She wanted to throw up. The piece wasn't covered with horsehair. The hair was Sibylle's.

## Chapter 38

Jenn's head lay on her folded arms. The horror was too great to fathom so she blanked her mind. A beautiful young woman was dead, killed by a fellow student. A thin groan escaped her throat.

Jake hadn't moved. Tears rolled down his face.

Shaking off the shock, she looked up at the clock on the wall: five-fifteen. The chief and the detective should still be working, although with the VIPs' arrival, she didn't know where they'd be.

The fiasco that morning in the chief's office popped into her head. She'd looked like a fool once, and the situation was too serious to experience a repeat. After considering all witness statements and concrete evidence, her heart sank. They had nothing.

"Jake, do you know of any real proof that Tiffany did this? Everything we have is circumstantial."

Rocking back and forth, Jake seemed not to hear Jenn, but she waited. He had, after all, just learned who killed his girlfriend. The words stumbled out of his mouth. "The black-striped piece—your proof—has Tiffany's fingerprint indentations. She gripped the piece so tight ... her fingertips pressed into the dried glaze. I saw them when I checked out everyone's pieces on the shelves after I unloaded the kiln. I didn't know then exactly how they came to be there."

Jenn rubbed her face as if the action would rid the killing blow from her mind's eye. "We have to go to the police station, Jake," she said in a soft voice. She reached for her coat and backpack.

Jake stood trembling by the door, staring at the wall. "They'll accuse me, won't they?"

"They may, but they don't have the answers." Jenn tried to put herself in Jake's shoes. He was the prime suspect in a murder. Innocent until proven guilty was a reassuring sentiment for the guilty, but provided little comfort for the innocent. Jake would have to present good evidence to clear himself.

As they trudged out of the Commons, Jenn noticed that parked cars lined the streets, yet an expectant hush draped the campus. An excited energy permeated the silence. Even the wind held its breath. In the distance, news vans framed crews setting up their gear. A crowd waited in front of HQ. All the attendees for the president's evening invitation-only icebreaker must be in place well ahead of time, she thought. A pang of regret stabbed at her heart because she'd likely miss the biggest event to hit the campus in decades. She reminded herself she was directly involved in a story just as big.

Behind her, Jake walked like he was headed to the gallows, and she slowed often for him to catch up.

As they entered the police station, Jenn avoided looking for Brida. She didn't want to talk to anyone except the detective or the chief. The Secret Service agent in the side room appeared to tick off a checklist while he spoke to his thumb. Jake stopped by the entry door and leaned against the wall, expressionless.

The chief's door stood open. He and another black suit stood leaning on his desk as they compared a map and a chart.

"Wait here," Jenn whispered to Jake who didn't acknowledge her. She patted his back in reassurance then walked to Kerry's office. His back was to the door as he typed on his computer; its screen faced the door; a report, she guessed, from the look of the form on the screen until he leaned over to spin a dial on a radio and spoke low into the microphone. "Copy, sector four." *He must be coordinating the overall crowd and traffic control on campus.* The calls through the radio were subdued, calm but expectant.

She glanced back at Jake to make sure he hadn't run away. Brida's phone rang. No one answered it. Jenn glanced around. Brida must have stepped out. She turned back to Kerry's office and flinched.

In those seconds he had turned, saw her hand on the jamb, and waited. She blushed. "I'm sorry to bother you, Sergeant, but this is urgent."

Kerry tapped his fingers on his desk, a slow rhythm as if he were angry at the interruption or bored at her appearance. "Miss Roby, the bones are still replicas."

Something inside Jenn's psyche snapped. Fury replaced her fatigue and apprehension. She marched into his office, placed her hands on the center of his desk, and leaned toward him. She thought about climbing on top of his desk to make him listen. "Stop it already. Stop the lies."

Kerry stood and leaned on his desk. Their faces were close. His lips were in a tight line, his eyes narrowed. "Miss Roby, should I throw your ass out, or should I arrest you for being a pain in mine?"

Jenn blinked first, but she decided to spell it out for Kerry like she had with the police chief. There would be no denying the murder or the cover-up. "Sergeant, I know about the skeleton in the kiln. I know her name. I know about the cover-up, and I know who killed her." Jenn refused to budge and forced herself to stare into his eyes.

Kerry still leaned on his desk. "What in the hell are you talking about?"

With his tenuous emotional state, she felt relief that Jake hadn't come in with her. He didn't need to hear this. She would make Kerry listen then bring in Jake for confirmation.

She turned on her heels, took a step toward the doorway, and grabbed the door, slamming it shut as hard as she could. Kerry's plaques rattled on the wall. She turned back to Kerry, her voice loud. "Damn you. I'm sick and tired of being lied to by the very people we're supposed to trust." She brought up her hand to indicate Kerry. "I'm sick of it."

He stepped around his desk and stopped close to Jenn. He opened his mouth, but before he uttered a sound, she pointed her finger inches from his nose. "Deny it once more, and so help me I'll scream it at the top of my lungs about the murder at Hamilton, and how you covered it up!"

Kerry said nothing. He stared at her like she had sprouted horns.

"On top of that, someone's been trying to kill me to stop my investigation. Not only that, Sergeant, Jake Barton is out there," She pointed at the door. "He's the one you've been looking for. He's here to answer your questions. We have proof of the real killer." Jenn stopped talking, if only to catch her breath. "Are you going to still deny it?"

"What in the hell are you talking about?"

"Fine. See you on CNN, Sergeant."

Jenn spun on her heels and flung open the office door. The crash of the door as it hit the wall rattled the windows. Jenn stalked to the chief's office. She ignored the shocked face of Brida and the scrutiny of the Secret Service agent as he stepped to the room entrance. Even Jake stared at her.

She stopped short of the chief's door, barely realizing the scene she'd made. No doubt Kerry would slap handcuffs on her. It was too late now. She pounded on the doorjamb. The chief and the agent looked up with some irritation. She stepped in the chief's office, looked directly at him, and in a voice that failed to cover her anger she said, "Chief, I have to talk with you ... now. It's urgent." She felt like she had a spine of steel. To the agent she demanded, "Will you excuse us please? Thank you."

The agent, apparently not used to being spoken to in a directive tone by a snippet of a civilian girl, retorted, "The President of the United States arrives in an hour. I'm sure the chief will have time for you later." Jenn did not mistake the sneer in the agent's "later".

Jenn snapped, "This is Wyoming. The only dangerous things we have are federal officers carrying rifles during hunting season." Bannister dropped his head and covered his smile with his hand.

The chief gathered the maps and handed the bundle to the agent in dismissal. In a condescending tone, he said, "Agent

Polk, take a minute's break. Everything's in place. We're ready and twiddling our thumbs. We can talk about this later." The chief emphasized "later".

Polk snatched the maps and strode out. Jenn, amazed with herself that she would talk to a federal agent that way, thought the man memorized her face as he stalked past.

Kerry blocked the doorway. "I'm sorry she bothered you, Chief. Miss Roby seems to be delusional. I'll call for an ambulance to take her in for a psych eval." He grabbed her arm and pulled her toward the door.

She jerked her arm out of Kerry's hand. "There's nothing wrong with me except for the cover-up going on at this college. Chief, I know who killed Sibylle, and I can prove it." She pounded her hand on his desk.

Kerry stepped into the room. "Chief, she was in my office talking about the bones in the kiln, that it was an actual murder." He reached again for her arm, but Jenn ran to the far interior of Bannister's office. The chief straightened; his eyes bulged.

Desperate, terrified that her world was spinning out of control, she wanted to scream to the chief, to anyone, "help me!" Kerry seized her arm. She struggled, but couldn't wrest her arm free. "Chief, Jake Barton's here. He knows who did it too," Jenn cried.

Kerry twisted her still-injured arm behind her back in a come-along hold. She screamed as damaged shoulder muscles and tendons stretched almost to the tearing point.

"Sergeant!" The bellow exploded from Bannister.

Kerry immediately released his grip. In pain, she fell against the chief's desk, gasping for air. She fought not to cry, but she lost that battle. Bending over to collapse on a chair, her cap fell off and her hair covered her face.

"Sergeant, return to your office. Stay there until I come for you."

"But, Chief—"

"Get your backup, Stephens in sector twelve, to take over your post, pronto. They're overmanned anyway and can spare him back there. Call in Assistant Chief Baker to move over with Agent Polk in the command post. He knows everything and that it's all in place, so it's just a matter of answering any questions Polk might have."

"Yes, sir."

Jenn hadn't looked up to see the exchange between Bannister and Kerry, but chose to hide behind her hair's silver curtain. The office's door closed. Her hair fluttered in the draft of air as Bannister walked beside her. His hand picked up her cap from the floor and held it out. He said nothing while she took it, and mashed the cap on her head. Bannister handed her a couple tissues.

A whispered "Thanks" was all she could manage. She should be more grateful since he'd stopped Kerry from hurting her and arresting her, but she was incapable of more.

"Miss Roby, I'm sorry. Are you all right?"

Jenn nodded, but wanted to shake her head. In pain and terrified she'd ruined any chances for her future at the college, she was not all right.

"What did you tell Sergeant Kerry?"

Jenn cleared her throat. "I told him I knew who committed the murder at Hamilton. He kept telling me the bones were a sham, like I was demented. I admit it, Chief, I lost it. I couldn't take the lies anymore. That's why I came to you."

Bannister covered his face with his hands. Jenn heard a soft "Damn."

He mumbled, "So what's your latest theory?"

Jenn remembered Jake in the hallway. She worried he had run away after the commotion. "Jake Barton's outside."

Bannister uncovered his face. "He's here?"

Yes, sir. Your main suspect, Jake Barton, is in the hallway. He came with me."

He shot out of his seat, moved fast around his desk and Jenn's chair, and flung open the door. Jenn followed, relieved to see Jake against the wall. She leaned through the doorway and motioned to him. His face was puffy, bloated from crying. His eyes were large with fear. Jake, with the chief close behind, stumbled into the office. The chief closed the door.

"Chief, Jake Barton. Jake, Chief Bannister." Jenn sat—fell was more like it—on one of the chief's chairs, fearing what was to follow.

Bannister studied Jake for a moment. "Will you two follow me please? Let's go into the squad room. There's more room there. Plus we won't distract the agents or officers."

Jenn followed Jake and Bannister down a narrow flight of stairs. They walked the length of the hallway to the squad room. Bannister flicked on the fluorescent lights.

The former home's basement was cold and the dampness drove the chill into her body. The ceiling height was at a claustrophobic level, about seven feet high. Desks with computers lined one wall. Heaps of traffic cones were piled in a corner. A conference table stood in the center. The off-white walls radiated a dull atmosphere.

The chief motioned for them to sit. Jenn and Jake sat on one side of the table. The chief's face had a gray cast. "Let me get you some water." Like he was sleepwalking, he lurched from the room. A minute later, he returned with two bottles of water, ice cold.

"Thank you, Chief," Jenn said. Jake said nothing as he reached for the bottle.

"Wait here." Bannister ordered before he disappeared.

Jenn spun off the bottle cap and took a long drink. Never had anything tasted so good in her life.

Jake leaned into Jenn. "What happened? All that screaming scared the hell outta me. I thought you were going to get arrested." He spun off his bottle cap and gulped the bottle empty.

She shook her head. "Kerry thought I was nuts. I lost it." She took another big gulp of water and held out her shaking hands. "I thought I'd get arrested too. That may happen yet."

## Chapter 39

"Are they waiting for the president to leave campus? What's taking them so long?" Jenn squirmed in her chair then stood up. Flexing her shoulders to relax, she stepped around the room, tempted to poke the keys on a couple of the keyboards to wake up the computers just for something to do. She guessed they'd been waiting fifteen minutes. The chief did say they had replacements taking over their responsibilities.

"I don't know. You'd think they'd be in here right away to hear how you solved the murder."

"How we solved it." Jenn turned to Jake to emphasize her point. "We pieced together what happened. Each of us couldn't have figured it out without the other." She admitted to herself that she didn't want to be alone in believing who killed Sibylle and how.

"Jenn, you get the credit. If it weren't for you, no one would have figured this out. You found out who did this to my Sibylle." Jake threw his arms around her. She hugged him back, touched by his sincerity.

She pulled away and paced in silence, like a tiger in its cage.

"Man, I need some air. Plus, I need to go to the bathroom." Jake rose from the chair.

Clomps of approaching footsteps vibrated the room. *The chief's coming.* During the wait for him to return, her nervousness had faded. Now, anxiety returned in full force. *Oh good. Thanks to Jake mentioning it, now I need to use the restroom.*

As Bannister and Kerry entered, Jenn sat, her arms tight to her sides, afraid Kerry would grab her again. She felt unsettled to see what seemed to be shock in their eyes. Their faces appeared to have been chipped from gray granite. Kerry caught Jenn's eye. She looked down at the table.

"Miss Roby."

At the sound of Kerry's voice, Jenn clutched her arms with her hands and hugged herself.

"Please accept my apology for hurting you. I'm sorry."

Jenn maintained her focus on the table and nodded. She was afraid to look at him.

"Miss Roby, you said you and Mister Barton know who committed this crime and can prove it." Bannister sat heavily in the chair opposite of Jenn.

Her grip relaxed. She could breath. At least they hadn't read the Miranda rights like she was a criminal for acting insane. She avoided looking at Kerry. She wagged a finger at Jake and herself. "Yes, sir, we know who killed Sibylle Beaufort, how, and why."

Bannister and Kerry didn't look at each other, but remained focused on her. Jake stared at the table, silent.

Not sure if Jake could talk, she addressed Bannister. "Tiffany Arnold killed Sibylle. Friday, about ten days ago, during a field trip to an art opening at the Jackson Hole Fine Art by Arnold gallery, Sibylle saw the sculptures Tiffany passes off as her own in ceramics class." Jenn nodded at Jake. "Jake's in that class. He's seen them. The real artist is Ty Albert."

"Ty Albert is Tiffany's brother," Jake's voice held no emotion. "His real last name is Arnold. Convenient having the same initials since artists always carve their initials somewhere on their sculptures."

Jenn continued. "Susan Hawley said she found a brochure for the opening in Sibylle's room. You were there, Chief." At this, Bannister's face turned red. "Tiffany told me that her father owned many of Albert's—Arnold's—works."

"Sibylle told me Friday night she would turn Tiffany in for cheating," Jake said.

Jenn rummaged through her backpack. She pulled out a sheaf of papers and handed them to the chief. "These are photos from the gallery's website."

"Those are what Tiffany passed off as her work in class." Jake pointed with his chin at the papers. "Plus, I saw Tiffany go into the ceramics studio Sunday morning ... when the kiln ... was loaded." Jake almost choked from the remembrance. He rubbed his eyes as if to push out the image.

"So did Carmen Ortega Aurelia de la Vega," Jenn added. The chief had spoken with Carmen, and she wanted to show him that Jake's statement had corroboration. "Sibylle must have been loading the kiln as she usually did on Sundays. When Tiffany showed up, Sibylle probably admitted she would turn Tiffany in for cheating. Tiffany knows she would fail the class and get kicked out of college. She struck Sibylle in the head with Ty's sculpture, and Sibylle's hair stuck to it. Tiffany pushed Sibylle in the kiln, and put the piece inside too.

"Tiffany knew Carmen would arrive soon, so she only partially loaded the kiln to hide the body. Carmen would finish loading it and start the fire. Then Tiffany left before anyone saw her, or at least, she thought no one had seen her."

Jenn reached for Jake's hand. What she would say next would be hard for him to hear. With a soft voice she said, "During a proper firing, the body and any evidence would burn away. With so many students handling the kiln, some wearing gloves, some not, it was just too easy to hide who actually loaded or operated it."

She looked squarely at the chief. "Carmen saw Tiffany leave the studio Sunday morning. Tiffany denied that fact during my interview. She told me Carmen lied. Chief, I never told her who told me. How would she know Carmen told me? Then, because of gas flow problems, the kiln didn't get hot enough to incinerate all the evidence." Jenn glanced at Jake.

"The piece that Tiffany used to ... hurt ... Sibylle has the black marks of ... her hair on it." Jake choked on the horror as he spoke. He rubbed his eyes so hard, Jenn thought he'd push his eyeballs into his skull. "It has Arnold's fingerprints on it. There were indentations in the glaze."

"Doesn't the glaze melt? Wouldn't that remove any fingerprints?" Bannister asked.

"Normally, yes," Jake shook his head. "But the kiln didn't get hot enough to vitrify the glaze—"

"Vitrify?" Bannister asked.

"The glaze turns to glass. Basically, it's to melt the glaze. The lower heat only solidified the marks or indentations. Me, Hannah May, and Tiffany," Jake spit out Tiffany's name like he spit a gnat out of his mouth. "We unloaded the kiln. She disappeared when we almost had the kiln empty so she wouldn't be around when we pulled the bottom shelf. She could act like it was news to her."

The chief glanced at the sergeant. Kerry remained fixated on Jake's face. Bannister turned to Jake, "Where do you suppose this alleged murder weapon is now?"

Jenn didn't like Bannister using the word "alleged" as if he didn't believe them.

"Our work is supposed to stay in the studio until we have our class critique, so it should still be in the ceramics studio."

"I saw it there yesterday when I talked with Professor Redgrave," Jenn said. From her peripheral vision, Kerry turned to look at her.

Bannister stroked his mustache as he stared at Jake. The silence lengthened. "I can't comprehend that a cheater would kill a human being in order to stop that person from reporting them. Cheating is bad, but it's not such a grave offense as to murder someone over it."

After a moment, Jake nodded. "I understand your point, Chief. I agree, but then I'm not a cheater. I'd've turned her in too. But consider this: Tiffany's parents are owners of major art galleries in two wealthy cities. How would Tiffany and her parents look if the art world knew that as a family they have to cheat to be successful?"

"Tiffany admitted to me that she felt a lot of pressure about that," Jenn said. "I thought she was going to start crying."

The chief stared at Jake, continuing to stroke his mustache. "Can you explain your activities and your presence in the ceramics studio that Sunday morning?"

"I was at the print studio that morning for class work. It's next door to the ceramics studio. Then I went to the ceramics studio to apologize to Sibylle, but Carmen told me she didn't show up that morning. That didn't make any sense because I saw Sibylle go in, but I didn't see her leave." Jake's chin quivered and his eyes filled with tears. "I've been looking for her ever since."

Bannister nodded. "We've been searching for you, young man. Explain to me why you hid."

Relief flooded Jenn, and she believed that the chief and the sergeant were open to his innocence. Jake blinked back tears, but looked directly at the chief. "I made an ass of myself when Sibylle told me she was pregnant. We had a huge fight. Then she disappeared. People thought I must have chased her away." He swallowed hard. "Sometimes I thought the worst. I worried that the bones in the kiln ... were hers. I heard the police were looking for me. Who would believe me? I have no witnesses to clear me, no alibi." Jake ran his hands through his hair. "I know hiding was stupid, but I didn't know what else to do. When I heard Jenn was looking into it, I thought I'd go to her."

The chief's gaze never left Jake's face. "Are you willing to make a written statement?"

"Yes, sir," Jake said, his voice adamant. "Anything you need."

"Are you willing to take a polygraph test?" Kerry asked a question for the first time. *Some detective.*

"Yes, sir," Jake said, unwavering. "Anything."

The chief nodded. "You'll need to work here with Detective Kerry as his office is being used for traffic and crowd monitoring. He may have more questions for you to answer, but I'd like for you to write out your statement."

He stood and tilted his head for Jenn to follow. She stepped behind Jake's chair and placed her hands on his shoulders. She gave him a slight smile and he patted her hands. Jake watched Kerry, who only stared at the table.

"Chief, do you need a statement from me?" Jenn asked as she lifted her pack.

"Absolutely." They hustled out of the squad room, then up the stairs toward Bannister's office. She deeply inhaled the fresh air. The air in the squad room had gotten stale.

The chief stepped into the side office, spoke a few moments with the agents and another man Jenn suspected was the assistant chief. After much nodding by all the men, the chief returned to his office.

"When the sergeant is finished with Mister Barton, he'll get with you for your statement. He may have more questions for you. I'd take your statement now, but as you can imagine I'm a bit busy."

As Bannister fell back into his office chair, Jenn lingered at his door, unsure of where to go or what to do.

He opened his center desk drawer, removed an envelope and set it on his desk. He stared at it for seconds then looked up at her. "So, Miss Reporter, this will be your first scoop?"

Startled, a lightning-bolt shock charged through her. The events of the evening had happened so fast, she didn't write notes or even think about writing the story. The chief must have believed her theory; she took his question as approval of her efforts and findings. Most significantly, he didn't forbid her from publicizing the story or demand she keep it quiet.

"Yes," Jenn managed to squeak. She stood in the doorway, dazed at the thought. "Can I leave for awhile? I promise I'll be back soon to write out my statement."

"Be back as soon as you can though. With all the activity tonight, don't make us come looking for you."

She headed to the main door. Behind her she heard the chief punch telephone buttons. "This is Chief Bannister. Get Dee Forbes immediately. Urgent."

Jenn stepped out of the building and gasped from the shock of cold air. The stress of the evening, the scare of the whole affair with Kerry, and being questioned in the closed squad room had made her sweat. Her damp skin heightened the shock. She shivered.

She felt sorry for Jake and terrible for Sibylle. A bright, young woman's life had been cut short in a horrific way all because another woman was too weak to stand on her own. Jenn shook her head, disgusted.

To calm herself, she strolled toward the intersection of Maguire and 11th Streets. Snow crystals crunched with every step. Deep breaths of the cold, dry air burned her lungs, yet the fiery sensation helped to shake off the strain of the evening. Her nostrils stuck together with each deep breath. Beyond the streetlights, the falling snowflakes glittered in the darkness. In the quiet, the flakes lighted on the ground with the softest taps.

She and Jake had been through the wringer today and had triumphed. True, some unknown fact could blow her theory apart, but this time they had proof—the ceramics piece with imbedded fingerprints. Even if the killer turned out to be someone other than Tiffany, the fingerprints would prove it. No matter what, her part was over. She had no more investigating. Only writing was left.

*I'll break the story tomorrow — my first scoop!* Her spirits lifted as she imagined Dad and Grampa being proud of her accomplishments.

Manny would crush her story. The deflating realization meant that even if she wrote it, he wouldn't publish it. She'd need every minute before the deadline to write it and plead her case.

With the case solved, the guilty couldn't run away or cause any damage because Tiffany was as good as caught. There was no need for panic on campus; the murder was an isolated case.

Jenn's pace picked up speed as she turned the Third Street corner and headed toward the Commons. Distant sirens broke her musing. With a glance over her shoulder, the lights of the approaching motorcade sparkled, dazzling the trees, the buildings, and the faces of the crowd lining the streets.

*"Get Dee Forbes immediately."* Is that what the chief said? But, the chief's boss wasn't Forbes; he was notifying the college's PR rep directly, the person who ordered anyone involved with the murder to keep silent. Soon, Forbes would know that the murder was solved and would guess that the

paper would try to print the story. She would not let the *Lariat* publish the exposé.

Jenn broke into a run.

## Chapter 40

President Paul Hulet felt like a king presiding over his court. In his dark-paneled conference room in the Headquarters, delicacies, fine wines and spirits decorated the antique sideboards. Ice cubes clinked in crystal tumblers. Bach caressed the gathering. Wyoming's distinguished and wealthy alumni mingled in three-piece suits and cocktail dresses. Expectations and excitement were high.

Moments earlier, he had welcomed President Edward Ives and Senator Finis Maguire to the sumptuous conference room for the VIPs' icebreaker. Hulet turned them loose to mingle, but he always knew where they were in the crowd; he only had to listen for the laughter. Vigilant and anxious, he noted the positions of the Secret Service agents, ensuring that they weren't being too intrusive. After all, most of these guests were wealthier than the president.

Hulet imagined how sophisticated he must look to Wyoming's favorite sons. To gather the wealthiest and most famous alumni together was a triumph, one that would take him to a bigger, wealthier university.

Dee Forbes sidled up to Hulet, her face pale and damp. "Pardon me, Mr. President. I must speak to you."

"Not now." Hulet's frozen smile didn't budge.

She drew close to him. Panting, she spoke low. "It's about the Hamilton Incident."

"Can't it wait?" he hissed.

"No, sir."

They slipped into Hulet's office through a side door. Bach faded as the door closed.

"Mr. President, the chief called." Forbes' voice cracked. "He's had a break in the murder case. College police are picking up a suspect for questioning, one Tiffany Arnold."

"Tiffany Arnold, of the Denver Arnolds?" Hulet asked, incredulous. "Stephan Arnold is a fraternity brother of mine from Yale. Impossible."

"I don't know if his Arnold is the same as your Arnold, Mr. President, but the chief mentioned Denver and Jackson Hole art galleries." Forbes swiped at a bead of sweat that trickled down her forehead. "He believes Arnold killed Beaufort because Beaufort caught her cheating. Jake Barton's probably in the clear. The police still have to collect and verify evidence, but he believes they have the right person."

Hulet shook his head. "The chief is wrong. The Arnolds are an artistic family. They are certainly not a family inclined for such pedestrian activities as cheating, or murder." He exhaled. "He's on the wrong track, but I'll deal with him tomorrow. At least his current theory corroborates the murder was an isolated incident. Most importantly, I don't have to worry about the story breaking in the newspaper since my police figured it out. Who broke the case? Kerry? Bannister?"

Forbes trembled. "The situation is graver than you realize, sir. Jennifer Roby, the reporter, figured it out. She's on her way back to the press office. I'm sure of it."

His face turned cold and felt as pale as hers looked. Hulet's body twisted violently. He hurried to the phone and stabbed the number for CSC's police dispatch. "This is President Hulet. Have police officers immediately head to the office of the *Lariat*. Throw out every student. Shut down their computers. Lock their offices."

He glared at Forbes while he spoke. "Do what you must to stop them. Now."

# Chapter 41

Long legs propelled Jenn up the stairs three at a time to the Commons' third floor. The newsroom light shone through the open door where Manny put the finishing touches on the next morning's issue.

"Manny!" Jenn screamed as she ran toward the newsroom.

As she charged through the door, he scolded, "Damn it, Jennifer, you scared —"

"Manny," Jenn cut him off, breathless. "The murder is solved. I solved it."

"Augh!" Manny leaned forward and put his face in his hands.

"For God's sake, listen to me!" Jenn wheezed, her asthma on the verge of closing her throat.

"Jenn ..." Manny grabbed his scalp as if he wanted to pull his hair out.

"There's no threat to the campus now. The killer can't run away or hurt anyone else."

"You don't understand. I can't." Manny stood up, his hands clenched in tight fists.

"I, one of your reporters, solved a murder. Is this how you'll operate when you're an editor of a real newspaper? Burn the First Amendment later, but what about your integrity? How did they get to you? How'd they get you to censor the presses? To suppress the truth?" Jenn rambled, desperate to say anything profound to get him to understand what he was giving up by giving in.

"They're blackmailing me."

She fell into a chair, stunned. *How huge is this thing? And why?* Jenn shook off the shock. "Blackmail only works if you let it, Manny. You are the press. You hold the power, not them," Jenn panted. "If you give in right now, at this moment, you're just as wrong and as guilty as them."

"You don't understand. Stroll will prevent me from getting a newspaper job where my father is."

Jenn knew of his father's condition and their limited time together. She knew the pain caused by the loss of a parent. She pushed the thoughts aside. "Think, Manny; Stroll and Forbes are involved in this cover-up. That's their choice. They have to live with it. If you choose to suppress this story, you will regret it." She grabbed Manny's forearms. "You will never recover from this mistake, but if you publish against Stroll's orders, his blackmail means nothing. By exposing a murder and a cover-up, you'll get any newspaper job in the country."

*Give him time to think.* The minutes on the clock advanced. "We have to do this now."

Manny glanced at the clock on his desk. Less than an hour remained until the deadline to email tomorrow's edition to the publisher. He closed his eyes. When he opened them, they were clear. A fire burned within. "Tell me."

"I'll tell you what happened as I'm writing it. You can make up the headline and layout while I'm talking." Jenn ran to a computer and started to type. She stopped. "Manny, the police chief's involved too. He just called Dee Forbes."

Manny nodded in understanding of Jenn's unspoken message. Forbes would notify everyone involved with the cover-up. Stroll would shut down the *Lariat* before the story could break.

Jenn talked while typing, but the accepted sequence for a newspaper article differed from the actual chronology. She confused him a few times, costing precious moments.

Manny faced his computer. The screen displayed page one of tomorrow's special edition. He moved page one's feature article and its headline, *Ives On Campus, Kicks Off Fundraiser Extravaganza*, below the fold. In its place, he typed *Campus Murder Uncovered*.

~ * ~

Twenty minutes before the deadline, Jenn and Manny polished her article. They felt the tension, spoke in choppy sentences, and responded with one-syllable words. Her hands shook, and her fingers hit the wrong keys. She still had to run spell check on her document then scrutinize the article for any errors. Manny warned her not to include the information of those who spoke off the record. "Don't jeopardize your story."

Heavy footsteps vibrated the stairs as they climbed toward the third floor. They didn't belong to Alejandro or Willy. Manny mumbled, "Damn it."

Jenn typed faster and her breathing became labored.

The door at the top of the stairs creaked open. Boot thumps and the squeak of stiff leather echoed in the hallway. Jenn and Manny tried to ignore the sounds. There was no reason to stop typing if the footsteps belonged to a lost student.

"Stop what you're doing, and please leave the premises," a stern voice rang out behind them.

Jenn and Manny jumped at the loud command. They spun in their chairs to see the newsroom doorway blocked by two college police officers. Dee Forbes stood behind them, her eyes glittering with hatred. Jenn's throat tightened. She and Manny exchanged terrified glances.

Astonished at the request, Manny blurted, "Who would order us to leave?"

"Sir, let me be clear," firmness tightened the shorter officer's voice. "The president asks you to leave the premises immediately."

"The college president?" Manny's eyes bulged in surprise.

A wave of dizziness washed over Jenn as she realized the scope of the cover-up.

"Please gather your things and leave," the taller one said.

Jenn and Manny paused. The officers advanced.

Dee Forbes followed close. "That's right. Get the hell out or I'll drag you out myself." Her face was purple, which highlighted the paleness of her white mouth, clenched so tight no blood flowed to her lips.

"Miss Forbes," the taller officer held up a hand toward her. "Step back. Please, let us handle this."

Forbes waved the hand away.

"We've done nothing unethical or illegal." Manny jutted his chin in defiance.

"The president has given a lawful order for you to vacate the premises." The shorter officer slipped his thumbs behind his gun belt. "You haven't violated any statute. The college attorney advised us to ask you to comply with that lawful order."

"Why do we have to leave the campus?" Manny's voice shook.

"Not the campus; our instructions are for you to shut down your computers and leave these offices, and you cannot return," the taller officer said.

"We refuse to have the press silenced by—"

"Jenn, don't argue," Manny cut her off. He turned to the officers and glanced toward Forbes. "We'll save our work, and we'll leave right away."

Jenn's eyes widened. She leaned toward Manny and whispered harshly. "Don't cave in now! Fight this! We've done nothing wrong! The deadline—"

"Save it. Close it. Now." Manny turned to the officers. "We'll comply with the president's directive." He closed his computer file and gathered his coat.

Jenn's eyes filled with tears of rage. The public had a right to know about the murder and cover-up. Manny had acquiesced to the suppressive forces, trampling the First Amendment on his way to hell. Her hands shook so hard she had difficulty closing the file. She gave one final push. "Manny—"

"Do it, Jenn, and let's get out of here," Manny barked. His military-experienced voice ordered Jenn to desist further protest. He turned. The officers and Forbes stood only two feet away.

While they grabbed their back packs and turned off the lights, Jenn's frustration dripped down her face. She wanted to kill Manny or at least beat the devil out of him, but she didn't have the strength to do either.

"Make sure the offices are locked," Forbes' voice was sharp. "They can't come back."

The officers double-checked the locked newsroom at her command then followed Jenn, Manny, and Forbes down the stairs. Halfway down one flight of stairs, Jenn felt weak. Her legs gave out. Manny grabbed her arm. Pain shot through the pulled muscles in her arm and shoulder where Kerry had performed his come-along hold. She moaned, pushed away Manny's hand, and gripped her right shoulder.

As snow fell, they stood on the stoop outside the Commons' main entrance. Forbes hovered behind the officers, shifting her weight from one foot to the other.

The taller officer ordered, "You cannot return to those offices. If you attempt to enter them, you violate the lawful order of the president, and you will be arrested for trespassing. Do you understand this order?" He looked to Manny. Manny nodded. He turned to Jenn. She also nodded.

The officers walked down the steps. Before Forbes followed, she fixed Manny and Jenn with a glare of wrath and triumph.

Manny zipped his jacket as the officers climbed into their cruiser. Jenn watched Forbes open the car door of a little red Audi. Jenn gaped at the license plate.

As the vehicles disappeared around the corner, Manny spun away and broke into a run down the stairs. "C'mon!"

Jenn stood rooted, still too terrified to move. Manny looked over his shoulder for her, slipped on the ice, and screamed again, furious. "Move your ass!"

Confusion evaporated her fear. Careful not to slip, within seconds her long legs caught up to Manny. "Where?"

"Science building," Manny puffed. Colter's thin air and his sprinting sapped his breath. "Our files ... are on ... the server. We might have ... enough time to ... revise the story."

# Chapter 42

In the Science Building's computer lab, Manny retrieved their file from the college's server. Jenn wanted to squeal with delight, but time was running out. Together, they hurried through changes. "Keep an eye on the clock so I can concentrate on this. Tell me when I have one minute left," Manny ordered.

With seconds to spare, Manny clicked "send" to e-mail the next morning's edition to the publisher.

"Just to make sure," he mumbled as he checked the sent-box to verify the edition was away. He pulled up the in-box to ensure the message hadn't been returned for some reason.

With the edition sent, they caught their breath in the abandoned computer lab and stared at each other. "Jenn, you can't tell a soul about this ... your article."

Her eyes grew wide.

"Hulet's got a big influence in this state and the states around us. You know everybody's got ties to everybody else. Anyone could be a friend or relative of Hulet or Stroll. Those people could contact either of them, not believing what they're hearing or reading. If it's the publisher who calls, Hulet would order him to squelch the story."

Jenn nodded. She vented to Manny, punctuating her frustration and fear from the day's activities with light jabs at his arms. She laughed until her eyes filled with tears that the files and editing software were on servers, not on individual computers, and that Manny had complied completely with the president's directive.

"What happened to your shoulder?"

Hesitating, Jenn told him about her bicycle brakes being disconnected and her close call with the dump truck. She described Dee Forbes' Audi as the one that almost ran her down that morning. "I'm trying to be logical, Manny, but that was too coincidental. This sounds overly dramatic, but what if she's really trying to hurt me? I'm scared. What if she tries again? You saw her tonight. She's crazy and unstable." She shivered and hugged herself.

He grew somber and stared at the wall, lost in thought. "If this relieves your mind any, she thinks we've been shut down. She thinks it's all over and she won. I don't think you have to worry about her."

She told him how she had stormed into Kerry's office and cursed him, and how he followed her into Bannister's office and twisted her sore arm behind her back. "Speaking of which," she checked the time. "I need to go to the station to give my statement." Bannister's warning made her anxious to get back.

They bolted out of the Science Building together, in silence. Neither felt jubilant in their success at outwitting the president or sending the exposé to the publisher. Repercussions from the story being printed in the morning, or from being squelched tonight, were to come.

"See you in the morning," Manny gave her a light embrace. As Jenn rushed toward the police station, she expected Forbes to leap at her from behind every tree.

The only people she encountered were lone officers or agents standing their posts. Beyond campus, receding sirens pinpointed the location of the departing motorcade. In the next block, the glare of floodlights illuminated the lingering crowd in front of the Headquarters. Police cars still blocked the streets, but the strobing lights revealed the officers moving the barricades aside. They'd remain in place, ready for the president's next visit.

At the police station, Jenn opened the door. Usually this late at night, the lights were off and the station was deserted. Tonight, although every door stood open and all the lights were on, the building felt strangely quiet. Two agents in the side room glanced at Jenn then turned back to a table spread with clipboards and electronic equipment. Though the place was hushed, an air of excitement swept through her. *At least I shouldn't have to worry about Forbes here.*

Creeping through the hall, wincing at the creaking floors she'd never noticed before, Jenn looked into every open door. An officer stepped out from Kerry's office and headed down the basement steps. The chief's office was vacant. The building was quiet except for the creaking and the soft thumps of her heels as they struck the plank floor.

She didn't want to wander too far into the bowels of the station where she may not be allowed. She decided to go to the Maguire Building and leave a note with the dispatcher, but first she'd tape a note on Bannister's door. She reached over Brida's desk and pulled off a sheet of paper from her block of notes. Puppies frolicked in the corner of the notepad. She leaned on the desk to write.

*Chief,*

*Returned to give my statement at 9:05 p.m. No one here. Will return in the morning.*

*Jennifer Roby.*

Jenn read over her note then added *Lariat reporter.* Satisfied, she folded the paper then stood to place the note in Bannister's door. She gasped.

Kerry watched her as he leaned against the hallway wall and drank from a mug.

Feeling like she'd been caught doing something wrong, she didn't want to look at him. She was still upset over his continued lying to her, his part in the cover-up, and his roughness in the chief's office. Worse, her face grew hot.

"Miss Roby."

"Sergeant." She fought to keep the sneer from her voice. With all her focus on her story through the past hour, she had forgotten he would be conducting an interview. "Where's Jake?"

Kerry pushed himself off the wall, and sauntered toward her. "Mister Barton left a half hour ago."

Jenn's muscles relaxed from the tension that had built up all afternoon and evening. She pulled out Brida's office chair and sat. Tears burned her dry eyes. Grateful that Kerry believed their side of the story and released Jake, she wondered where he was now. "Tiffany?"

"Officers will be heading to the Delta Omega Gamma house momentarily."

That was the last activity in confirming the truth. Sibylle's murder would be solved. Jenn's shoulders heaved and she started to sob. Feeling, more than hearing, Kerry approach around Brida's desk, she stood and backed away. Collecting herself, she wiped her face. She didn't want him close or, worse, touching her.

"Miss Roby, I ..." Kerry backed off, hands raised. "Tell you what, let's go to the squad room. You can spread out there." He stepped away from Brida's desk and raised his right hand toward the hallway.

In the squad room, Jenn set her backpack on the chair that Jake had sat on and eased onto the chair she'd used earlier. She folded her hands on the table and focused on them. Kerry appeared with a notepad and pen.

"Again," he said. "I'm sorry for my conduct earlier. I didn't know ..." His voice trailed off.

"What?" Jenn didn't try to hide the anger in her voice. "What didn't you know, Detective?"

"Skip it." Kerry pushed the notepad toward Jenn and slapped the pen on top of it. "Write down everything you know or did concerning this case ... who you talked to, when, and what they said. Questions?"

"No questions." Zipping open her backpack, she retrieved her interview pad. Pleased she'd taken good notes, writing her statement would be easier — long, but still easier. She reached for the pen and the pad.

"What is that?" Kerry pointed to her notebook.

"My interview notes."

"You'll need to leave them behind."

"Why?" For the first time that night Jenn stared into Kerry's eyes, daring him to confiscate her papers. How tired he looked—demoralized actually. He should be. A young reporter solved a capital crime before a seasoned detective had, she groused to herself.

"You may have something in your notebook that is pertinent to this investigation, something you may not be aware of."

*Never give up your interview notes. If you do, your sources will neither forget—nor forgive—that you violated their trust.* This situation is what Edison Sinclair was talking about. Jenn felt faint, just when she thought she was finished arguing with the police. *"A true journalist will choose prison and trust over liberty and violation."* Grampa's words resounded in her mind. "I'm sorry, Sergeant. I can't let you have my notes." Nervous, Jenn's eyes worked their way up Kerry's uniform to his face.

His face reddened. "Are you determined to make this investigation difficult?"

"No. I'm very sorry, but as a journalist, I can't reveal what my sources said." An odd sensation of power spread through her body. She sat straighter, her pen poised over the notepad. "So you're investigating the case now?" Jenn wanted to change the subject and to poke at him.

Kerry rubbed his eyes and stood up. "Write." He left the room.

*Or did he say "Right"?* Jenn shrugged, and turned her attention to the notepad. Her hand moved quickly across the page as she wrote the sequence of her activities, referring occasionally to her notes. *Only write what I did and was told, not who told me, in order to protect my sources,* she reminded herself.

~ * ~

After an hour, her hand cramped. She inhaled deeply and leaned back in her chair. *I haven't eaten since ... when?* She grabbed her coat with her wallet in its pocket and headed up the stairs to search for a snack machine. If there wasn't one, she would have to leave the building. Jenn shook her right hand to loosen it.

Passing the sergeant's office, she noticed the parlor room was dark behind the closed French doors. Turning back, she saw Kerry leaning back in his chair, staring at the ceiling. Jenn wasn't going to ask him anything, but intended to walk down the hall to find a break room. Her movement caught his attention, and he spun his chair.

"Can I help you?"

"I'm just looking for a vending machine. Is there one here?"

"No, but we have a break room with lots of stale doughnuts and day-old coffee."

Jenn didn't laugh. She pulled on her coat, feeling nauseous. Her thoughts were cloudy.

"You think you're leaving?" Kerry's voice was tight.

"Yes. I'm starving. I haven't eaten since lunch." She zipped up her jacket.

"Sorry. You can't leave."

She felt the shakes coming on. "Am I under arrest?"

Kerry closed his eyes and took a deep breath. He fixed Jenn with a stern eye. "No. Once you start your statement, we prefer you to remain until we have no other questions. We don't want witnesses wandering in and out at will. Tell you what …" He sat up in his chair. "I had a pizza delivered earlier. I'll be happy to share it with you. You can wash it down with the bottle of soda they tossed in."

Pizza and soda sounded delicious. She was so hungry the stale doughnuts and day-old coffee had sounded tempting. His offer to share his meal took the edge off her anger.

"Thank you. That's most kind." Jenn removed her coat and draped it over her arm. Kerry disappeared down the hall. Within seconds she heard what sounded like a microwave humming. She followed the noise into the basement. Down the passageway from the squad room, the break room was lined with beadboard cabinets and 1970s-vintage mahogany countertops. The room was clean, but battered from decades of use. The tang of burnt coffee tickled her nose. Kerry removed two plates from a microwave that looked like it had been installed about the same time as the countertops. The chrome was worn off the rotary knobs.

The aroma of hot pizza made Jenn's stomach growl, loud in the quiet room. If Kerry heard, he made no acknowledgement.

He tugged open a drawer, pulled out two forks and inspected them. Satisfied they were clean, he set them by the plates. From the avocado-green refrigerator he pulled out a big plastic bottle of soda. "Get started while it's hot."

Jenn didn't waste time. She scooped up a fork and started to cut her huge slice of pizza, cooked too long at too high a temperature. The cheese had melted off the slice. Kerry cooked liked Dad and Grampa, they wanted it cooked *now*. She smiled at the memory.

She set down her fork, determined to wait for Kerry. Despite her increasing dizziness from hunger and a hot meal under her nose, waiting was the polite thing to do since he was sharing his late-night dinner with her.

Kerry set the glasses on the table, one by each plate.

"Thank you."

"You bet." He picked up his fork, delaying until she dug in. She tried not to scarf the pizza.

"I didn't know I was so hungry myself," Kerry said between mouthfuls.

"Funny how that works." Jenn covered her mouth while she spoke, and washed down the mass with soda. The huge mouthful of pizza was too big for her esophagus. She fought back a grimace as the lump forced its way down.

In silence, they cleaned their plates then sat, sipping their soda. Each tried not to look at the other. Soda bubble pressure built up in her stomach, but she didn't want to burp in front of him. She managed to slip out a long, but silence release. "Pardon me." She tapped her chest.

After another moment, her shakiness was gone. Her thinking cleared. "You didn't get to work the presidential detail."

Kerry shook his head. "No. I would've liked to." He shrugged. "But real life calls. That's the way it is. He'll be back on Saturday, so there's another chance I can see him. With luck, it'll be quieter on campus." He flicked a quick smile at her. "You didn't work his visit either? No pestering hardworking people with inane questions?" His grin broadened.

A small smile curled her lips. "No. I'm afraid all this business with the bones really messed up my editor's trust in me." The smile faded. She stood up and pushed the chair to the table. "Thank you, Sergeant. I really needed that. I appreciate it."

"You're welcome." Kerry held Jenn's gaze.

"I should get back to it."

"I'll take care of the dishes."

"Thank you."

Resting in her chair in the squad room, she burped again. "Excuse me," she said to the empty room. Would she see Tiffany brought in? Maybe they'd take her to another room. It didn't matter. She whipped off her cap and let her hair fall then combed her hair with her fingers, savoring the scalp massage. She then picked up the pen.

~ * ~

Nearing the end of her statement, Jenn shook off the renewed cramping in her hand. When she finished, she reviewed the pile of papers.

Kerry walked into the room. She didn't acknowledge him, but remained focused on her task. After reviewing her last page, she signed her name.

She looked up at Kerry and noticed he blushed. Wondering why, Jenn remembered her cap was off and her hair was down. Now he could see what she really looked like. It was her turn to smile.

"I'm done, finally." Jenn gave the notepad a nudge.

"Let me review it to see if I have any questions." Kerry slid the notepad toward him then thumbed the stack of handwritten papers, curled from her pen's pressure. "There's a lot here."

"A lot happened."

She sat quietly as Kerry read her report. A few times, she noticed his forehead furrowed. Sneaking a peek at the page, he was reading where she had interviewed him in his office. The deepest creases were for the page where she had screamed at him in his office and where he had grabbed her in Bannister's office. Jenn felt ashamed that her emotions controlled her actions, which led to those episodes, but frustration had swept her away.

Kerry leaned his forearms on the table, and flipped the pages closed. His fingers tapped the top page. She waited while he thought of any questions. Once released, she didn't want to come back … well, except to share another meal with him.

"There are a lot of blanks in your report."

"That's where I spoke to people. I can't divulge my sources." Jenn felt like a child playing a grown-up game.

"Withholding information can make you an accomplice." Kerry's threat was conversational.

"How do you figure that I'm an accomplice because I withheld my sources' names?" The infuriating detective had returned. "If it weren't for me, Jake Barton wouldn't have showed up here in the first place, and you sure wouldn't have the real killer!"

Kerry's eyes stared at his tapping fingertips.

"My notes stay with me." Righteousness flowed through Jenn's body. A feeling of lightness as a moral, higher power took over, buoyed her spirits. *Now I know why reporters go to jail for protecting their notes and their sources.*

She sat up in her chair and looked Kerry in his eyes. He tapped the note pad for a moment longer. "Well, then, I don't have any questions. You're free to go." Kerry's voice was so soft she could barely hear him. He didn't look at her.

# Chapter 43

While Jenn scooped up her backpack, the radio hooked to Kerry's black epaulet squawked to life. The muffled message spewed a couple ten-codes. Without a word or a glance, he gathered Jenn's report and left the room.

Relieved to be excused, she was too intrigued to leave. She didn't want to return to Morris Hall, and wake her roommate who had been nervous to extremes over an upcoming demonstration in her Modern Physics class. She couldn't go to the staff room. Regardless, she had no energy to do either. Until she figured out where to go, Jenn decided to linger in the squad room. She'd have a long night ahead and a longer day tomorrow.

"Well," she said to the empty room. "I can't just sit here." She didn't move. "Here I go." She giggled, punch-drunk from fatigue. In slow motion, she dragged her backpack to the tabletop. She slapped her ball cap on her head then shrugged on her coat.

Metallic noises echoed down the hall. Jenn wondered if Kerry was cleaning the kitchen, but the noises weren't right. A deep voice shouted but he sounded far away. Alert, the sound frightened her. She didn't know if she should search for the source or ignore it. A higher-pitched voice yelped, closer than the first sound, piercing the darkness. Jenn's heart rate picked up.

"Don't touch me!"

Jenn gasped at the emotion that echoed around the corner in the hallway. Taking place in front of her was real-life police action, something she had been sheltered from her whole life.

The screamer could be Tiffany. Jenn moved away from the squad room, aware that the police might need it. She stopped at the end of the hallway near the stairs. Here, she was close enough to watch.

"Miss Arnold, thump me again, and I'll slap you in cuffs," Kerry's voice warned Tiffany as they approached. The thought of Tiffany striking Kerry flustered Jenn. Irritation at herself flared for feeling protective.

His back to Jenn, Kerry appeared as he steered Tiffany toward the squad room. Her white face contrasted with hot pink pajamas. She staggered and retched. Stomach contents spattered onto the floor and Kerry's pants and shoes.

Jenn covered her mouth in shock and mirth. She tried to remain silent at the end of the hall, unseen, but a snort escaped.

He turned at the sound and grimaced as Jenn clamped her hand over her mouth. She couldn't help but giggle. He raised his hands as if to protect them from the mess.

"Get in there." Kerry pointed into the squad room. Tiffany lurched into the room. He stared at his legs, as if he moved the mess would seep through his pants and onto his skin.

Jenn tossed her backpack on the floor and approached him. "I'll give you a hand, Sergeant. Where are the cleaning supplies?"

Kerry leaned over and closed the door to the squad room. He pointed down the hall toward the right. She strode down the hall and opened the door. Boxes of soaps, paper towels, and jugs of cleaning supplies filled shelves that lined the closet. From the hallway's dim light, two cleaning buckets looked like big yellow lollipops with sticks of mop handles. Jenn snatched a box of rubber gloves and pulled out two.

She grabbed the supplies she needed and headed back to Kerry. He seized the towels she held out. What was it with her cleaning off men lately? First it was for Jake to wash his face and now to wipe off Kerry's legs and shoes. She bent to wipe the mess. Thankfully, it was mostly liquid, soda from the smell. She sopped it up and tossed the garbage in the bucket.

She sprayed the floor with the sanitizer; it would have to stay wet for ten minutes.

The clean towels were still clenched in Kerry's hand. *He's not a very good detective and is afraid of a little mess.* She grabbed a rag then wiped his shoes, if only to get him moving again so he could do his job. *This investigation will never get finished.* He'd have to take care of the mess on his legs himself.

Without a word, Jenn gathered the supplies and took them into the women's lavatory, across from the closet. She dumped the bucket contents into the trashcan, and, with a snap, whipped off the rubber gloves. Scooping up the cleaning equipment, she replaced them in the closet.

The hallway was empty. She guessed Kerry sat across the table in the squad room, letting Tiffany get a whiff of her late-night drink.

Wide-awake now and curious of what was happening, she sat on a chair at the end of the hall to wait.

Footfalls approached. Kerry stopped outside the squad room to eye the wet floor. His pant legs were soggy, but looked cleaner. He flinched as he noticed Jenn. "Miss Roby, you're still here." He sauntered toward her. He raised his hand to indicate the wet spot on the floor. "I'm sorry you had to see that. Thank you. I can handle of lot of things with this job; unfortunately, that's not one of them." His grin was sheepish, and he rolled his eyes.

She waved her hand in dismissal. "Not a problem. That doesn't bother me."

"You're heading home?"

Jenn nodded then shook her head, "I'm too tired to go home, plus I don't want to wake up my roommate. She has a big presentation tomorrow — today — and she's really nervous about it."

"You're a considerate roommate."

Jenn appreciated his compliment. "I've also been barred from the *Lariat* offices."

"I heard. You could go to the Commons. You're not barred from there."

True, but Jenn couldn't explain her need for comfort and feeling protected. Lying on a couch in the deserted Commons, unlike lying on the couch in the newsroom, she'd only feel vulnerable.

Kerry seemed to read her mind. "There's a comfortable couch in the break room. It's seen lots of sleepy heads. If you can't sleep, there's usually a pot of coffee on." Jenn remembered the stink of burnt coffee.

"Thanks for the offer. I'll do that. Plus, I could be here if you want me." At Kerry's slight smile Jenn realized the double entendre. "For any help or to answer any question," she stammered. *Good thing the hall light is dim so he can't see my face.* "Well, Sergeant, I guess I'd better let you get back to her." Jenn made a motion toward the squad room, although she didn't want him to go.

"It's good for her to stew for a while."

"Is that what you and Chief Bannister did? Let Jake and me stew for a while?"

Kerry looked angry at the question and glanced up to where the chief's office would be on the main floor. "No."

"I won't be mad if that's what you did. I'm just curious." Jenn caught his irritation.

He turned toward the squad room. "Good night, Miss Roby."

"Good night, Sergeant."

"Call me Matt."

~ * ~

Jenn slouched on the hall chair after Kerry closed the door behind him. She wanted to go to the *Lariat* staff office, her home away from home. She thought of Dad and Grampa and wondered how things were going in the Red Desert. *I hope they're having a good time.*

The murmurings in the squad room aroused her curiosity. She gathered her coat and backpack then crept down the hall, straining to eavesdrop. She kept moving so that if someone caught her, they might think she happened to be walking past.

A shriek erupted from the squad room. As she neared the door, a chair scraped the floor. The door opened and immediately slammed shut as if Tiffany tried to run away, but Kerry stopped her. Jenn jumped back. Her heart rate quickened. Pieces of the conversation filtered through the door.

"I want to call my Daddy!" Tiffany's shriek made Jenn flinch.

"Miss Arnold, you're an adult. You can do this without Daddy." Matt's voice had a condescending tone.

"I won't say anything."

"We asked you here, Miss Arnold, so that if you choose to answer these questions, you can clear up this situation."

"You just want me to confess." Jenn leaned closer to the door, anxious to hear Tiffany's confession and put an end to this case.

"For what crime do you think I want you to confess?"

"Am I under arrest?"

"Not at all. You'll recall at your sorority house you agreed to come here to talk with us. All I'm requesting is for you to answer some questions. Will you do that?" His voice's timbre altered, and Jenn knew he was smiling as he spoke.

The silence lengthened. Jenn stepped toward the door. She heard a faint, "I guess."

"What can you tell me about Sibylle Beaufort?"

Jenn listened to the faint sounds of settling in the old building. She glared at the door as if her stare would generate a response from Tiffany.

"Go to hell!" Tiffany screamed. Jenn gasped.

"Why don't you just relax for awhile? Let me bring you a bottle of water."

Jenn's mouth flew open. On tiptoes, she raced through the hall toward the break room. She flung herself on the couch just as Matt closed the squad room's door. She closed her eyes and pretended to be asleep. His footsteps entered the break room. The refrigerator door made a kissing sound as he pulled it open then clicked closed. His footsteps headed out of the break room. "Good night, Miss Roby."

Busted, she smiled as his footfalls retreated down the hall. Softly, she said, "Call me Jennifer."

## Chapter 44

As the sun peeked over the Granite Mountains, Jenn bit into her hard-fried egg on a toasted cheese bagel. The caffeine in her extra-large cup of coffee failed to lift the grogginess weighing down her head. Lit class loomed in a few hours, but she wasn't sure if she could get through the class without falling asleep. Unsure if she were talking herself into or out of skipping class, she shook her head. She'd never debated skipping a class before. According to the clock on the wall, the *Lariat* was due for delivery.

She rubbed her neck. Since she'd left the police station an hour ago the crick had finally loosened. For most of the night she lay on the squad room's couch. Never sleeping, she floated in and out of consciousness. The two officers who ordered her and Manny out of the *Lariat* office came in for a fresh pot of coffee and their night lunch. They stared at her as if wondering why this girl lay on their couch. She smiled at them and shrugged. "I can't sleep on the staff room couch."

The officers exchanged glances then ignored her. Moments later, Matt's voice on their radios called them to the squad room. She listened carefully. Moments later they escorted a whimpering Tiffany to the interior of the police station. Matt never returned to the break room.

Finished with her breakfast, Jenn dared to sneak up the stairs toward the *Lariat*'s floor, expecting Dee Forbes to pounce from the shadows. She tried to walk quietly. On the third floor landing, she nudged open the door and peeked down the hall.

Manny leaned against the wall watching the maintenance man change the lock on the newsroom door. President Hulet made good on his threat to close the newspaper. Metallic clicks of the man's screwdriver were the only sound. She pushed the door open. The maintenance man glanced up, nodded then returned to his work.

She and Manny didn't speak while they exchanged a long look. She guessed that he hadn't slept all night either. His eyes were glassy and he hadn't bothered to shave. "Any time now," Manny murmured.

Jenn nodded. "I can't believe all the other places on campus get the *Lariat* delivery before we do." Within moments, they would know whether their adventure was either over or had just begun. They would either be fools or heroes. "We could just go to a place that has their papers," she said flatly at the absurdity of them standing in the empty hall.

A small smile flicked across Manny's mouth. "I'm hiding." He looked at Jenn. "You're welcome to go get some."

"I'd rather hide here with you," Jenn said and suppressed a giggle. The chuckle faded as she said, "I wrote my statement for the police, Manny." If she made a mistake by withholding her notes, it was better to fix it right away. On the other hand, she was exhausted from constant nervousness about the repercussions of her article and arguing with the police. If she had done something right she needed a pat on the back.

"The detective demanded my interview notes. I refused to give them up. I still have them. When I wrote my statement, I didn't include my sources' names. Is … that right?"

Manny stared into Jenn's eyes while he considered her words. A somber look crossed his face. "You refused to turn over your notes to the police?"

Jenn's heart pounded for his verdict.

A small smile flickered across his mouth. "Sorry to tell you, Jenn, but no fiction for you. You're a real journalist after all. You did exactly the right thing. "Uncle Walt" would be proud of you."

At the mention of her idol, Walter Cronkite, tears welled and she sniffled. She nodded her head in gratitude at the highest compliment of her journalistic life then leaned against the wall beside Manny. He reached his arm over, pulled her to him, and gave her a tight squeeze. The gesture touched Jenn, physically and emotionally exhausted to her core, and she started to weep. Manny held her, patted her back, and rocked her.

Fighting to control herself, Jenn leaned back and whispered, "Thanks, I needed that." She was surprised to see tears in Manny's eyes.

"Me, too. It was a hell of a run, huh?"

Jenn giggled, grateful for the release of tension. "Yeah, literally and figuratively." She knew Manny meant her chase of the truth, but she recalled last night's run.

Manny laughed, too hard. Last night, as he ran to the Science Building he slipped on the ice and landed flat on his back. Unable to catch his breath, he gasped like a big fish in a goose down coat and motioned for Jenn to keep running. Time was not on their side.

The maintenance man tested the new keys in the lock. They both worked.

"When can I get new keys for my reporters?" Manny asked.

He shook his head. "Dunno. My instructions were to tell you that you're to ask your department head. See ya." He gathered his tools and trundled down the hall. The approaching elevator's hum traveled the silent hallway. The double doors opened just as he reached them.

Jake dashed from the elevator and headed for her. "Jennifer!"

Delighted to see him, her joy was cut short by his strained expression. He walked like a panting somnambulist toward them.

"Jake?" Jenn trembled.

"I ran all the way here … from the art building." His voice was ragged as he struggled to catch his breath. "They're delivered there first." From under his arm, he pulled out a folded newspaper. With shaking hands, he unfolded it and held it up to display the *Lariat*'s headline.

*Murder at Hamilton*
*Cover-Up at HQ*

Jenn screamed. "Oh, my God! Oh, my God!"

Manny whooped. They hugged each other and spun in circles. Tension faded from her body. Jenn broke away from Manny and turned toward Jake, who gave her a tight hug and burst into tears. "At last, the truth. Thank you. Thank you, Jenn," he managed to say between sobs.

Jenn pulled away. She wiped his tears. He'd been through so much horror, she thought.

"It's over." Jake sniffled. "I can't believe it's over."

Manny put his hands on her shoulders. "But it's just beginning. All hell's fixin' to break loose."

"Yeah. Yeah," Jake mumbled. "Uh, listen, about that. I gotta get out of here, but I had to see you first." He reached for Jenn and she returned the embrace.

"I'm glad you did because I've been worried about you. I'm thankful you were the one who brought us the first copy."

Jake kissed Jenn on the cheek, nodded at Manny then retreated down the hall. The elevator doors opened as the cranky old man who delivered their *Lariat* editions appeared pushing his loaded dolly. As always, his belly and the front of his thighs were ink-smeared from heaving the heavy bundles. He threw the stacks on the floor. In a practiced maneuver, he broke the seals then dragged his empty dolly behind him to the elevator.

Manny threw his arm around Jenn's shoulder, and they walked together toward the stack. They stared at the pile of papers emblazoned with their headline. With both hands, Manny grabbed newspapers and handed half to Jenn. "For your portfolio."

Her laugh trembled as much as his hands. They returned to the locked door of the newsroom and leaned against it. With the looming possibility that their newspaper careers were over, simply pressing against the doorway provided comfort.

Jenn snapped the paper flat and read the article's opening sentences. "'A gruesome murder was discovered on March three by fellow students in the Art Department ceramics studio. The Shoshone County coroner confirmed the homicide and identified the victim as CSC student Sibylle Beaufort.

Because of a sequence of misinformation orchestrated by Public Relations Director Dee Forbes, the *Lariat* previously reported the incident as a prank'." Breathless, she held the newspaper at arm's length and stared at the page.

Manny continued reading. "'At press time, information on the identity of the alleged killer was presented to the campus police. After being informed of this information, Forbes and CSC President Paul Hulet barred this reporter'—that's you, Jenn—' and *Lariat* editor Manuel Whitaker from the newsroom in an attempt to conceal the exposure of the homicide.'"

He took a deep breath at end of the exposé's opening paragraph. His hands trembled as he folded the paper.

Inside the newsroom, the phone rang. Before that caller gave up, the phone in the staff room rang. *Everybody knows now.*

"Manny, are you scared?" Jenn shivered and gripped her bundle of newspapers tighter.

"Yeah."

"What do we do now?"

"Wait."

Both phones in the newsroom and staff room stopped ringing. The staff room phone began again.

"Are we in trouble?"

"Probably."

All manner of repercussions ran through Jenn's mind. She may be fired from the *Lariat*, dismissed from CSC, or prosecuted for interference with a police investigation. Ridicule from the media drifted in her mind. Jenn quaked with fear. *What have I done?*

The elevator door opened. Dee Forbes flew out and raced for them, her eyes wild with rage. "You bitch! I'll kill you for what you have done!"

Jenn felt faint. She forced down a sob at the fast-approaching fury.

Manny's face paled. He stepped in front of Jenn, arms outstretched, to block Forbes' charge. "Now, Dee ..."

"You son of a bitch! You've ruined me!" Forbes' uncontrolled rage powered her attack. Manny's head snapped back at the snake-fast strike of an uppercut before she slammed into him. He flew backward. His head struck the tile floor with a sickening crack.

Jenn leaped back to avoid Forbes' reaching arms. Forbes stamped on Manny's motionless body and lunged. Grabbing Jenn's shoulders with both hands, Forbes shrieked, "You blamed me!"

Panicking, Jenn screamed. Forbes struck Jenn across her cheek with her fist. A white haze blocked Jenn's vision.

"You wouldn't stop!" Forbes seized Jenn's throat with both hands.

Jenn flailed, but off-balance from Forbes' force she fell backward to the floor. The fall knocked out her breath. Forbes landed on top. The madwoman's hands gripped Jenn's throat tighter.

Choking, no sound escaped. Jenn's fist repeatedly hit Forbes in the face but her strength faded. Her arms wouldn't move. Her legs refused to kick. As Jenn's world faded to black, shouting sounded far away. She barely heard a faint slapping sound. Then Forbes was off Jenn.

Jenn wheezed. Precious air filled her lungs. Rolling to her side, she fought to breathe. Coughing and choking, pain seared her throat. Too afraid to open her eyes, Jenn slithered with the little strength she had to retreat from the spot where Forbes might be.

A hand grabbed her shoulder. Jenn screamed. She swung a fist and connected with a hard face.

"Miss Roby!"

Jenn's eyes popped open.

Detective Matt Kerry knelt beside her and patted her shoulder. "You're safe. It's all over."

~ * ~

"Mom, I don't want to go to school," Manny protested.

The emergency medical technicians pulled tight the last strap encircling him as he lay on the gurney.

A smile flitted across Jenn's mouth. "Okay, but you're going to the hospital. Son." She laid a hand on his shoulder. Tears welled as she remembered how he tried to protect her from Forbes' attack and the gruesome crack of his head hitting the floor.

The EMT glanced at Jenn. "Sign of a concussion."

She nodded, sniffled then wiped her running nose on her sleeve. She patted Manny's shoulder as he was rolled away.

Earlier, the police officers had dragged the handcuffed and cursing Dee Forbes from the scene. Now, except for Jenn and Detective Matt Kerry, the *Lariat* hallway was vacant. Silence weighed heavy in her ears.

Too exhausted to stand, she sank to the floor. Her throat and face throbbed. She fingered the butterfly bandage near her left eye and flexed her bandaged right hand. She must have struck Forbes harder than she thought. *Good.*

Matt folded his legs to sit on the floor beside her and studied her face. With a gentle voice, he asked, "Will you reconsider going to the hospital? Choking can cause unseen damage. It can be serious."

Jenn winced as she tried to speak. A croak escaped from her bruised throat. "Maybe I should."

"I'll take you when you're ready."

Jenn returned his gaze. His uniform's normally crisp edges were droopy and wrinkled. His five o'clock shadow matched his dark hair and his glassy eyes were bloodshot. She fought the urge to stroke his face.

He examined the scattered newspapers on the floor. "You certainly popped the cap off this bottle of beer." A small smile creased the exhaustion on his face.

Clearing her throat, she mumbled, "How did you know to come here?"

"Last night, the chief told me about someone tampering with your bike's brakes and your near hit-and-run with Forbes." He reached for a copy. "When I saw your headline and the cover-up accusation this morning, I had a hunch she wasn't finished."

## Chapter 45

"When would your resignation have been effective if the president had accepted it?"

Chief Tom Bannister deeply inhaled. "If President Hulet had approved my resignation, he would have made it effective as soon as the college hired my replacement." His voice cracked. "He made me realize I have more to offer the college."

Jenn leaned against the back wall in Hulet's conference room and watched the throng of national news reporters shout questions. The lectern and the bouquet of microphones hid him up to his mustache.

"Do you, personally, believe in Miss Arnold's guilt?"

"Only a jury can decide guilt. Right now, we're still collecting and verifying evidence." He pointed to another reporter in the audience.

Bannister kept his cool with that ridiculous question, Jenn thought, although he looks like he wants out of here in the worst way.

"Who in the police department knew the truth of the murder?"

Bannister and Kerry, Jenn answered the question in her head.

"Only I knew of the murder. I kept the information from all the others." Bannister's clipped words slipped from between tight lips.

Jenn's jaw jutted in anger. *He's lying! Kerry knew it — he just didn't act on it.*

"When did you tell your detective the truth about the murder?"

"I informed Detective Kerry after Jennifer Roby approached him with the information that broke open the case."

The mob of reporters turned as one to stare at Jenn. Mortified by the sea of staring eyes, she hung her head and raised her left hand to hide the bandage on her cheek and her blossoming black eye.

A jolt of realization startled her. She met the chief's eyes. Their gaze held.

Kerry hadn't known the truth. She thought back to the events of that night when she and Jake went to the police station to make their report. From Matt's perspective what she said and how she acted was crazy. That also explained why she and Jake were left in the squad room so long: Bannister had to come clean to Matt. Their awkward behavior and the fact that Matt couldn't look at Bannister made sense.

A small smile flitted across Jenn's mouth. Matt never divulged that Bannister hid the truth. His professionalism and loyalty was impressive, she thought.

"I have nothing else to say, folks. We'll keep you updated as information becomes available." Bannister held up a hand in farewell, and turned from the lectern.

The tide of reporters rose and rushed to intercept her. Jenn gasped at the onrushing mob and escaped out the rear door to the cacophony of "Miss Roby" and shouted questions.

Safely back in the staff room, Jenn slowly sank into her chair. Across the room, Alejandro hunched his shoulders trapping a telephone receiver to each ear. His face gleamed from sweat. He shouted over the din of other ringing phones, "She has no comment."

He slammed both receivers on their bases and ignored the rings of other calls. Finally the callers hung up. "Our ace reporter, how are you feeling?" He hurried to Jenn and placed a hand lightly on her shoulder.

"I think I would have felt better if that dump truck had run over me and my bicycle," she joked and grimaced from the pain of her bruised throat. "The ER doc said I had a contused larynx. I was lucky though. Poor Manny." She shook her head.

"Oh, Manuel was just here. He is looking for you," Alejandro said.

"Here? They only kept him overnight?"

"Yes. The hospital released him this morning."

Just then, Manny stepped stiffly into the staff room. "Well, there you are. If it isn't—almost—the biggest pain in my backside." He grinned, placed his hands on his buttocks then grimaced. A black swollen patch on his chin skewed his face.

Jenn stood to accept his embrace. Manny stepped back and lightly cupped her face with his hands. He studied her bruise and the bandage by her eye. "This is all my fault. I'm so sorry this happened. All of it."

Tears welled at his heartfelt apology. "It's not your fault, Manny, and I'm sorry too." She wiped her nose with the back of hand. "Shouldn't you be home recuperating?"

"The hospital said to rest for a week." Manny waved aside her concerns. "Between the president's visit and the flood of national news reporters on campus about the scandal, this is a chance of a lifetime. There's no way I'm missing this." At Jenn's focused stare he touched her arm. "I'll take it easy. I promise."

"Too bad Willard quit the newspaper," Alejandro said. "He was supposed to interview the president tomorrow when they return from fundraising in Jackson."

Manny rolled his eyes. "The questions Willy submitted were designed to embarrass Ives and Maguire. I told him to change the questions and he refused. He said he would have the 'prez' cornered and intended to make him squirm. On top of that, he insulted the Secret Service agents to their faces. He didn't quit. I fired him."

He turned to face Jenn. "Which reminds me, you need to hustle." An intense look came over his face. "Jennifer, you must complete a Secret Service form for your background check and submit a list of questions for my approval. Tomorrow, you will interview President Ives and Senator Maguire."

## Chapter 46

Jenn sang at the top of her voice accompanied by Johnny Cash. Euphoria and her father's Dodge propelled her toward home. She pressed the steering wheel's volume button until the interior vibrated.

On Friday after their camping trip, Dad and Grampa picked up their home delivery of the Colter *Cabernet*. At seeing "Murder" in the headline and a photo of their bruised Jennifer, they had raced to campus. Soothing their panic that she would be fine and that she needed to prep for the president's interview, the men reluctantly left. Before leaving, her father handed her the keys to his new truck with stern instructions to head home as soon as she could. Nervous about driving such an expensive and huge vehicle, she soon relaxed with the aid of the stereo's power.

As she turned the wheel to take the sharp curve around Red Canyon, an image of a skeleton bathed in a ring of fire popped in her mind's eye. Grimacing, she lowered the volume and poked the button to switch the station.

"Investigators from the U.S. Department of Education, the agency responsible for ensuring compliance with the Clery Act, are set to arrive on the CSC campus next week. Their arrival coincides with the special prosecutor assigned by the Wyoming governor, although college president Paul Hulet insists no federal laws were broken," the reporter out of Casper intoned.

"Liar!"

"Meanwhile, the college's Board of Trustees gave President Hulet a provisional seven-to-five vote of confidence. The board's vote comes on the heels of the Edward Ives and Finis Maguire fundraiser kickoff, which alone is expected to bring in thirty-six million dollars."

"Woo hoo! Wyomingites comin' through!" She yelled and jammed a fist into the air.

"After her arrest for the alleged assault on the student reporter who broke the story, President Hulet terminated Public Relations Director Dee Forbes' employment contract. In his statement, he expressed his lack of confidence in her ability. Now for the weather."

Jenn poked the "power" button. In the sudden silence, she felt breathless and lightheaded. Hearing such personal information mentioned in a public forum brought back all the terror of the assault. She inhaled deeply then exhaled slowly to rid her body of the stress. "I just want to get home," she murmured, suddenly longing for the comfort of Dad and Grampa.

She glanced at the *Lariat* papers stacked on the passenger seat. The top copy displayed her headline *Ives and Maguire Trade Barbs* and the article from their interview. Turning back to watch the road, she smiled. During her interview, Ives and Maguire's relaxed camaraderie generated a ping-pong of stories, most of which might be true and all at the other's expense.

She slowed for the turns onto the South Pass City Road and the ranch road. "Somebody's here," she muttered. A mud-spattered Willys Jeep pickup stood in front of the house. Suddenly nervous it belonged to either Dad or Grampa's girlfriend, her euphoria dampened.

"Hello, my boys!" Jenn held out her arms to the two galloping Australian shepherds. She giggled at their throaty welcoming grumbles and wriggling back ends. "Come on! Moose stew's waiting," she wheedled as she stepped into the house.

"Sorry I'm late," she called out to beyond the empty living room. "People kept stopping me to talk."

Dad called from the dining room. "Better hurry while the biscuits are hot."

"Thanks for trusting me with your truck, Dad. I'm so glad to be home—" She halted in the doorway.

Four settings circled the table. Her spot was untouched. Dad and Grampa sat at their places, and chewed their stew.

Matt Kerry wiped his mouth with a napkin, pushed back his chair and stood, grinning.

She glanced at his denim shirt and the short-sleeve hems tight across his biceps. Dumbfounded, she bowed her head, but not before she noticed his tight Levi's. Heat burned her cheeks. The fading bruise under her eye throbbed. She ignored Grampa's high-pitched giggle.

"Hello." Matt studied Jenn.

"Hi." Jenn glanced at her father.

"Okay," Dad broke the uncomfortable silence. "Since I knew you were finally going to get a couple days home for spring break, I called the sergeant to have a surprise lunch with us if he was free." He focused on Kerry with an intent expression. "He saved the life of my only child." His voice cracked. "I wanted to thank him for his service in a social setting, even if it's over something as simple as moose stew and biscuits." He took a big bite of biscuit. Apparently self-conscious at his sudden emotion, he hung his head as he chewed and blinked back tears.

At his heartfelt words, Jenn's throat tightened. "It's been a tough week for all of us." She leaned over to embrace her father's shoulders and kissed his cheek. As she straightened, she patted his hand.

"If my reward for saving a damsel in distress is this stew, I'll follow Jennifer everywhere," Matt said as he sat down. Everyone laughed, grateful to be rid of the tension.

Dad sprang from his chair. "Jenny, take your seat. We wanted to wait, but the biscuits were cooling. We had just started." He ladled a bowl full of stew, grabbed another heaping platter of biscuits from the counter and set both on the table. As Jenn scooted her chair forward, he planted a kiss on her head.

In the awkward silence, she tore apart a biscuit and spread butter on the halves. She picked up the spoon and stirred the stew.

"I don't think either one of us will forget how terrified we were when we came back from our camping trip." Grampa indicated Dad. The twinkle in his eyes faded. He cleared his throat and brightened. "We thought having your savior here would be a nice surprise for you." The gleam returned. He snickered as he studied Matt, then Jenn.

"Do you mind my being here?" Matt leaned in, placed his elbows on the table as his smile broadened.

Jenn felt her nervousness fade. "No. It's a great surprise. Thank you for coming." They dropped their gaze to take a bite of stew.

"I brought some *Lariat* copies for your dad and grandfather." A soft redness bloomed on his cheeks.

Jenn's lips twisted in a smirk at his discomfort. "That's kind of you. I brought several too."

They ate in a hush, though they all cast furtive peeks at the others.

"Campus quiet?" Dad asked, slathering butter onto a biscuit.

"No. A lot of reporters are still around. I think just as many college people ran away as there are hanging around hoping to get their faces on TV. It's been crazy."

Sated, one by one they pushed back their bowls and plates, and sighed.

"So, your investigation's going well?" Grampa looked to Matt.

"Yes," Matt straightened in his chair, suddenly the police officer. "The college has formally expelled Tiffany Arnold. The order barring her from campus came across my desk yesterday. If she's ever released from jail, she can't come back." He glanced at Jenn. "I did find something surprising on Tiffany's cell phone. She had several close-up snapshots of Sibylle's pieces. I gathered from those she had intended to continue her copying."

"Coffee?" Dad reached for the full pot.

"Please." Matt held up his cup. "Thank you," he said as Dad filled it.

Grampa held a hand over his cup. Jenn shook her head. Dad set the pot on the table in front of Matt and sat, scooting his chair closer. "I'm still trying to figure why the college covered this up in the first place." Dad sipped his coffee.

Jenn recalled the radio announcement of the fundraiser kickoff. She relayed the information. To the men's whistles, she held up her hands in disbelief, "Thirty-six million dollars, and there's still weeks to go for all the fundraising events!"

The light of the answer blinded Jenn: "Money! That's got to be the reason. The skeleton was found just at the start of the fundraising campaign." She steepled her hands under her chin. "The president ordered the cover-up because he believed a crime this terrible would stop contributions. The cover-up was simply to keep the money flowing in." She looked to each of the men.

"Hmm," Matt grunted. "Interesting."

"If that's the case, Hulet certainly doesn't know Wyoming people." Grampa reached for the coffee pot and topped off his cup.

"She makes sense, Dad." Her father nodded. "Unless someone spills the truth, doubtful we'll ever know for sure."

Jenn plucked another biscuit off the platter. "Not likely anyone involved will tell me. I already know there are folks on campus who won't talk to me."

"*Persona non grata*," Matt grinned. "Like when you come to my office."

Jenn pulled off a bit of biscuit and flicked it at him. He dodged the piece and laughed.

"Did you find the ceramic piece?" Jenn blurted. The men sobered and turned their attention to her. "I mean, I heard you couldn't find it. I'm really nervous because that's really our only concrete evidence."

Matt nodded. "Finally. It wasn't in the studio like I'd expected. I had to wait for a search warrant to go through Tiffany's sorority room or the house, but it wasn't there either.

Then I searched her car—her parents' car." His nose wrinkled. "It was in a bag of her soiled underwear."

A low groan spread around the table.

"I'm relieved," Jenn breathed.

Matt reached for another biscuit and tore off a chunk. "The Wyoming Department of Criminal Investigations has the sculpture now. The tech is a friend of mine. He called this morning after a preliminary look. The prints are there, sealed into the glaze. He's not sure how clear the whorls and lines will be." He popped the bread into his mouth. After he swallowed, he said, "I relayed this information to the county attorney this morning. He and Chief Bannister had just come back from Tiffany's arraignment. The judge set bail at half a million dollars."

At Grampa's soft whistle, Jenn's stomach clenched. "I'll have to testify, won't I?"

"Well, Jenny, you are a key witness." Grampa set his cup on the table. "We can help you practice your testimony, if you like."

She groaned and gingerly rubbed her face. "I have to admit I feel bad about pointing a finger at anybody for something so horrible, even when professionals believed me. I actually feel bad over this. I'm still scared I screwed up." She tore off a piece of biscuit and studied it. "Getting that guilty verdict is the only way I can move beyond this."

"Well, if that's what it'll take for you to move on, then I'm afraid I have disappointing news for you," Matt's voice grew somber. "You deserve be told this face-to-face, since you brought about all this."

His mouth tightened. "Information was disclosed after the judge rapped his gavel."

Jenn's eyes grew wide. She clenched her fists.

A smile flitted across Matt's lips. His eyes twinkled. "Tiffany confessed."

## About The Author

Barbara Townsend's writing journey began at the University of Wyoming. During her first fiction writing class she felt compelled to write a mystery. The thought of twists, turns, red herrings, clues and making them all fit into one story fascinated her. That first short story, *Murder at Wainwright,* she later wrote into *CACE.*

An internship in the Toppan Rare Books Library led her in another direction. With books dating from the 1800s, she wrote a thesis that examined women in nineteenth-century Mormon polygyny. That paper won a student competition at the university's American Heritage Center. Her accumulated research led to *Blood Atonement*, a historical mystery.

Her writing credits include the university's newspaper and Air Force newspapers. She was first a student and then a faculty member of the Wyoming Writing Project. She graduated *summa cum laude* with a Bachelor of Arts degree.

She lives with her husband in Wyoming's Wind River Mountains.

## Books by Barbara Townsend

*Clear and Convincing Evidence*
*Blood Atonement: A Pioneer Trail Mystery*
*Tarnished Gold*